QB KEEPER

BOSTON BLIZZARD SERIES
BOOK 3

C.L. ROSE

Cover Design: C.L. Rose

Editing and Proofreading: Breanne at Breezy Book Edits

Chapter Break and Character Artwork: Breanne at Breezy Book Art

To all the Tanner girls…

Daddy's home.

TRIGGER WARNING

This book contains scenes of a couple exploring BDSM in an unsafe and uneducated way. While unintentional, there is an instance of the dom injuring his sub during play.

There is a scene that involves cheating, but not by either of the main characters.

It also contains a scene with light face slapping by the MMC during oral, which is completely consensual and discussed ahead of time between the characters. Please take care of yourselves, and if these situations are triggers for you, take caution when moving forward.

Always research thoroughly and discuss your limits before engaging in any type of kink with an experienced partner.

Love,
Candice

PLAYLIST

1. Didn't See It Coming - My Brothers And I
2. Summer Secret - Connor Price
3. Watermelon Moonshine - Lainey Wilson
4. better off without me - Matt Hansen
5. that way - Tate Mc Rae
6. Religiously - Bailey Zimmerman
7. Falling - Harry Styles
8. Million Ways - HRVY
9. Ghost - Justin Bieber
10. Drown - Justin Timberlake
11. Kissing Strangers - USHER
12. Pull the Plug - VOILÀ
13. regrets - Stevie Howie
14. Wine Into Whiskey - Tucker Wetmore
15. The One That Got Away - Boyce Avenue
16. It's You - Ali Gatie
17. your place - Ashley Cooke

18. This Heart - Corey Kent
19. BIRDS OF A FEATHER - Billie Eilish
20. Loved You First - One Direction
21. I Can Do It With a Broken Heart - Taylor Swift
22. i hate u, i love u - gnash, Olivia O'Brien
23. 18 - One Direction
24. Lose Control - Teddy Swims
25. Freak Like That - Austin George
26. Therapy - VOILÀ
27. If the World Was Ending - JP Saxe, Julia Michaels
28. Hey Daddy (Daddy's Home) - USHER
29. Can We Pretend That We're Good? - Daniel Seavey
30. Good Girl - Slaz
31. Breathe - Kansh
32. She Thinks of Me - Landon Tewers
33. Red Room - Bryce Savage
34. prove it - 21 Savage, Summer Walker
35. Get On Your Knees - Nicki Minaj, Ariana Grande

PROLOGUE

TANNER

I HOLD the thick paper in my hand, reading it for the tenth time while standing at my mailbox. I don't know what I was expecting when I took a quick run down my mile-long driveway this morning, but this definitely wasn't it.

YOU ARE CORDIALLY INVITED TO THE 40TH-ANNIVERSARY CELEBRATION OF BILL AND

LIBBY VALENTINE

SATURDAY, APRIL 2ND AT 2 O'CLOCK

1111 JOURNEY LANE, HOPE HARBOR, MASSACHUSETTS 01125

I wish I could say I was excited to celebrate such a huge milestone for my childhood best friend's parents. Forty years of marriage is a big deal, and their love has always been an inspiration to the people who know them, but the only thing going through my mind as I think about what attending this party would mean is *her*.

Grace Valentine.

My Grace.

The girl whose anguished cries haunt my dreams every single night.

There was a short time in my life where I held her and

nothing else mattered. Not football, not school, not my future. It was just us, learning, exploring…falling.

And then I fucked it all up.

I knew better than to have a secret fling with my best friend's younger sister. It started as me wanting to protect her, as I had done since the day she was born. I was only three, but our parents always joked that I was Grace's personal bodyguard. If another kid tried to play with her or touch her toys, little Tanner had no problem letting them know that wasn't an option. And as we got older, my instinct to make sure she was safe and happy only intensified. I can't tell you how many douchebags her brother Riggs and I scared off in high school so they'd stay away from her. Wrong? Maybe. But I'd have done anything to protect her heart.

Then I turned around and ripped it out with my own two hands.

What I thought was the right thing at the time ended up being my biggest regret. It's been five years, and every time I get invited to an event in Hope Harbor, I decline like a little bitch. I make some shit excuse about having practice or workouts so I can get out of them, convincing my family to come visit me in Boston instead. I even had this house built with a fully equipped guest suite so they would feel like it was a little vacation when they came here. For half a decade, everything I've done has been for Grace…or to avoid her.

Riggs and I still talk occasionally, but he's currently playing professional baseball in Florida, so our conversations rarely make it long enough for his sister to come up. Especially since, to this day, he has no idea what happened between her and me that summer.

I don't want to know what she's up to now. My guess is that she's in a relationship, if not married. Girls like Grace Valentine don't stay single for long. If her beautiful blue eyes and silky blonde hair don't reel a guy in, her kind heart and amazing sense of humor will. Some lucky son of a bitch is probably holding her right now. And I can tell you with absolute certainty that whoever he is, he doesn't deserve her.

No one does.

The day I walked away, I deleted all my social media accounts, drove myself from Hope Harbor back to Harvard, and vowed to stay away for good. I had done enough damage. The least I could do was let her have our hometown as her safe space. Let her chase her dreams in Los Angeles, being able to return whenever her heart missed home, and give her a fair chance at a happy life. Because I knew that without her, that would never be an option for me.

The thick cardstock feels like a brick in my hand as I try to tell myself to stay away. That I'm only invited because Riggs and his parents have no idea that I'm the cause of Grace's first broken heart. That for one whole summer, she gave me every single piece of herself, and I humiliated her by acting like the way she felt was just some stupid schoolgirl crush. Then I told her she meant nothing to me and walked away while she cried and begged me not to.

I decide right here that it's time to go back and face the consequences of my actions. I deserve to see how happy and successful she's become in spite of the way I broke her. That she's thriving while she unknowingly still carries my heart in her hands.

And she deserves to see how empty my life has been all these years, knowing that I'm the only one to blame.

ONE
TANNER
5 YEARS AGO

"YO, DICKHEAD! YOU HOME?" I yell up the stairs to Riggs. I just got home for the summer, and I didn't even bother going to my house before I came to see my best friend. My junior year at Harvard is officially over. I had to stay on campus an extra two weeks after finals for meetings with my coach, but now I'm ready to see what kind of trouble we can find back in our hometown. Classes, football, and workouts took up so much of my time during school, that I rarely got a chance to wind down. I was able to save up enough money to not need a summer job, so the possibilities are endless for the next three months.

"Riggs! Where you at?" I yell after he doesn't answer. He's probably in his room with his headphones on. I haven't spoken to him since before finals because we've both been so busy, but I know UMass finished earlier than we did, so I assume he's been home for a while.

"Put your dick away. I'm coming i—" I say, immediately freezing when I see that his room, which used to be decorated in navy blue and gray has been transformed into a pink and white wonderland. Boy band posters hang on the wall, but they aren't what catch my gaze. Because sprawled out on the bed is Riggs' little sister, Grace Valentine. Only, the woman lying there with her earbuds in and eyes closed is anything but the cute, awkward girl I remember from last summer.

I shouldn't notice how long and smooth her legs look in her pajama shorts. I also shouldn't notice the supple swells of her tits peeking out from the neckline of her tank top. And I *definitely* shouldn't notice the way my dick is thickening inside my boxers at the sight of her lying there, still completely unaware of my presence.

As if she can sense me staring like a goddamn peeping Tom, her eyes fly open, immediately landing on me in the doorway. I'm like a deer in headlights, sure she's going to notice the bulge in my shorts that she absolutely caused, so I'm caught off guard when a giant smile stretches across her face.

"Tanner!" she squeals, pulling her earbuds out and tossing them to the bed before launching herself at me. I almost don't catch her, opening my arms at the very last second while she wraps around me like a koala bear. This is one hundred percent normal behavior from Grace. I was there the day she came home from the hospital. Our parents have been friends since their years at Hope Harbor High and bought houses next door to each other shortly after college. Our moms were pregnant with me and Riggs at the same time, with Grace following three years later. I've experienced almost every one of her major life milestones right alongside her. The only difference between then and now is that she was like a little sister to me. But now, holding her tightly against me with her soft curves pressed against my hard muscles, the thoughts I'm having are so far from brotherly—it's not even funny.

"Hey, Gracie," I say, inhaling her signature vanilla scent. "I didn't mean to barge in. I was looking for your brother."

"Oh!" she giggles, sliding down my body. "This room has a bathroom, so we swapped after last summer. He has my old room, but he's not here. His coach is making them stay on campus until the season is over, so he won't be here for at least another month. I'm surprised he didn't text you."

Riggs is on a full ride to UMass Amherst, which is about two hours from Hope Harbor. He's one of the top MLB prospects for the next draft, so baseball is his first priority from February to June. I knew he'd be traveling a lot during the NCAA playoffs, but I thought he'd be spending his off time at home.

Well, fuck. Now what am I going to do? Our parents are spending their annual 'childless vacation' in Nantucket. They do this every year at the beginning of summer, going away to a cabin for the week, soaking up all the peace and quiet before us kids wreak havoc on their lives for three months straight.

"My phone died on the way here and my charger is packed. I just figured I'd see him here," I tell her as she hops back on her bed, sitting cross-legged while facing me. I avert my eyes when I notice the white lace of her panties as it peeks out from under her shorts. I'm hyperaware of the fact that if she weren't wearing underwear, I'd be able to see her pussy. Do I *want* to see her pussy?

No.

I don't.

I can't.

What the fuck is going on with me? Maybe I need to get laid. Between my full-time course schedule and daily work-outs with the team, I haven't had the time to hook up in a while. Sophomore year was different. I allowed myself some time to enjoy the parties and girls, but I needed to lock in this past year so NFL team scouts could see that I'm a dedicated quarterback all year long.

A lot of guys opt out of their senior year to declare for the draft, but I was a backup until last season, so I need to play this year to show my chops. The only dream I've ever had is to play for the Boston Blizzard, so I'm going to squeeze every moment out of my college career to prepare for it. Plus, how many people can say they have a degree from Harvard? It's a once-in-a-lifetime thing, and I've earned the right to walk across that stage next May.

"Looks like it's just us for the week," she says cheerfully. "Do you have plans?"

"No," I tell her. "I was hoping to just chill and unwind. What about you, Miss High School Graduate? I'm sure you have all sorts of parties lined up. Got a boyfriend to hang with this summer?" I'm fishing. And I don't know why. So what if she has a boyfriend? It's not like I could make a move on her even if she didn't. She's my best friend's sister, and she's only eighteen.

She scoffs. "Yeah, right. You've seen the boys at that school. If your boyfriend doesn't know how to change a tire and wears tighter jeans than you do, then ma'am, throw the whole man away."

God, I missed her sassy, quirky little attitude. Grace has absolutely no filter. She says whatever she's thinking, no matter how outlandish it sounds. Nine times out of ten, it's something fucking hilarious. It's one of my favorite things about her.

"What about grad parties?" I ask. "Are you going to any?"

She shakes her head. "Almost everyone is traveling right now and waiting until the hotter weather to have theirs. You know the rich kids and their pool parties." She rolls her eyes like *we* don't come from wealthy families. My father and mother are both successful real estate agents, and the Valentines own a commercial construction company that's worth millions. But we weren't raised with silver spoons in our mouths. Our parents taught us the value of a dollar and that we were expected to earn our places in this world just the way they had.

Of course, having money afforded us certain luxuries when

it came to opportunities. Riggs and I both spent summers going from football camps to baseball camps all over the country. We had the best coaches money could buy, but that didn't mean we could coast our way into college. We used the skills we learned and perfected our crafts so that we'd stand out to scouts. Which, we did. Riggs had his choice of several schools, while I had a shorter list of options, but a couple were Ivy League. Harvard was a no-brainer since it was a quick drive from home, and they have a good football team.

Making the football team as a freshman wasn't hard, but working my way to being the starter took a while. I was second string until our last quarterback graduated when I was a sophomore. Then, it was a battle to become QB1. I thought I was home free since I was his backup the year prior, but we had an incoming junior transfer from Kent State right before last season, so I had to prove that I was the right man for the job. In the end, I came out on top. I have to return to campus for practices next month, but it's a short drive, so I plan on commuting. I want to soak up as much of the summer as possible in Hope Harbor.

"So, what are you going to do this week, then?" I ask. It's hard not to see Grace as the little girl who used to follow us everywhere because she was scared monsters would eat her if we left her by herself, but it's clear that she's all grown up now and has a life of her own. The last thing she wants is to tell her brother's overprotective best friend what kind of trouble she's planning on getting into while her parents are away.

She shrugs. "I don't know. I'll probably just stay here and watch movies or something. I don't really want to go out and party. I'm kind of over it."

"You're going to just hang here alone?" I ask.

"Unless you want to keep me company," she says with an adorable grin.

I smirk. "You sure you want me here cramping your style? I'm practically an old man now."

She looks me up and down, and I have to be honest, it makes me feel hot all over as she drags her bright blue eyes from my feet to my face. She stops for just a split second when she gets to my dick, which I'm trying very intensely to stop from getting hard under her gaze.

Fuck, this is bad. I need to end this dry spell so I can stop looking at Riggs' little sister as something I can have, when I definitely know I can't.

She raises a brow, her eyes twinkling as she looks into mine. "You don't look like an old man to me."

I try to act unaffected, but alarm bells are blaring in my head, telling me to keep some distance between us until I can find a warm hole to stick my dick in. One that doesn't belong to Grace Valentine. Because apparently, he isn't getting the memo that she's the furthest thing from available to us.

"What do you say, hot shot?" she asks. "Want to come back over later and watch a movie? Unless you have plans," she hurries out. "I don't want you to feel like you have to hang out with me or anything."

I should tell her I can't. I should call some friends or a girl and do anything else. But Grace has always had me wrapped around her finger, and I just can't say no.

I blow out a breath. "Nope, no plans. I'll go home, unpack, run to the store for snacks, and be back at eight."

She bounces on the bed, clearly excited. "You're the best, Tan. I really did miss you."

"I missed you too, Bunny," I say, using her childhood nickname. We gave it to her the year her parents caved, after a lot of begging, and got us a trampoline. Riggs and I would jump and do flips for a while, but we'd eventually get sick of it and move on to some other activity. Unlike Grace, who would bounce for hours on end, never tiring of it. She looked like a little bunny rabbit, just hopping around, singing to herself while her golden pigtails blew around her face.

I tell her goodbye, making my way down the stairs and out the door toward my house. I'm not sure if I should be as excited as I am to come back tonight, but I find myself counting down the hours until I get to see her again. I just need to make sure I keep reminding myself that no matter how different she looks and sounds, there is no universe where my best friend's little sister could ever be more to me than just that.

TWO
GRACE

I LOUNGE ON THE COUCH, flipping through the options on the streaming app while I wait for Tanner to arrive with our snacks. I don't know what kind of movie I'm in the mood for, but if I don't pick something quick, he'll talk me into some shitty action movie that'll bore me to tears within ten minutes. There are a few new releases this week, so hopefully we can settle on a rom-com or drama that can keep my attention.

I narrow it down to two new ones, waiting for him to get here so we can decide. Although I have a feeling he's going to throw one of them off the table quick, fast, and in a hurry. It's a drama about a billionaire who has a crazy sex dungeon in his house and moves a young, inexperienced woman in to be at his kinky beck and call. I've been dying to see it, but I doubt Tanner would be comfortable watching it with the girl he knows as an annoying little sister. I'm sure he thinks I'm some non-sexual being who couldn't possibly imagine herself in any type of situation where a penis is involved.

He'd be half right. Even though I can and have imagined it, I'm still a virgin. I know it's not the end of the world, but I hate the fact that I'm about to go to college in the fall with my v-card intact. As excited as I am that I got into the California College of the Arts Fashion Design program, I highly doubt that I'll find a guy that'll tick all my boxes when I get there.

I have a type. I like tall, masculine, and athletic guys. Which is going to be pretty hard to find at school since CCA doesn't have any sports teams.

Damn my brother for always having the hottest teammates. They made me this way.

I dated the captain of the football team last year and had every intention of having sex with him, but when the time came, I chickened out. He wasn't forceful or anything, but I could tell by the way he kissed and touched me that he didn't care if it actually felt good or not. I've heard horror stories about how the first time can be uncomfortable or even painful, and I knew I couldn't trust him to take care of me. So here I am. An eighteen-year-old almost college freshman who will be making the trip to California in the fall as a certified virgin.

Pitiful.

I'm snapped back to reality when the front door opens and closes. I hear Tanner in the foyer as he removes his shoes, sliding them across the floor to the mat my mom insists we use. She's tripped over flip-flops and sneakers enough times to make that one of her rules. Everyone who comes here regularly knows better than to leave their shit lying around.

I turn my head just as Tanner enters the living room. He's wearing a tight crimson Harvard Football t-shirt and a pair of grey sweatpants. His black baseball cap is turned backward and every hormone in my body is holding up a little sign that reads '10', as if they're scoring an Olympic event. He's always been hot, but right now? He's drool-worthy with his ocean blue eyes and sand colored hair that's perfectly tousled. Maybe it's all the thinking about sex that went on before he got here, but I'm suddenly picturing Tanner as he sinks into me for the first time. Obviously, that would never happen, but I'm allowed to fantasize about him naked.

Not like I haven't done it before.

"I got your disgusting Sour Patch Kids," he says, tossing a family-sized bag of the best candy in the world into my lap as he rounds the couch. I try not to notice the way his bicep strains against the sleeve of his shirt with the motion. "I also grabbed us a pizza from Henry's, in case you haven't eaten yet."

That makes my ears perk up. "First of all, they're not disgusting. You just have terrible taste," I joke as I set the bag beside me and sit up on my knees, reaching for the top of the pizza box once he's standing in front of me. "I hope you got the—" I lift it up to see my favorite toppings, sausage and mushrooms. I can't hide the wide smile as it stretches across my face.

He raises a brow. "Did you really think I'd enter this home with any other kind of pizza, Bunny? You're a nightmare when you're hangry."

My jaw drops in mock exasperation. "I am *not*," I argue. I pause, shrugging. "Okay, maybe I am." I take a slice from the box, turning to the TV and going back to the new releases as Tanner settles in next to me.

"So," I say with a mouthful of food, "here are our movie choices. You can pick."

He sets the box on the coffee table before choosing a slice of pizza for himself and sitting back. I watch his mouth as he takes a bite, noticing his plump lips and strong jaw muscles as they work to chew his food. I have a weird urge to reach out and touch the side of his face, but I ignore it because who the fuck would ever do that? I quickly turn back toward the television as he angles his head my way, trying my best to act like I wasn't just drooling over the way he masticates.

This is Tanner Lake, Grace. He's so far out of your league, it's laughable. Get a grip.

"How about that one?" he says, pointing at the photo of the exact movie I thought he'd want to avoid.

I slowly turn to look at him, unable to keep my eyebrows from almost touching my hairline. "Really? Do you know what it's about?"

"No," he replies.

I laugh incredulously. "It's...how do I say this?" I pause. "Spicy."

He stops chewing for a moment. "*Spicy?* Is that like, sexy? Is this a kissing movie, Bunny?" he jokes.

My cheeks heat. God, this is embarrassing. Tanner has probably had sex thousands of times. Meanwhile, my hymen and I are practically besties. We're inseparable...*literally.* "Umm, yeah." It comes out as a squeak and *holy shit just bury me alive right now.*

He laughs. "We're watching it," he says, swiping the remote from my hand and hitting play. "You don't even have to tell me what it's about. I just want to watch you squirm during the sexy scenes."

"I hate you," I mumble, melting back into the couch cushions as he chuckles. He reaches forward, grabbing the remote that controls the lighting in the house. The room darkens just as the opening credits roll across the television screen. Suddenly, I'm no longer hungry, reaching forward to set what's left of my pizza back in the box.

The first twenty minutes of the movie is just introducing the characters to us. The guy is a rich CEO who hires the young girl to be his live-in housekeeper, not reading the fine print of the contract before she signs on the dotted line. If she had, she'd know that she's really agreeing to be his submissive for the next three months. Imagine her surprise when she's dusting the bookshelves and he enters the room, telling her to kneel. She resists, of course, but after considering her options, she eventually consents.

It isn't long before the slow, sultry music starts playing as the man undresses her completely. She stands there, trembling as he circles her like a hungry lion playing with his food before devouring it. I feel a delicious pull low in my belly when the camera zooms in to his hands as he ghosts them up her torso, stopping to pinch her hard nipples. I let out an almost inaudible gasp right along with her, and I'm thankful for the surround sound when I remember that I'm not alone.

I feel the couch cushions shift under me and look out of the corner of my eye as Tanner's legs become restless. And when I see his Adam's apple bob in his throat as he forces a swallow, my thighs press together on their own volition. I immediately notice the wet feeling in my panties that I know wouldn't be as prevalent if I wasn't sitting so close to this six-foot-four perfect specimen. It's uncomfortable, but also, I can't help but notice how good it feels when I clench my inner muscles while I sneak another peek at his profile that's illuminated by the glowing lights of the television.

I shouldn't be thinking of him like this, but it becomes increasingly hard not to when the man on the screen takes a handful of the woman's hair, forcing her into submission before him. Thankfully, since it's not actual porn, the camera fades away just as she leans in to take him into her mouth. I let out the breath I was definitely holding in as the movie returns to the everyday life of the billionaire and his new pet. I'm able to tamp down my arousal and stop thinking of my brother's best friend as if he were a juicy piece of meat waiting to be tasted.

He's not meaty, Grace. So stop it.

An hour and *several* kinky scenes later, the end credits roll, and the tension from enduring that movie next to a man who is arguably the hottest living being on the planet finally subsides from my muscles. I blow out a relieved breath.

He turns to me with a cocky smirk. "You good, Bunny?"

I paste a look of nonchalance across my face. "Why wouldn't I be?" I ask.

"I don't know," he says. "You just look a little embarrassed."

He's trying to rattle me. To pick on me. But I'm an adult who can watch a sexy movie with another person and stay cool. Fuck this guy, right?

"Embarrassed," I scoff, "I'm the furthest thing from embarrassed." I sit back, crossing my legs and mustering up every ounce of fake confidence that I can find. "As a matter of fact, I think I'm going to do some of that stuff when I get to college."

Oh. My. God. I did not just say that.

"Is that so?" he asks, trying to hide his smile. "You gonna go find some guy to tie you up, Gracie girl?"

I can feel the tips of my ears getting hot because I'm so flustered. I'd rather get up close and personal with a Taco Bell toilet seat on a random Tuesday than finish this conversation, but I dug myself into this hole of humiliation, so someone pass me a shovel. "Totally," I squeak out. "I think it would be really hot."

His brows shoot up. "Hot?"

"Mhmm," I say. "I've just been waiting until I go to LA because the guys here don't really rev my engine, you know?"

"Yeah," he says, but his expression has changed. At first, he was playful, trying to get a rise out of me. Now, he almost looks pissed off. I guess it's not really a surprise since Tanner has always seen me as a younger sister and probably doesn't want to think of me getting tied up and spanked. I probably grossed him out.

He stands, wiping his hands on his sweats. "It's uhh, late. I'd better get going," he says, avoiding eye contact. *Yep, I definitely grossed him out.* "Good night, Grace."

And then he's gone, leaving me to wallow in my own desolation.

THREE
TANNER

I PICK UP MY PACE, feet pounding on the pavement beneath me as I open up into a full sprint. After a night of tossing and turning, I decided before the sun was even up to go for a run. My hope was that I'd get a little bit of clarity on why I'm feeling so messed up right now.

What the fuck is wrong with me? I flew out the Valentines' front door like a bat out of hell after Grace told me her plan to find a guy and explore BDSM with him. I paced my kitchen for an hour, practically wearing a hole in the hardwood floors, ready to tear this whole town to shreds...and I don't even understand why.

I pretended like I didn't know what that movie was about because I thought it would be funny to watch her get all flustered. I honestly didn't expect it to have so many graphic sex scenes, but after the initial shock, I was able to focus on Grace's reactions. I didn't miss a single one of her gasps and quiet moans as the man on screen dominated his girl. The way her thighs clenched together as the couple fucked roughly. I saw everything.

Is that really what she's into? Or was she just trying to

throw me off? I'll be completely real. I've never once even considered that Grace could be out there having sex. But she's eighteen. Clearly, she wasn't going to stay a virgin forever. I've been her protector for so long that I guess I just pushed those thoughts from my mind. Now that I'm being forced to really consider it all, I understand that was a pretty good defense mechanism, because the way it's all making me feel isn't something I expected.

I also don't expect to end up back on her doorstep before dawn, knocking loudly when I know there's no way she's up. But fuck it. I won't be able to focus on anything else until we sort all of this out.

"Grace!" I yell, pounding my fist rapidly against the hard wood. "It's Tanner. Open up!" I change tactics, ringing the doorbell, listening between pushes of the button for any movement inside. "Grace!"

I hear footsteps followed by loud shuffling and then a *thud* against the door before it swings open. Grace is standing there wearing an oversized t-shirt and nothing else. Her smooth, creamy thighs are on display, and I only tear my eyes away from them when I see that she's cradling her forehead with her hand. "Tanner? What are you doing here? It's nighttime," she says groggily, wincing as she rubs her head.

I push into the house, shutting the door before placing my hands on her warm cheeks. "What happened?" I ask, concern lacing my tone as I tilt her head so I can see better.

She drops her hand to reveal a red mark on her skin, which is swelling just slightly. "I tripped over my shoes and hit my head on the door. It was dark and I forgot I didn't put them on the mat," she says. Without even thinking, I lean forward, gently pressing my lips to her forehead. I close my eyes, inhaling her vanilla shampoo, lingering there for a few seconds before pulling back. It's not the first time I've kissed one of her bumps or bruises. I can't even pretend to know how many times she fell off her bike or the trampoline when we were kids, screaming like she was being murdered until I checked it and kissed it better. But we aren't kids anymore, and it's been years since I've done it, so why was that my first instinct?

"You okay?" I say, inspecting the bump again by ghosting the pad of my thumb across it. It's raised, but not enough for me to freak out over.

"I'm fine," she says quietly. "Why are you here? What time is it?" she asks, squinting as she tries to focus on the wall clock across the room.

"It's four thirty," I answer. "We need to talk."

She furrows her eyebrows in confusion but says nothing as she leads the way to the living room. She rounds the couch, stopping to turn on a table lamp before she sits down. I follow, keeping enough space between us so I can think without reaching over out of my own frustration and shaking some sense into her.

"What couldn't wait until daylight, hot shot?" she sasses, bringing her knees up to her chest and pulling her t-shirt over them. I take a few seconds to figure out what I'm going to say, because even though my mind has been racing since I left her last night, I'm not completely sure why this is affecting me and what I plan to do about it.

I've always had an overwhelming need to protect Grace. I honestly think I'm more intense about it than Riggs is. It's just the way it's always been.

I clear my throat, which suddenly feels like the Sahara. "What you said last night," I say, "about finding a guy when you get to LA to—" I can't even finish the sentence without feeling the burning embers of rage threaten to spark to life within me. "Did you mean it?"

She looks completely bewildered at first, the skin between her eyebrows bunching together as she tries to recall the exchange. I see the moment when it all clicks into place. "Oh," she says, "I mean, kinda. After watching that movie, it made me curious." She pauses, shaking her head as if she's just realizing how weird this whole conversation is. "Why are we talking about this?"

I ignore her question. "You know how dangerous that is? Choosing a random stranger to explore kink with? What if you get hurt, Grace?" My stomach twists with anxiety at the thought of some asshole being rougher than she wants or crossing the line from pleasure to pain. The more I let the scenarios play out in my head, the more my rage starts to bubble up, threatening to come to the surface.

She lets out an incredulous laugh. "I'm not just going to sling my honey pot at any ol' guy, Tan. I'll get to know him first to make sure he's a suitable candidate."

"I—your *what*?" I ask, raising a brow. "Did you just refer to your vagina as a *honey pot*?"

She sits up straighter. "Yes. Is that not an acceptable pseudonym? Would you rather I say *pussy*? Or *cunt*? Is that better?" She winces just the tiniest bit at that last one and I can tell she's trying to steel her expression to prove a point.

I cringe. "Jesus Christ, Grace." I don't even know why it's affecting me. I've said those words a million times. But coming from her innocent lips? They sound…*filthy*.

She smirks. "You look flustered. Was it something I said?" *Little fucking brat.* "Anyway," she says, changing directions, "what I do with my body isn't yours or Riggs' concern. I'm an adult. So, unless you're volunteering as tribute, you can cut the protective brother act. My hands are already full with the one I have."

For some reason, I black out and don't even consider the repercussions before blurting out my next words.

"Okay. Then I volunteer."

Her smug expression morphs into one of befuddlement

before she chokes out a forced laugh. Only seconds later, she bursts into hysterics, popping her knees from under her t-shirt and leaning forward with a side-splitting howl. Tears fall from her eyes as she blinks at me, continuing to laugh as if I'm the funniest motherfucker to ever walk the earth. I just stare, waiting for her to get herself together as she lets out an adorable little snort before wiping her cheeks.

"Oh, that was good," she says. "I can always count on you for a chuckle, Tanner."

I stare, completely straight faced. "I'm not kidding, Bunny. If you want to explore that stuff, fine. But it's going to be with me."

What the fuck am I doing? This is Grace fucking Valentine. My best friend's little sister. The girl who used to beg us to leave the lights on in the tent when we'd go camping because she was afraid of the dark. And now I'm going to, what? Cuff her to the bed and spank her until she begs me to fuck her?

My cock twitches at the thought.

I'm not really thinking of doing this, am I?

What choice do I have? Either she goes off to school, finds some random guy who probably has zero experience with this, and ends up hurting her or forcing her to go too far before she's ready…or she can use me. At least this way, I'll know she's safe, cared for, and her boundaries aren't being pushed or crossed. It's the only option.

Her face turns serious. "Why does it seem like you're not messing with me?" she says, nervously playing with the hem of her t-shirt.

"Because I'm not," I answer with a shrug. "You have two choices, Gracie girl. You can do this with me, or I can show up at the worst possible times when you get to school and make sure you aren't doing anything I told you not to." I raise a brow, daring her to defy me.

Her shoulders sag in defeat as she swallows roughly. "Okay."

"Good girl," I say, reaching up to ghost my fingertips over her jaw. She lets out a sharp breath, her eyes fluttering closed as she leans into me. "I have some stuff to do today. I'll be back around eight tonight and we'll get started." I don't even give her a chance to reply before I press my lips to her forehead and stand, heading out her door.

FOUR
GRACE

WHAT THE HELL JUST HAPPENED? Did I pass out? Am I dead? Because I could've sworn Tanner Lake, the hottest guy I've ever seen in my entire life, just told me he's coming back tonight to do unmentionable things to me. But that can't be right.

Right?

As much as I'd like to say my thoughts for him have always been pure, I'm not dumb, and my vision is perfect. So, of course I've fantasized about Tanner. More times than I'm proud to admit, but whatever. He's always been so protective and caring toward me. Pair that with his gorgeous blue eyes and sharp jawline...*ok, fine. And his eight-pack abs*...who wouldn't make him the star of their dirty daydreams?

But that's all it was. Just a fantasy. A way to get from point A to point O when my usual audio porn app wasn't doing the trick. Never in a million years did I even consider making those thoughts into a reality.

First of all, both Tanner and my brother have never had a shortage of girls vying for their attention. I've seen the revolving door of cleat chasers that they've gotten to experience since everyone in school realized they both had futures as professional athletes. They've always been open and honest, never promising more than a night of fun, but the girls are always all too happy to take whatever they can get. From the outside, it looks a little desperate, but also, good for them getting that dick.

Well, not my brother's. That's gross.

Another reason why I never thought anything could ever happen between Tanner and me is our age difference. He's three years older than me, and when you're a freshman in high school lusting over a senior, the last thing you'd ever expect is for them to look your way. But now, I'm eighteen and he's twenty-one. That seems like less of an age gap, even though it's the same as it's always been.

And lastly, I know Tanner has always seen me as a little sister. He's never been shy about the way he's so protective of me. All through high school, he and Riggs scared away every single boy that looked my way. They may think they were sneaky about it, but I knew. I guess they're both partially to blame for the fact that I've never had sex. Kind of hard to find a guy who would be willing to risk four broken limbs in exchange for deflowering me.

And then, there's *that* problem. It was easy for Tanner to be all up in my business when we went to the same school, but I'm sure he assumes I found a way to hook up with guys since he graduated. And I mean, I *could have*, but it just never felt right. So, I never did.

I'm going to guess that he thinks he's coming over tonight to let me further explore my sexuality, but he probably has no clue that there will be no *further* involved, since the only thing I've ever done with a guy is kiss and let him put his hands in my pants. It was last year with my ex-boyfriend. We were at a party after one of his football games and I decided to let him go further than we ever had. But when he wedged his hand between my legs, it felt more like he was trying to double-click his mouse in the computer lab than he was trying to actually massage my clit. Needless to say, it was a subpar experience, and probably the main reason I decided against having sex with him. If he couldn't give enough of a shit to see if what he was doing felt good in that situation, he certainly wasn't going to take care of me during sex. There was one other instance with an older guy a couple months ago, but it never even moved below the belt.

Will Tanner even go through with this when he finds out? Maybe he won't want to have to deal with my inexperience. Maybe he'll be turned off when he realizes I'm a virgin.

Maybe I should call him and call this off.

But fuck, I want to get this over with. And who better to do it with than the one person in this world who I know will make sure I'm okay. As confident as I pretend to be, I'm terrified of having sex for the first time. From what I've heard, it hurts, you bleed, and you don't even get to have an orgasm. You just have to wait for the guy to stop thrusting and grunting so you can push him off and hope the next time is better.

But it's the means to an end, right? You can't have good sex without having bad sex first.

Not to mention, if we actually get to the point where we get into all the kinky stuff, it'll all be worth it. Because I wasn't lying. Watching that movie really did make me curious. I've always had a pretty high pain tolerance, and this isn't the first time I've wondered how close I'd be able to toe the line between pleasure and pain. With any luck, we'll really go through with this, and Tanner will help me find out.

I head upstairs, stopping by my room to grab some clothes before walking into my attached bathroom. I'm too wired to go back to bed, so I may as well shower and get ready for the day. I undress, catching my reflection in the mirror as I peel off my clothes. It hits me in this moment that hopefully, after tonight, the next time I see myself, I'll be different. Will there be a visible change? Will my skin have that glow I've heard so many people talk about? Will I look older? More *womanly*? If anyone could have that effect, it would be Tanner. He's so hot, I can't even imagine what it'll be like watching his face as he pushes inside me for the first time. It's almost too much to think about.

I step into the shower, turning the water temperature up as high as I can handle. After a few minutes of letting it run down my body, relaxing my tense muscles, I shave from head to toe. Normally, I keep my bikini area cleaned up, but I decide to go completely bare. I've watched a lot of porn, and it always seems like that's how the women are. I know Tanner has been with a lot of girls, so I don't want to look like an amateur compared to them, even though I am. It takes me a while to make sure everything is clean, but once I'm done, I'm feeling confident that I'll at least look the part.

I turn off the water and step out, drying my entire body with a warm fluffy towel. Instead of putting on the clothes that I brought in, I walk back out to my room and lie down on the bed. I don't know why, but for some reason my hands begin to roam my body. I turn my head, looking into the full-length mirror that sits in the corner of the room. I let my fingertips drift down my stomach, stopping to ghost along the newly exposed skin of my mound. I watch my face in the reflection as I put pressure on my clit and start rubbing in slow circles. I try to focus on my expression as pleasure sparks to life in my core, wondering if this is exactly what Tanner will see when he finally does make me come. Even though I know everything will happen naturally, I try to practice looking sexy as the most delicious pressure builds within me.

When I can no longer keep my eyes on the mirror, I close them, imagining Tanner's face instead. I try to conjure up the noises he would make as he thrusts into me, using my body to make himself feel good. Will he just moan and grunt? Will he talk dirty like the guys in the videos I watch?

I'm equal parts scared as fuck and turned on at the possibilities.

I envision him between my thighs, his tight abs and that delicious V that sits below them, rubbing against my clit as I grind it against his skin. I can almost feel his large hands squeezing my hips to hold me in place while he moves. I want it so badly. I want to feel his fingertips digging in hard enough to leave behind bruises that I can look at every time I want to remember how he felt inside me.

"Fuck, Tanner," I moan. "Just like that." I barely recognize the sound of my own voice as my orgasm hits like a speeding train, making me still as my muscles contract and shake. When the waves of euphoria finally fizzle out, I sink into the bed, waiting for my breathing and heart rate to slow.

When I can finally put my thoughts together, I expect to feel a little bit of shame for thinking of him in this way. Every other time I've fantasized about him, I've had a little twinge of regret after because I knew I shouldn't think of Tanner as anything more than my brother's best friend. But it seems as though he's given me the okay by offering to help me explore my sexuality, so maybe that's why I'm not feeling bad about what I just did. The only thing on my mind is actually getting him under me. Hopefully, after everything is said and done tonight, I can find out what it feels like to be fucked by the most gorgeous guy I've ever seen.

By the time I'm back up and dressed, the sun is peeking through the morning clouds. I make myself some avocado toast and a cup of coffee, retreating to the backyard to eat. I'm mesmerized by the lapping of the water in our pool as I enjoy the peace and quiet. It's not a rare thing for me to be home alone, but after so many years of Riggs and his friends running around being obnoxious all summer long, it did take some getting used to. Now I love the silence. Most girls my age are always on the go, but I'm perfectly happy just sitting in my backyard, thinking about all the things I have to be grateful for in this life. I graduated high school with honors, and I'm going off to college across the country to pursue a career in fashion design, which has always been my passion. Now, I have one more thing to be thankful for, because by the end of tonight, I'll get to live out something that has only ever been a fantasy.

And it's just the beginning of our summer together.

FIVE
TANNER

MY MIND IS GOING a million miles a minute as I get ready to head back over to the Valentines' house. I've spent the entire day thinking about the pros and cons of what I proposed to Grace earlier, and unfortunately for me, the pros won out. Obviously, she's my best friend's sister and I already know he would fucking murder me if he knew I touched her, but other than that, I can't think of another good reason why I shouldn't be the one to do this with her.

She made it clear earlier that this was something she wanted to explore, so I feel like it's the right thing to do to offer to be the one that she uses while she learns. I want her to do this in the safest possible way, and I just don't trust anybody else to take care of her the way I would. The more I went back and forth on it, the more I realized that I'm doing the right thing here. Of course, we'll have to keep things a secret for as long as this is going on, because the last thing I want is to lose Riggs over any of this. If I was in love with Grace and planned on being with her, I might risk it all, but that isn't what we're doing here. I'm just providing her with a safe place to explore the things she's curious about. Plus, I'll be headed to the draft next spring and Grace will only be finishing up her freshman year at college. Out of all the things I'm uncertain about with this plan, I'm confident that we'll be able to keep our feelings out of it. We have to.

Now that my mind is made up, I need to figure out how I'm going to do this. Obviously, Grace wants a man to be dominating, so I know I can't go in there and ask what she wants to do. I have to *demand* it. The thought makes my cock thicken inside my briefs.

I've been with girls who liked it a little rough before. I've pulled hair and delivered a few light spankings. I've held wrists above heads. But that was all at their request. They wanted it and I gave it. With Grace, it might be different. I don't even know what kind of experience she has sexually. She's eighteen and drop-dead gorgeous. I know she's dated a couple guys from the football team over the past year or so, one of which seemed pretty serious, so I'm sure she's done stuff, but *how much* is the question. Where do I start? This is something we'll need to talk about before anything goes down because the one thing I absolutely won't do is hurt her. Physically or emotionally. That's the whole reason I proposed this in the first place—to protect her. And I'll cut my own dick off before I ever cause her pain.

I twist the doorknob, exiting the house and crossing from my yard into hers. I'm slammed by nerves as I hit the first step of the porch, but I shove it down. I have to stay in control here. I can't show any signs of hesitation or fear. If I let my mask slip, the whole illusion will be ruined for her.

I take a breath, shaking out my shoulders and lifting my chin before reaching out and ringing the doorbell. Normally, I'd just walk in like I have every other time in the past twenty-one years, but for some reason, this feels different. Maybe I'm trying to make things less personal so we can keep what we're about to do separate from our normal relationship. I realize how dumb that is, because the reality of the situation is that once Grace and I cross this line, we can't go back. We'll always have this secret.

I can hear her on the other side of the door as she approaches. I'm half-expecting her to trip again because, despite her name, she's always been anything but graceful. As a matter of fact, Riggs and I have gotten plenty of laughs at her expense due to her incoordination. Of course, I always make sure she isn't actually hurt, but then I can't stop myself from grinning at how adorably clumsy she always is.

She makes it through the entryway unscathed before pulling the door open. "Why didn't you just come in?" she asks, her brows pulled together in confusion.

I stare like a fucking idiot, taking in her outfit. She's wearing a pair of cut-off jean shorts that are so short, I'd be telling her to march her ass right back upstairs and change if it were anyone else but me seeing her in them. The white frays tickle her creamy thighs when she pops a hip out, her sassy attitude on full display. I move my eyes up, dragging them across her stomach and up toward her tits, which are only covered by the small triangles of her pale blue bikini top. I've seen Grace in this exact outfit hundreds of times. So why, all of a sudden, is my throat closing up, making it impossible to swallow?

"You're being weird," she says, pulling my attention back to her face, making me painfully aware of the fact that I have no idea how long I was blatantly staring at her body like a fucking creep. I need to pull myself together. This is the same girl that I taught to throw a punch when Foster Bailey kept throwing sand in her hair on the playground in second grade. That little fucker had it coming when she finally hit her limit and knocked two of his baby teeth right out.

"Where's the rest of your outfit?" I ask, trying my best not to let her know how her bare skin is affecting me right now.

She rolls her eyes. "Seriously, Tanner? I'm an adult, in case you hadn't noticed. I can wear whatever I want. Plus, it was hot out and I was swimming earlier. Is that alright with you, *daddy*?" she says, a small smirk tipping up one corner of her mouth.

Motherfucking fuckety-fuck. How is she so calm and collected and I'm sweating in places I didn't even realize you could sweat from? It's like the roles are already reversed and she's in charge while I stand here silently.

Nope. We can't have that. If I can't give her what she's looking for, she's going to end up in California being tied up by some guy named Starshine who has a soul patch and survives on a diet of tofu and rainwater. *Not fucking happening.*

I collect myself, erasing the space between us in three large strides. My six-four frame towers over her by nearly a foot as I wrap my hand around her throat and lock my eyes onto hers, which are now the size of saucers. I lean in, feeling her small pants puff against my lips as I speak lowly. "Not really into the whole daddy kink thing, Bunny. But you can call me *sir*." I definitely don't miss the way her body melts into mine as I hold her neck. I can feel the way she trusts me, which just solidifies the fact that it has to be me that does this with her. And even though the scent of her vanilla perfume is making my head spin, I lean in even closer, pressing a soft kiss to her cheek. It would normally be an innocent gesture, but this one feels monumental. Like things between us are shifting into completely forbidden territory. But we're here, and we're doing this, so I may as well give her everything I can.

Grace looks up at me through her long, thick lashes. I can feel her throat work to swallow under my hand as I wait to see if she'll speak. She doesn't disappoint when she finally does.

"Yes, sir," she breathes quietly. My cock goes from six to fucking twelve at the sound, and it takes everything in me not to pin her to the wall and kiss her so hard that she'll feel me for weeks. But I can't do that yet. Not until we discuss things a little more. So, as much as I don't want to, I step back, creating enough space for us both to collect our thoughts.

"We need to talk about this before we jump in," I say, kicking off my shoes and using my foot to push them onto the mat by the door. "I will remain in charge here, so don't think for a second that you'll be getting away with trying to tell me what to do. But I need to know what you've done before and what you have or haven't liked. I want this to be enjoyable for you." The thought of hearing how far she's gone with those dickbags she dated makes me want to put my fist through a wall, but I need every shitty detail if I'm going to do this right. "So, tell me everything," I say, stepping a little closer because I can't help myself. "Tell me what they did to this tight little body, Bunny," I grit out through clenched teeth.

I wait for her answer, watching as she visibly stiffens. I also notice how she's looking everywhere but at me, which is a total one-eighty from when she was jokingly calling me daddy five minutes ago.

"Come on, Grace," I urge. "Don't clam up on me now. If we're going to do this, you can't be afraid to talk about your past experiences with me." Before I even realize what's happening, she turns, taking off toward the stairs. I dart after her, reaching her just as she hits the bottom step, and wrap my hand around her arm, halting her.

"Let go, Tanner," she says, trying to pull away, but I don't let her. Her back is still to me, her eyes locked on the top of the stairs like there's nowhere else she wants to be than up there, away from me and this conversation.

"Hey," I say, still firmly gripping her arm. "What the fuck is going on? Did somebody hurt you?" Every bad scenario goes through my head as I think of how I'm going to murder whoever touched her in a way she didn't like. Fuck a career in the NFL. I'm going to prison for life, and it'll be worth it.

She steps back onto the hardwood floor before she turns to

me. The longer she stands there with her eyes glued to her feet, the more I feel my blood boiling in my veins. Just as I'm ready to run out the door and beat the shit out of every guy I've ever seen her within ten feet of, she finally answers me.

"Nobody touched me. Like, *ever*," she whispers. A wave of relief washes over me until I go over exactly what she just said. Because the way I heard it can't be right.

"One more time," I say. "Because you're making it sound like you're a virgin." I need her to clear this up because if that's really the case, it changes everything.

She finally looks up at me, trying her best to stand tall. The confident expression on her face is fake, but it's a hell of a lot better than her running away from me. "Well, I am," she says. "And it's not a big deal."

I can't fucking believe it. I always hoped she'd stay a virgin forever, mainly because I know there isn't a man on this earth that could ever be worthy of her, but I didn't actually expect that she would. Grace was one of the most popular girls in her grade. She was the homecoming queen and captain of the cheerleading team. She never pulled anything less than straight A's and she's always been so kind to everyone. I just don't understand how she's never been touched before. I'm certain it's not from a lack of options because Riggs and I spent the better part of our time at Hope Harbor High warning guys away from her. But after we graduated, I figured she'd have her pick of anyone there.

"First of all," I say softly, "it's a very big deal. You've obviously hung on to your virginity this long for a reason. So, why now? And why jump into the deep end of the pool without even telling me? What if I hadn't found out and ended up hurting you?"

She rolls her eyes, pulling her arm from my loosened grip. "You would never hurt me. And it *isn't* a big deal to me. It's not like I was saving myself for my future husband. I came close to doing it a few times, but I chickened out at the last second. It just never felt right. And now I just want to get it over with."

She turns, walking toward the living room and plopping down on the couch like she didn't just drop a bomb on me. It takes me a minute, but I finally follow her, sinking into the plush cushions before rubbing my hands down my face. Everything in me is saying *abort mission*, but with the info Grace just gave me, I feel like the stakes are even higher. She said she came close to having sex before, but that it didn't feel right. Then, in the next breath, she said confidently that she knew I wouldn't hurt her. She wants it to be me…and I don't think I could bear the guilt if I walked out on her tonight, and she ended up with someone else who didn't take care of her.

I turn my head, my eyes locking on hers that are full of so many emotions, and I can read every single one of them. She's embarrassed, likely from the fact that I called her out for not telling me she's a virgin. She's worried, either that I'm turned off by it or that it's a complete dealbreaker for me. And she's hopeful. Hopeful that I won't call this whole thing off and leave her to explore her sexuality with someone else.

I don't make her wait long before I put all those emotions to rest.

"We still doing this, or what?"

SIX
GRACE

"WAIT. WHAT?" I say, doing a double take at Tanner sitting next to me on the couch. "You'll still do it?"

He raises a brow. "This whole thing was so I could protect you from creeps who wouldn't take care of you. The fact that you have no sexual experience doesn't really change that for me, Bunny. If anything, it makes me want to do it more," he says with a shrug.

There's a lot to unpack with that statement, starting with the fact that he isn't going to do this because he wants me, but because he's always had this incessant need to make sure I don't get hurt. But if it means finally being able to say I'm not a virgin anymore, and getting to try out some of the kinky things that had me throbbing between my legs while watching that movie, I'm willing to overlook that particular tidbit.

*Already setting that bar up nice and high, Grace. Well done. *slow clap**

I wasn't lying when I told Tanner that my v-card wasn't a big deal to me. I don't care about hearts and roses. I just want someone who will care if I like it or not. Someone who won't treat me like I'm just another hole for them to use. It's not a lot to ask, but I've *heard things*. I'm the last in my friend group to have sex, and I think hearing about their experiences made me pull back when I had the opportunity to do it with past boyfriends. That's why I'm not nervous in the slightest to do this with Tanner. I trust him and I know he'll make it good for me.

"Okay," I say, standing up from the couch and pulling my hair into a messy bun with the elastic I always wear around my wrist. "Let's fuck."

He chokes out a gasp. "Jesus, Grace!" His eyes are wide, and he looks like I just asked him if he wanted to help me bury a body. "No, we aren't just going to *fuck*. If we're doing this, we're going slow."

I stomp my foot on the floor like a child. "We don't have time to go slow, Tan. We have a week before our parents come home. Let's just," I wave my hand vaguely above my head, "get the ball rolling."

He stands, towering over me and forcing me to crane my neck up to see his face. He drags the back of his pointer finger from my collarbone down, ghosting it between my breasts, past my belly button, and hooks it under the waistband of my shorts. "You're not in charge here, Grace. I am. And we'll go as fast or as slow as I say we will. Understood?"

"Mhmm," I squeak out. My chest feels like all the air is being forced from it, just from the way his eyes are burning through my skin.

"Excuse me?" he says, looking down at me with dark eyes and the cockiest smirk I've ever seen. "What did you say? Couldn't hear you." He turns his head, putting one finger behind his ear as if trying to listen better.

I inhale sharply. "Yes…*sir*."

"That's my good girl, Bunny," he replies, pressing a ghost of a kiss to my lips. Before I even get a chance to taste him, he backs up out of my reach. I stretch up onto my tippy toes, hoping to suddenly be about a foot taller, but he's back to his full height and his lips are too far away. I don't mean to, but I let out a small whine as I lower back onto the flats of my feet.

Tanner chuckles. "Don't worry. I promise you'll get all the kisses you can handle tonight." He looks toward the front door. "But not here. Let's go to your room in case someone comes home early. I can't talk my way out of what I'm about to do to you."

My core clenches at his words and it all feels so foreign. Don't get me wrong. I've been turned on before. I've felt the aching need to orgasm, but it's never been like this. I feel like I need him inside me. Like I'm so empty right now. I want to feel him fill me up, stretching me to my absolute limit. And I don't know how much longer I can wait.

I nod my head rapidly, swallowing the lump in my throat as I grab his hand and practically run toward the stairs. He follows, laughing quietly at my eagerness to be behind a closed door with him so we can get this thing going. If I wasn't so desperate right now, I'd be embarrassed as I take the stairs two at a time and yank this man, that outweighs me by almost a hundred pounds, through the doorway to my room. I drop his hand, turning just in time to see him kick the door shut.

We stand there, just staring for a moment. I watch as his blue eyes somehow darken and the corner of his mouth tips up in a wicked smirk. I'm frozen in place, realizing that my nerves have finally entered the chat. I feel my insides trembling and I'm just praying my outsides don't join in as well. Even though Tanner knows I haven't had much experience being touched, I don't want to look like a complete loser. My normal confidence and who-gives-a-fuck attitude are nowhere to be found as he walks toward me, closing the distance between us in just a couple strides of his long, thick legs. By the time he reaches out, settling his hand on my hip, I'm ready to melt into a puddle at his feet.

"Like I said," he rasps, "we're going to go slow, but I need to know what you've done and what you haven't, okay? And you have to be honest with me."

It takes me a few seconds to remember that there are, in fact, other guys that exist on this planet. And that, despite the fact that something as simple as a light touch to my side is making me feel like his are the first hands that have ever been on my body, they aren't.

"Umm," I say, trying to gather myself. "My ex-boyfriend put his hand in my pants last year, but I stopped him because it didn't really feel good. And...and," I start to lose my train of thought as I breathe him in, but somehow manage to keep it together, "Cash Hadley got me out of my bra a couple months ago at a party. I let him, umm..." I stutter as Tanner's grip tightens.

"You let him *what*, Grace?" he grits through clenched teeth.

Fuck. I don't even want to say it. I'd actually prefer for the floor to open up and swallow me right now.

"I let him put his mouth on me. On my boobs," I whisper, unable to look him in the eyes.

"Cash fucking Hadley?" he asks, clearly angry. "My fucking backup quarterback? Why was he even at a high school party in the first place? He graduated two years ago."

I furrow my brows in confusion. "I don't know. He went to Hope Harbor Community College and still lives here, I guess. We were dancing and he kissed me. One thing led to another and—"

I'm cut off when Tanner crashes his lips to mine in a bruising kiss. My eyes go wide at first, because it's the last thing I was expecting, but it only takes a few seconds before I'm giving it right back. I've never been kissed this thoroughly before. It's never felt so...*charged*.

His hands find their way into my hair, gripping firmly to hold my head in place as he forces my mouth open with his tongue, plunging it inside. I let him dominate me, taking whatever he wants as I get used to the way he feels. I don't even realize I'm white-knuckling the soft fabric of his t-shirt until my fists begin to cramp, but I don't let go. I can't. I want to keep him right here, kissing me, forever.

I feel the growl coming from his throat as he moves his hands down, tilting my neck to the side before he begins trailing his lips and tongue downward. He takes time to suck gently at my skin, eliciting a moan that's a lot louder than I intend, but I can't fucking control it. I'm at Tanner's mercy right now. My body is his to command and he hasn't really even touched it yet.

I'm reveling in the feel of his mouth on me when my bathing suit top goes slack around my back. His hand, that just untied the string wrapped around me, slides to the front of my body, where my breasts are now completely bare between us. He pulls my top over my head, tossing it aside before taking a small step back to look at me as I stand topless in front of him.

"Fuck, Bunny," he chokes out. "Your tits are perfect."

All the embarrassment I should probably be experiencing right now takes a back seat to the ache between my legs. I can feel my bikini bottoms becoming damp under my shorts, and all I want to do is reach my hand inside to quell the throbbing. I have to ball my fists at my sides to stop myself, because I'm desperate to see what he does next.

Returning his hands back to my hips, Tanner squeezes before dipping his head down and licking around my nipple. I suck in a quick breath at the contact, because even though I've done this before, it didn't feel like it does with him.

"Mmmm," he hums. "Your skin is my new favorite flavor." He sucks gently on my puckered bud, making a bolt of electricity shoot down between my legs so fast, my knees almost buckle. They might if he wasn't holding me up.

"Tell me, Gracie girl. Did that douchebag Cash make your

clit throb when he did this? Did he make your body shake like it is right now?"

Fuck. I *am* shaking. I just now notice the adrenaline spreading throughout my body, causing involuntary tremors to rack all of my limbs. I try my best to pull myself together, so I don't look like a complete amateur in front of him, but it's no use. I'm losing control and we've only just started.

I remember that he asked me a question, but I'm unable to make more than a pathetic squeaking sound at the moment, so I just shake my head. Because, no, Cash definitely didn't make me feel this way. In this moment, I'm convinced nobody else in the world ever could. Only Tanner.

"Yeah, I figured as much. You poor girl. I'm going to take care of you," he coos. The tone of his voice makes me feel like I could combust, and even if he stopped and walked away from me right now, it would still be the single hottest moment of my life.

Holding my hips, he walks me backward until the backs of my thighs hit my bed. He pushes gently, and I land on the mattress with a soft *thud*. Tanner has always been a lot taller than me, but now that I'm sitting in front of him, I realize just how vast the size difference is. He is so imposing and dominating in the most delicious way, and I haven't even experienced the full effect of it yet.

He brings his hands to my face, tilting it upward so that we're looking into each other's eyes. I try my best not to be completely entranced by just how beautiful he is and the amount of tenderness I see in his expression as he stares down at me. I know it's only been seconds, but it feels like he's been studying me for hours before he leans back down and kisses me again.

"Is it okay if I take off your shorts?" he asks. "We're still going to go slow, but I want them out of the way."

I can barely find my breath long enough to reply. I haven't even moved, yet I feel like I just ran a marathon. "Yes, please," I whisper. I don't trust my voice to speak any louder right now.

"Lie back for a second," he says. I obey, and he immediately trails his fingers from my face down my body until he reaches the button of my shorts. He goes at an agonizingly slow pace as he unfastens them, sliding the zipper down before pulling the denim down my legs. I'm left in my white bathing suit bottom with light blue ties at the sides. I'm afraid that when I open my legs, he'll be able to see just how much this is turning me on. Even though they have extra padding in the gusset, I'm completely sure I'm starting to soak through them already. I don't know if I should be embarrassed about it or not, but I can't find it in me to give a shit while he's hovering over me like this.

With my shorts tossed aside, Tanner grabs around my waist and hoists me up the bed so my head is on the pillow. He lies beside me and returns his lips to mine as his hands roam freely all over my body. I'm still shaking, but it's not because I'm cold. I can't put my finger on exactly which emotion has me trembling, but if I had to try, I'd say it's a mixture between nerves, desperation, and excitement. I've never felt so much all at once.

I get lost in the kiss. I'm consumed by the way his tongue explores the inside of my mouth, the little movements causing sparks to prick all over my body. When he moves his hand down, putting pressure on the mound above my clit, I let out a loud moan. That seems to spur him on further as he continues his descent and presses the pad of his middle finger on my bundle of nerves through my bathing suit. I'm not sure if he's taking things slowly because he thinks I need it, or because he's just enjoying teasing me, but either way, I can't take it anymore. My hips begin to move on their own accord, trying to create some friction between his fingers and the part of me that's aching to have him.

"Needy little girl," he chides, letting me continue to rub

on him as he presses to the fabric. Normally, him calling me a little girl would piss me off, but right now, it just might be the hottest thing I've ever heard. Especially knowing that once we get all of this beginner stuff out of the way, he'll be completely in charge of everything when we're together. I can't wait to know what it's like to let him dominate me. The thought has me making larger circles with my hips and whining in frustration because I can't quite get what I need.

As if he knows what I'm thinking, Tanner finally takes mercy on me and slides his hand up just enough to slip it between my bottoms and my most intimate part. A part that, up until now, has always felt wrong when a guy touched it. I should have known it would be different with him. Just feeling the calluses on his fingertips against my newly bare flesh is enough to make me want to orgasm without him even touching my clit. We are every bit the contradiction that I feel with his rough skin against my soft skin, but I've never felt more connected to another human being in my whole life.

He finally gives me what I've been silently begging for when he begins to rub tight circles over my aching bud. I can't control the volume of the moans coming out of my body, not that I want to. I want him to know how good this feels. I want him to know that I'll do anything as long as he doesn't stop.

Just when I think it can't possibly feel any better, he inches down just a little bit more and gently pushes the tip of his middle finger between my lips.

"Fuck, Bunny. You're soaking wet. All this just from a little kissing and rubbing?" he teases. "You're going to be a lot of fun."

"I've never felt like this before," I say on a breath just as he enters me up to the first knuckle. It isn't uncomfortable because I've gotten this far by myself, but I've always been too nervous to go any further. He takes his time, pumping gently in and out as he uses his thumb to rub my clit back and forth. I'm a writhing mess next to him as he carefully coaxes me toward my release. It's the most euphoric thing I've ever felt, and we're not even done yet.

"I'm going to go in a little farther, okay?" he asks. "Tell me if it hurts, and I'll stop."

I huff a breathy laugh. "Tanner, you could hit me with your car right now and I wouldn't want you to stop. Please keep going. I want to feel you inside me." I'm sure I sound beyond desperate right now, but I really want this.

He chuckles before leaning back down to take my lips again. Just as I'm falling into the kiss, he pushes his finger further into my pussy. There's a bit of a sting, but the pleasure definitely outweighs any type of discomfort. I don't hold back the satisfied sounds as they come out of my mouth, wanting him to know that I like what he's doing to me.

"Look at you," he says, pulling his head back so he can drag his eyes down my body. "Taking my finger so well. What a good fucking girl you are."

I know the moment he feels my muscles clench at his words because his eyes widen. That makes him double down and pick up his pace, finally bottoming out with his middle finger inside me. He doesn't stop or slow as I feel my release begin to tighten in my core. My pants and moans have become so loud, I would be worried that Tanner's parents could hear them from next door if they were home. Thankfully for us, there's no one within earshot. I let it all out for him.

"Your pussy is getting so tight. It's practically strangling my finger. You going to come for me, baby?" he asks. I nod my head rapidly because I'm already there, every muscle in my body seizing as he buries his finger to the hilt. My orgasm takes over and my back bows from the bed. I can't think. I can't breathe. I can't do anything but surrender to the waves of pleasure as they crash into me over and over again. It feels like minutes have gone by before my body finally loosens. I sink into the mattress, my heart pounding wildly behind my ribcage as I try to catch my breath.

My eyes are still closed, but I feel Tanner's lips press against my cheek. "You look like an angel when you come. Did you know that?" he breathes into my skin. I want more of him.

I want *all* of him. Like, right now.

I fist his shirt, pulling him to me and crashing my mouth to his. Even though I just got off, I can already feel the need building inside me again, but I don't want all of this to be just about me. I want to make him feel good too. I want to touch him everywhere and taste his skin. I want to know what it feels like to take his cock into my mouth and hear the sounds he makes as I do it. I want all of that.

I push him back just enough to roll onto my side, snaking my hand up his shirt. The muscles of his abs flex under my touch, and I'm already so turned on again that I can barely think straight. I trace my fingertips through the dips above his sweats, and when I eagerly start to lower my shaky hand under the waistband, he grabs my wrist and stops me.

"I said we were taking things slow, Grace. As much as I want you to touch me everywhere, I think that's enough for tonight," he says softly.

Everything in my body deflates. "Oh. Okay," I say, trying to conjure up as much confidence as I can. I don't want to seem clingy, but I can't say it doesn't hurt that we just did that and now he wants to go. It's a little embarrassing now that I have the wherewithal to think about it.

I push myself into a sitting position before swinging my legs off the bed. Just as I go to stand so I can gather my clothes and not be so exposed in front of him, a strong arm bands around my waist.

"Whoa, Bunny. Where are you running off to so fast?" he says. I turn to look over my shoulder at him, seeing his cocky smirk. "Not going to lie, I'm feeling pretty used right now. Didn't take you for the *love 'em and leave 'em* type."

I give him a weak smile. "You said—" I begin, "I thought you wanted to go." The last thing I want is for him to think he has to stay if he doesn't want to. I understand what we're doing here. I know this isn't a relationship and that he's just helping me explore my sexuality. So, I don't want him to feel like he's on the hook for anything once we're done.

"Of course I don't want to go," he says on a laugh. "Do you really think I would do what we just did and then not spend time with you afterward?"

I don't know what I think. I only know what I want, and I definitely want him to stay here with me. Even though being fingered is probably not a big deal for most girls my age, that was my first time and I'm feeling all kinds of things. Mostly, I just feel happy and satisfied. And I'm glad it was with Tanner. I knew he would take care of me, but everything that just happened felt so right. I'm kind of relieved after all the times I tried doing things with other guys and just couldn't go through with it. I guess all it took was finding someone I trusted.

I smile at him. "Are you telling me you want to cuddle, hot shot?"

He scoffs. "Duh, Gracie girl. It's the least you can do after I just gave you a mind-blowing orgasm."

I laugh, lying back down next to him and letting him wrap his arms around me. "It was okay," I shrug. I'm obviously teasing him because he's right. That absolutely blew my mind. But I'm not going to let his ego get any bigger by telling him that.

He rolls us over so he's on top of me before digging his fingertips into my side to tickle me. "Just okay?" he says, continuing his assault. I let out a very unladylike snort as I laugh hysterically while he pins me down.

After proving his point, he stops tickling me and leans

down to press a chaste kiss to my lips. "Keep it up with that smart mouth and we're going to fast-forward to the punishment part of this little experiment," he says with a raised brow. I feel my insides clench, imagining what it'll be like when he has me tied up and makes me pay for being a brat—which I inevitably will because it's who I am as a person.

Tanner knows me so well, that I'm sure he can tell the dopey look on my face was brought on by those exact dirty thoughts.

He smirks again before reaching over me to grab the remote control off my nightstand. He pulls me into him as he turns on the TV and opens the streaming app. "You better pick something to watch this time, Bunny. You saw what happened when you let me choose," he says with a wink.

I laugh quietly, knowing that letting him decide on that movie last night is going to make for the most epic summer ever.

SEVEN
TANNER

I WAKE SLOWLY, immediately loving the way I've got Grace wrapped in my arms. Sometime in the middle of the night, I removed my shirt, so we're skin-to-skin from the waist up. She's curled into me, her slow, soft breaths puffing against my bare chest.

I keep trying to sort through the mess of emotions I'm feeling about what went down last night. We both know this can't go further than just a physical thing for the summer, but I refuse to do this without also showing her that she deserves to be cared for and appreciated at the same time. The reason I insisted that she do this with me was because I wanted to protect her. That includes her heart. I have a chance to set the bar for what she accepts from any guy that comes after me, and I'm planning on setting that fucker to the goddamn moon. Making sure we don't cross any lines is going to be hard, but that's how it has to be. I just have to keep my eyes on the goal here, which is to give her a safe place to try everything she wants to try before she heads to California.

I look down, tightening my hold on her just a little bit. I can't stop myself from carefully burying my nose in her hair and inhaling her soft, vanilla scent. And when I press my lips to her head, she stirs, a small whine coming from her tired body. I laugh to myself because Grace is definitely *not* a morning person. She never has been. Even as a kid, she'd stomp into the kitchen like a pissed off gremlin, scowling and grunting at us while we laughed at her messy hair and half-closed eyes. She was still cute as hell, though. Just like she is now.

"Morning, Bunny," I say quietly.

"No," she rasps, making me laugh. She's going to need a vat of coffee and a bag of Sour Patch Kids to fix her attitude. I can already tell. But first, I have an idea.

"Be right back," I say, slipping out of the bed and walking over to her sewing table where I spotted a spool of pink ribbon yesterday. It immediately got my wheels spinning, but I wanted to start vanilla and work our way to the kinkier stuff. But this is technically still beginner level...kinda, so why not?

I look back to the bed where Grace is still facing my side, her hands extended onto the warm spot I was lying in just a minute ago. I take her fabric scissors and cut about three feet of ribbon before walking back over and kneeling on the mattress. As I begin tying it around her wrists, binding them together, her eyes flutter open.

"What are you doing?" she asks, not pulling away in protest. I take that as her consent to continue.

"Tying you up so I can have my way with you," I say with a shit-eating grin.

It takes her a moment to process my words, but when she does, her eyes snap open wide. I can't help but laugh quietly as she stares up at me like a deer in headlights while I continue winding the ribbon around her wrists tightly enough so she won't be able to escape. I finish it off by pulling it into a pretty little pink bow, which makes me feel a fuck ton more deviant than I should right now.

I roll her to her back and pull the covers off her still naked body, taking a quick second to admire her soft skin and mouthwatering curves before I take her bound wrists and place them above her head "I want you to keep your arms there the whole time. No matter what I do to you or how good it feels, you're not to move them. Do you understand?" I ask.

"Yes," she says on an exhale.

I don't waste any more time, leaning down and taking her mouth in a heated kiss. There's no testing the waters this time. We're beyond that. So, when I flatten my tongue on her lips, she opens for me to push it inside. She moans at my forceful intrusion, letting me take what I want from her. My intention was to show a little more dominance than I did last night because I know that's what she ultimately wants from this arrangement, but I'd be lying if I said she was the only person I was trying to please here. I'm surprised by how hard I am just from kissing her right now, and how quickly I'm turning feral as our kiss becomes frantic and almost pornographic. My animal instincts are double daring me to rip off my boxer briefs, pin her down to the mattress, and spear my cock into her as hard as I can, but I know I need to push that away. Possibly forever. Grace isn't just some girl. I refuse to treat her like she is.

I lower my body onto her and settle between her legs that are already open, inviting me in. I didn't let myself feel her, even through my clothes, last night. So, when I press my dick against her exposed pussy, I have to grit my teeth at how it feels. I can feel her warmth and wetness as it seeps through the fabric between us. I thrust my hips forward, creating a friction that feels like too much and not enough all at once.

"You're already wet, aren't you, beautiful?" I say into her ear. "Such a good girl getting ready for me. Do you want my finger again?"

"Please," she whimpers.

I kiss her again as I reluctantly put space between us so I

can slide my hand down, rubbing gentle circles over her clit as it swells and hardens under my touch. I can tell she's struggling to keep her arms over her head by the way they twitch every time I increase the pressure. Part of me wants her to disobey to see how well she'd take a little punishment, but the other part knows how quickly I could lose control in that situation before she's ready.

When Grace's needy whines fill my mouth, I know she's wound up enough for me to go a little further. I run the pad of my middle finger along her slit, gathering as much of her wetness as I can to make it more comfortable for her when I slide in. Taking a chance to see how she reacts, I lower my finger just a little more, rubbing it against the sensitive skin between her pussy and asshole. And let me fucking tell you, she does *not* disappoint. Her fists clench above her head at the same time her hips lift off the mattress, causing me to push into that spot harder. The most beautiful moan slips from her lips when I do.

"Good to know," I say, trying to sound like I'm not ready to bust in my shorts at the thought of pushing into her forbidden hole as she cries out for more.

"Tan," she chokes out, "I need…I need,"

I smirk. "I know what you need, Bunny," I reply as I enter her warmth with one finger. She sighs in relief as I pump in and out as slowly as I can, hoping to get her even hornier than she already is. I want to hear her beg. I want her desperate for me to blow her mind.

"M-more. Please," she stutters. "*Please.*"

That was quick.

"Aww," I pout. "Being finger fucked slowly like this isn't enough for you?" I continue at the same pace, taking my time to speak as the sound of her wetness and heavy breaths fill the room. "How about I use my tongue? Would that be better?"

She doesn't say anything. She just nods her head rapidly as she whimpers.

"Gonna need you to say the words, Grace. Tell me you want me to taste this virgin pussy."

She opens her bright blue eyes, locking onto mine. I can see the hesitation. She's never been spoken to like this, and she's definitely never said those words before, other than when she was trying to rattle me earlier. Why would she? They're filthy and she's a fucking angel. But I'm ready to knock that halo of hers right off.

I raise a brow, nearly halting the movement of my finger inside her as I wait for her to submit.

C'mon, baby. Say it.

"I want you to," she pauses, swallowing thickly, "taste my virgin pussy."

"Fuck," I say on a forced exhale. I'm feeling as desperate as she sounds right now. "Remember to keep your arms above your head. If you move them, it all goes away and I won't let you come," I warn as I move down her body, taking time to trail open-mouthed kisses on her flushed skin. She writhes beneath me, clearly uncomfortable from being so turned on with no relief. She's taking it like a champ, though. I'm proud of her.

All I have to do is nudge under one knee with the back of my hand and she opens wider for me. Her smooth, creamy thighs lead right up to her apex, where she's actually dripping. Like, real wetness is running out of the bottom of her pussy, and my mouth waters with the urge to lean in and drink from her. I almost forget it's her first time doing this, which means I need to keep going slowly. As much as I want to feast on her, I don't want it to be overwhelming. There will be plenty of time for me to eat her the way I really want to later. For now, I need to focus on making all of this perfect for her.

I lean forward, dragging my tongue across her hot skin,

everywhere except where she's aching for me. And just as I go to press my tongue to her sweetness, I get an idea.

I quickly move back up her body, chuckling at the loud huff of annoyance that leaves her lips. I take the pillow from my side of the bed before wrapping my hand gently behind her neck so I can prop her head up.

"I want you to watch me," I say before dropping my lips to hers quickly. I crawl back down her body, never breaking eye contact as I do. When I finally lean in, licking her slit from bottom to top, her eyes flutter and roll back.

"Grace," I say, recapturing her attention, "watch it happen."

When she obeys, I flatten my tongue to her clit, flicking it quickly. An uncontrolled, guttural moan leaves her when I change tactics, drawing the sensitive bundle of nerves between my lips and sucking gently.

"Tanner," she gasps, and my name on her lips makes me feel like the luckiest motherfucker in the world that I'm the first to taste her. I'm torn between giving her everything I have so I can feel her explode around my tongue, and going so slowly that I never have to stop. I've only been down here a minute and I'm absolutely sure I'm addicted.

"That's it, baby. Let me make you feel good," I rasp. I use my tongue to massage every part of her, using varying patterns and pressures to find exactly what she likes. She begins moving her hips, trying to shove herself into my face, so I press harder, sinking my tongue inside. Now it's my turn for my eyes to roll back.

"Fuck, Grace," I mumble. I've never tasted anything better in my goddamn life. If I never have another meal, I'd be fine with that. This is all I need.

I take my time licking and fucking her with my tongue, feeling her muscles start to tighten as her orgasm builds. The sounds we're making fill the room and my restraint almost snaps as a small gush of wetness covers my lips. She's so close, she's leaking all over my face. My cock is painfully hard and all I want is to dip it inside her for just a second.

Soon.

"Mmmmm!" she whines, and I know it won't take much to push her over the edge. She's kept her arms over her head this whole time like such a good girl. She deserves to come her fucking brains out.

I keep my pace, looking up at her as she stares right into my eyes. And when I pull her clit into my mouth, sucking hard, she detonates. A loud scream leaves her as her whole body convulses, surrendering to the most intense orgasm I've ever witnessed. Only then does she bring her arms down, fisting my hair and holding me tightly to her. I grunt into her sensitive skin, not slowing or letting up until her muscles relax and she sinks into the mattress. I unlatch from her, gently licking around the outside of her cunt until she whimpers from the overstimulation. As much as I'd love to see what she could handle, I stop myself.

Kissing my way back up her body, I hover over her, taking in the satisfied look on her face. Her chest is heaving as she tries to catch her breath. Her skin is flushed a beautiful pink and glistening with a sheen of sweat. She's the most beautiful goddamn thing I've ever seen in my life, and I think I might be just a tiny bit fucked, because my heart squeezes in my chest at the sight of her lying under me.

Her eyes open and she gives me a lazy smile. "That was…" she says, shaking her head in disbelief. "Wow."

I laugh, leaning down and taking her mouth in a slow, sensual kiss. I give her the opportunity to lick her taste off my tongue, which she does. My hard cock twitches and even though I don't mean to, my hips thrust forward on instinct. It feels so good that I keep doing it, even after telling myself repeatedly to make this about her right now. Plus, I'm barely hanging on to my restraint as it is. I need to get my shit together before I accidentally push her too far, too soon.

"Tanner," she says into the kiss.

"Mmhmm," I reply, keeping my lips pressed to hers.

"I want to make you feel good."

I pull back, the internal conflict obviously apparent on my face because her expression deflates a little.

God, I want that. More than anything. But if we cross that line, where I'm the only one getting pleasure from something we do, it's no longer just for Grace. It's for me, too, and it obliterates the imaginary line I drew in the sand. The line where, if I stayed on the right side, I could justify this whole situation by saying I was just trying to protect her. Otherwise, I'm taking advantage of her *and* betraying my best friend.

"Please?" she says, her expression full of hope and determination. "Teach me to suck your cock, Tan."

Buh bye, self-control. It was so nice hanging with you for the last twelve hours.

You know what? Fuck it.

Fuck. It.

Either she learns here with me, or she learns with someone else. What if he's too rough and ruptures her esophagus or something?

That's probably not medically possible, but let's just say it is. For the sake of my delusions…and the fact that if I don't get in her mouth in about five seconds, she's going to watch me come in my pants like an idiot.

"You want to swallow me, baby?" I ask.

"Yes," she breathes. Her eyes twinkle as I stand from the bed, pulling her up and untying the ribbon on her wrists. I check to make sure there aren't any red marks from her pulling on it, but she's all good.

"On your knees then, Bunny. Let's see how fast of a learner you are."

EIGHT
GRACE

I SINK TO MY KNEES, settling in front of Tanner, looking up at him while I wait for further instruction. I've never done this before, but I've watched enough porn to know the basics. I'm not going to let him know that though. I want to see how he teaches me. I want to know exactly what he likes so I can make him feel as good as he made me feel.

I can't help but notice how strong and tall he looks, towering over me. Even though I just came, I can feel the coil of warmth start to bloom back to life inside me.

"Lick it through the fabric," he orders. I immediately obey, placing my hands on his thick, muscular thighs, and dart my tongue out to swipe over the small spot of wetness in the front of his boxer briefs. As impossible as I thought it was, his taste explodes on my tongue, and all I can think about is how badly I want more.

I press further into him, opening my mouth and putting my lips over the head of his cock. He hisses through his teeth and his hand grabs hold of my hair. He doesn't pull, he just holds me there as I move my mouth around, gauging his reactions.

"Fuck, baby," he says. "I'm not even in your mouth yet

and I'm already on the verge of coming." I preen under his praise and decide to make the next move as I grab his waistband and pull down enough for his cock to spring free. I could tell it was big by the way it felt rubbing against me a few minutes ago, but I certainly wasn't prepared for the real thing. Not only is it long, but it's so thick. Wide veins wrap around the length of it, and I swear I can see it pulsing with need. My mouth waters even more now that I know I get to taste it.

"Touch it, Grace," he commands. I'm too excited to hesitate, so I reach up, wrapping my hand around as much of it as I can. He's so big, I can't even connect my fingers while I hold him.

He sucks in a breath. "Fuck. Stroke me. Firm grip, up and down slowly."

I do as he says, tightening my hand until I see the muscles in his abs flex. And when I start stroking him up and down, his hips immediately begin to thrust into my grip. As much as I want to look at his dick, I'm completely entranced by the expression on his face as I jerk him off. His eyes are closed, and his mouth is hanging open as he sucks in deep breaths, exhaling forcefully every time I tighten my fist.

He opens his eyes and looks down at me. The intimate way we're staring into each other is almost too much for me, but I can't seem to tear myself away from it. I want him inside of me in every way.

"Put your mouth on me," he says, and I don't have to be told twice. I brace my hands back on his thighs and slowly lower down on him. He stays still, letting me explore him with my tongue. I run it along the thick veins, pulling back to the tip and giving a gentle suck. I know he likes the move by the way his breathing stops and his hand flexes in my hair.

I want to make him do that again.

I continue bobbing my head up and down, changing my pace and the amount of suction I have on him. I'm obviously doing a good job, because he's stopped giving me instructions and is just letting me do my own thing. When I abandon one thigh to cup his balls, giving them a gentle squeeze, he lets out a whimper that makes my thighs clench together.

I made him fucking *whimper*. And it was the hottest thing I've ever experienced in my entire life.

"Holy shit, baby," he says, barely able to catch his breath. "You're a natural. Keep doing that. You're going to make me come."

I can't think of anything I've ever wanted more than that, so I pick up my pace, continuing to gently flex my fingers around his balls as I suck him. I take him further back into my throat, and when the head of his cock brushes against my gag reflex, I constrict around him. At first, I'm embarrassed because that's *got to be* a turnoff for him. Isn't gagging while blowing a guy a rookie move?

"Oh, fuck," he chokes out. "Feels so good when you gag on me." Surprised, I repeat the motion, making him moan. And when his abs tighten, I know he's there. Warmth floods my tongue as he comes with a loud grunt. Whatever I was expecting, I was wrong. I thought I would hate it, but the taste of his pleasure, and the fact that I caused it makes my clit begin to throb between my thighs.

I pull my mouth from him, swallowing his load before I wipe the rest that's dripping from my lips. I can't help but suck it from my finger, making sure to look up at him as I do it.

"Fuck, Bunny. You're amazing," he says on a heavy breath. He reaches down and takes my hand, pulling me up to stand in front of him. Definitely not expecting what happens next, I'm almost knocked off my feet when he grabs my cheeks and kisses me hard. Apparently, he doesn't care that he just came in my mouth, because he parts my lips with his tongue and pushes it inside. I moan into his mouth, barely keeping myself together, but just as I'm about to beg him for more of whatever he's willing to offer, he pulls away.

"You did such a good job," he praises. "I can definitely see myself getting addicted to that pretty little mouth of yours."

"Really?" I say in disbelief. "I'm not bad at it?"

He huffs an incredulous laugh. "You just sucked my soul out of my body through my dick, Grace. No, you're not bad at it." He gives my ass a little pat and moves toward my dresser, pulling out a pair of shorts and a tank top. "Let's get dressed and get some breakfast. I'm sure all that sucking dick has you famished." I roll my eyes, allowing him to pull the tank over my head. I go to reach for my top drawer so I can take out a clean pair of panties, but he grabs my wrist, halting me. "Nope," he says. "I might need more of you later and I want easy access to that sweet cunt." My eyes go wide at his dirty mouth, but he just chuckles, bending down in front of me so I can step into the shorts. He pulls them up my legs, returning to his full height and placing a gentle kiss on my lips before he wordlessly walks out the door.

Well, fuck.

NINE
TANNER

"YOU CAN'T JUST EAT a bag of candy for breakfast, Bunny. You need nutrients," I say, pulling my bowl of oatmeal out of the microwave.

She scoffs. "I'd hardly call," she pauses, turning the bag of Sour Patch Kids so she can read the back, "twenty-nine grams of carbohydrates *innutritious*. That's eleven percent of my daily value, thank you very much."

I cock my head to the side, perplexed. "I'm not sure you understand any of what you just said." This girl is cute as hell and smart as a whip, but she will go toe-to-toe with anyone who tries to separate her from that disgusting candy.

"Sure I do," she replies, popping a red one in her mouth. "It means I could eat like, eight more bags of these today and still be fine."

"Riiiiiight," I say, giving up. This is a battle I know I won't win. Sitting down beside her at the island, I stir the boring ass food in my bowl and take a bite. It *does* taste like shit, but eating healthily is a priority right now so my body is ready when we start two-a-days next month. This is my last chance to show the Blizzard that I'm the absolute best choice for their organization. Next April, I can't imagine any other team saying my name at the draft. This has been my dream since the first time I set foot on a football field, and I'll do whatever it takes to get there.

"What do you have going on today?" she asks, brushing the sour sugar from her hands.

I swallow the almost flavorless mush before speaking. "Hanging out with you. What do you want to do?"

A blush creeps over her cheeks, and I can already tell what she's thinking. She wants to head back upstairs and fast-forward to the kinky shit. Call me crazy, but I actually like taking it slow. It's building tension, and when I finally do sink into her, it's going to be amazing for her. And for me, if I'm being honest.

I know everyone has their own thoughts on what their first time should be like. Mine was forgettable. In fact, I can't even remember the girl's name. I was a sophomore in high school, and we were at an away game. It was an overnight trip and some of our guys snuck the opposing team's cheer-leaders into the hotel. One of them was super clingy with me and when she asked to go somewhere private to talk, we went to my room. One thing led to another, and I came in approximately two pumps.

Not my finest thirty seconds.

Grace claims that losing her virginity is the means to an end, but there's no way I'm just going to go through the motions. I plan on making it special for her even though we aren't actually together. She deserves to be treated like a fucking princess, and that's what she's going to get. That's why it's so important for me to spend time with her when we aren't getting down and dirty with each other.

Believe it or not, boyfriend energy doesn't come easily to me. I had a couple girlfriends in high school, but as soon as I realized how much time I'd need to devote to football, I decided to be upfront with any of the girls I spent time with. I wanted to make sure they all knew going into our hookups, that I couldn't offer them anything more than sex and maybe me staying the night after. But once the sun came up, I left and didn't go back. Sleeping with someone more than once can result in blurred lines and hurt feelings, which I don't want. Every day, I'm closer to my goal of being in the NFL, and I can't fumble on this. *No pun intended.*

But this is different. This is just an arrangement between me and Grace. We're both very clear on the rules, and we both have a lot to lose if we don't follow them. First and foremost, Riggs would be pissed at us both. Me, especially. Then, there's our whole future. She's going off to college across the country. Tying herself down to anyone is a bad idea when she should be focusing on her career in fashion design. Not to mention, being with a professional athlete is emotionally draining, from what I've heard. I'm not even in the pros yet and women still throw themselves at me regularly. Even if I didn't take them up on the buffet of pussy that's constantly being offered up, anyone I'm with would have to be at home, worrying every time I walked out the door.

So even if I did, by some crazy stretch of the imagination, want to be with Grace, I could never do that to her. She deserves better, which is why it shouldn't be hard for me to do this and let her go in a few months, knowing we tried everything she wanted to.

"Want to go to the movies?" she asks. "We can go to the one right outside Boston and see a matinee, so there are less people around to see us together."

I cock a brow. "You embarrassed to be seen with me, Bunny?" I tease. We've hung out all our lives, with and without her brother. Everyone in town has seen me walk down the street with Grace tucked under my arm, and they wouldn't give it a second thought if they saw me drop a quick kiss to the top of her head. It's just…*us*. So, I'm wondering what's making her say this.

She shrugs, looking down at her hands, which are

fidgeting in her lap. "Not at all. I just didn't know if you'd want people thinking something is going on between us."

I bring my bowl over to the sink, rinsing it and placing it into the dishwasher before walking back over to where she sits on a backless barstool. From behind, I drape my arms around her, pulling her into my chest and kissing her jaw. She tilts her head, giving me easy access to her neck. I run my lips down past her ear, sucking the sensitive skin as her breathing quickens. "They won't," I say, trying to reassure her. "And even if they do," I pause to lick along her neck, "who cares? I want to take you somewhere." I should care, but we've been out together plenty of times. If people were going to suspect anything, they'd have done it already.

"Mmm," she mewls at the feel of me lightly sucking on her heated flesh. "Okay."

"There's my girl," I say, sneakily darting my hand forward and swiping the bag of candy that sits in front of her. "But you aren't bringing these. Eat some Sno-Caps like a normal moviegoer."

She reaches for the bag, but I pull it away, holding it high above my head.

"Tanner!" she whines, making me laugh. "Give me my kids back. I can't just leave them behind! We're a package deal, so get over it!"

I shake my head, pressing a chaste kiss to her lips before giving her the bag back. She looks inside as if I've injured her precious babies before looking at me with a scowl. "It's hard out here as a single mom."

"You're so weird," I reply, giving her ass a playful tap. "Let's get ready to go."

TEN
GRACE

I SLOWLY DRIFT AWAKE, immediately feeling Tanner's warm body pressed against my back. I have to keep reminding myself that I can't let my feelings get involved with this whole thing, but it hasn't been easy.

Yesterday, we went to the movies, trying our best to look like two pals hanging out until the lights dimmed, leaving us in the dark with only three other people in the large room, seated way up in front of us. It wasn't long before his hand slid down the front of my shorts, stroking my clit while he whispered dirty things into my ear until I quietly orgasmed.

I was hoping that when we got back, he'd finally make the move and take my virginity, but he didn't. Instead, he went down on me until I begged him to give me a break. I woke up in the middle of the night, seeing him lying there naked, and couldn't stop myself from kissing down his body and taking him into my mouth. He woke up, grinning down at me sleepily before digging his hand into my hair and controlling my movements until I was gagging and gasping for breath. By the time he finally came, my face was covered in tears and my throat was sore in the most delicious way.

I can tell he's starting to let go a little. At first, he was so careful, treating me like I might break if he was even the slightest bit rough. But each time, he's given me a little bit more of the dominance I'm dying to experience.

"Mmm," he hums, pressing his nose into my hair. "Morning, beautiful."

"Morning," I rasp, pressing my ass into his cock, which is already hard. He tightens his hold on me as I move slowly, grinding back into him. His fingers move up and down my bare stomach, reminding me that we're both completely naked and turned on.

Is this it? Could we *actually* do it this time?

Nerves take over my insides, but I want this so badly. In fact, I've never wanted anything more in my whole life. It's gone from just wishing it was over and done with, to actually longing to give my body to Tanner completely.

I roll to my back, and he immediately starts moving his lips all over my skin. My neck. My collarbone. My shoulder. And when he works his way to my tits, taking one tight, hard nipple into his mouth, I moan loudly. I can feel myself getting more aroused by the second as he sucks and bites on the sensitive peak. I have to squeeze my thighs together to quell the ache that's pulling at my core.

"Are you wet, baby?" he coos, lowering his hand between my thighs. I open for him immediately and my heart pounds in my chest as he rubs my slit, groaning at what he finds. I whimper, lifting my hips from the bed, trying to get him to push inside. I need him. I'm desperate for all of him.

He stills for a moment, looking into my eyes. "Are you sure you're ready, Grace? I need you to be absolutely positive. Once it's gone, you can't get it back," he says, his expression completely serious.

"I'm ready," I whisper. "I want to give it to you, Tanner. Please. Take it."

His brows pull in as though he's contemplating something. I start to get nervous, thinking maybe he won't go through with it, until his conflicted expression morphs into one of sincerity and acceptance. I exhale the breath I was holding in, thankful that he's not running out of here before we can go any further.

He swallows thickly, nodding his head before he cups my cheek in one hand. He lowers his lips to mine and slides on top of me, where my legs are already open and waiting for him. The feel of his bare, hard cock rubbing along my wetness is unlike anything I've ever felt before. And when he slowly thrusts his hips, rubbing his head at the perfect angle on my clit, I cry out. He's not even inside me and I'm already seeing stars. He feels like stone wrapped in velvet as he continues pumping himself over my most sensitive part, making me desperate for more.

"Please," I beg.

"We need a condom," he says, clearly pained by the idea of leaving the bed to get his wallet. I don't want him to go, either.

"I'm on the pill," I blurt. I've always had heavy periods, so when I was fourteen, my doctor prescribed birth control to combat the symptoms. Even though I've never had sex, I've been on it ever since.

He squeezes his eyes shut. "I can't come inside you, Grace. It's too risky."

"Then pull out," I tell him. "I want to feel you."

He rubs his thumb on my cheek, pressing his mouth to mine. When his tongue teases my bottom lip, I open for him. I feel tingles all over my body as he kisses me like his life depends on it. I'm not completely sure I wouldn't float away if he weren't pinning me to the mattress.

I'm brought back to the moment when he lines the head of his cock at my entrance and slowly begins to thrust forward, meeting resistance before he can even get inside. And just as he starts pushing harder, I hear it.

"Gracie!" a voice sings from the hallway, making us both

go completely stiff. My eyes go wide, pushing Tanner off of me with the strength of a goddamn gorilla on Red Bull, sending him over the edge and onto the floor between the bed and wall. He lands with a loud *thud*, groaning in pain.

"Shhhh!" I say, pulling the covers up over my body just in time for my mom to open the door and peek in.

"Hey, sweetie," she says cheerfully. "Just wanted to let you know that your dad had a work emergency, so we had to come home a few days early."

I do my best to look like I didn't just have an actual dick being pushed into me, and that the owner of said dick isn't butt-ass naked on the floor beside me. "Oh, man," I squeak, clearing my throat. *Fucking smooth, Grace.* "That sucks."

"Well, you know what they say," she says with a sigh. "If you want something done right, you have to do it yourself. And Bobby Archer doesn't know his ass from a hole in the ground. I told your father to just let the old coot retire early."

Great. Cool. Awesome.

Can we wrap this up so I can sneak our neighbor out of here before you find out he was just about to deflower your precious baby girl under your roof without protection? K, thanks.

"Are you okay?" she asks. "You look flushed. You don't have a fever, do you?" She opens the door fully and my eyes go wide with panic as she walks toward the bed.

"Mom, I'm fine," I rush out as she lays the back of her hand on my cheek, then my forehead. "I was just about to get up and take a shower."

She raises a suspicious brow, doing a scan of the room from where she stands. My heart is pounding so hard and fast, I feel like it might vibrate me right onto the floor with Tanner. I stare like a deer in headlights until she finally speaks.

"Okay. Pick all these clothes up off the floor. Just because you're eighteen doesn't mean house rules don't apply. I still have the authority to ground you," she teases, making me relax just slightly, until I realize the clothes she's talking about don't belong to me. I stiffen again, but thankfully, she's already walking out the door, closing it behind her with a quiet *snick*.

I huff a relieved breath, sinking into the pillow. I try to regulate my heart rate, completely forgetting about Tanner until he peeks up over the mattress. "Lock the door, Bunny!" he whisper-shouts. "My fucking cock is out!"

"Oh my God!" I say, scrambling out of bed and locking the door. I turn, leaning my back to it, watching as he stands and walks toward his boxer briefs that are bunched up at the foot of the bed. It's a fucking miracle my mom didn't notice them, but I guess they could've been mistaken for a tank top or something.

He quickly steps into them, pulling them up his muscled thighs, and I can't lie, I die a little inside. We were *so close*. He must see the despair in my expression because he laughs quietly as he walks over, dropping a quick kiss to my lips before moving to my ear.

"I wasn't even inside you and I can already tell I'm going to be obsessed with your cunt, baby," he rasps.

I whimper quietly as he pulls my lobe into his mouth, giving it a gentle suck. I'm all the way turned on again and there's nothing we can do about it.

"Tonight, you're mine," he whispers. "I'll figure it out and text you, okay?"

All I can do is nod as he throws on the rest of his clothes and turns away, opening the window and disappearing. There's a trellis right outside my room that he used to climb when Riggs still lived here, and thankfully he'll be able to sneak out unseen between our houses.

I walk over, closing the window and grabbing my clothes to shower. Now that I know we're in the clear, I have a little extra pep in my step as I think about what's going to happen tonight…and who it's going to happen with.

ELEVEN
TANNER

NEVER IN MY life have my balls actually shriveled up and retreated *into* my body, but when Libby's voice echoed outside Grace's room just as I was about to thrust into her for the first time, that's exactly what happened. I've never been so scared in my entire twenty-one years, and that's saying a lot, since Riggs and I were chased by a mama bear while we were camping one time. Thankfully, we made it to the car before she reached us, peeling out of the site as fast as we could and never returning for our tent. But even that wasn't as terrifying as almost getting caught naked and on top of Grace.

But do I still want to finish what we started?

Fuck. Yes.

Which is exactly why I've spent the entire day planning the perfect little hideaway for us. I was initially thinking we'd just go to my house since it's still empty, but then I started to worry that maybe my parents would cut their trip short since the Valentines weren't there anymore. There's no way I'll be able to focus on giving Grace the first-time experience she deserves if I'm worried about being caught the whole time. Plus, even if my parents don't come home, knowing hers are fifty yards away is kind of a boner killer in and of itself.

After considering our limited options, I came up with a plan that will hopefully make tonight one that she'll never forget. A night that, when the next guy comes along, she'll compare to before she decides to give herself to him.

Why does that thought piss me the fuck off?

TANNER:

Meet me at the cul-de-sac in fifteen minutes.
Tell your parents you're staying at a friend's tonight.

GRACE:

You want me to lie to my parents, Mr. Lake?
gasp What a terrible influence you are on my young, innocent mind.

TANNER:

If you want to tell them you'll be spending the evening riding my fingers, face, and cock...by all means, Bunny. Go ahead.

GRACE:

wide eyed emoji *sweating emoji*

I'll see you in a few.

Twenty-five minutes later, Grace comes running down the sidewalk toward my car with a white hoodie draped over her arm and an overnight bag on her shoulder. She's wearing a short, pink sundress with a pair of silver glitter Chucks. Her blonde hair falls in waves over her shoulders, and I realize then just how fucking breathtaking she is.

All my life, I put her in this box. I couldn't think of her in any way that wasn't completely platonic, so my brain never even registered how beautiful she got as the years went by. It wasn't until a couple of days ago when I accidentally barged into her room that I saw her as anything more than my best friend's little sister. But now that I'm seeing her in this new light, my head is all over the place.

I'm still on board with helping her explore her sexuality this summer, but I'd be lying if I said that the last two days haven't muddied the way I'm feeling about things. I thought I could separate the physical part of this from the emotional part. I honestly had my head on straight about what this was…until I was getting ready to push myself into her. For just a split second, she looked up at me and it was like we were connected. She was handing me the keys to her mind and body, trusting me fully to take care of her.

I need to remember why we're here. That I proposed this whole arrangement to keep her safe. There's no room for me to fuck around and mess things up by thinking what happens between us could ever be more than it is.

"Sorry," she says breathlessly as she throws herself into my passenger seat. "My mom had to ask me fifty questions about what I was doing tonight before she'd let me leave. I thought the inquisition would stop when I turned into a legal adult, but I was wrong." I chuckle as she closes the door and fastens her seatbelt before I pull around and head toward Main Street.

"Where are we going?" she asks, looking out the window.

"Somewhere we won't have to worry about being interrupted," I reply. "I want you all to myself tonight."

She smiles before exhaling contentedly, relaxing into the seat. We spend the ten-minute drive listening to Bella Simon, who Grace is ridiculously obsessed with. Last summer, she spent two hours waiting in a virtual queue to get concert tickets to see Bella on tour, but they ended up selling out before she even got a chance to get onto the actual website. I tried buying them from a resale site but couldn't find them for less than five grand apiece. Instead, we parked as close as we could to Blizzard stadium, or as the fans call it, *The Igloo*, on the night the tour came to Boston and listened from the front seat of my car with the windows down. Riggs and I were not into it at all since it's not really our type of music, but we'd have done anything to make Grace happy that night.

I turn down the gravel road toward our destination and look over at her, gauging her reaction.

"What are we doing at the lighthouse?" she asks, brows pinched together in confusion.

"Well," I begin, pulling into the driveway and putting the car in park. "My parents bought it about a year ago as an investment property, but it needed to be updated, so they've been renovating it. It's pretty much done, but they're waiting until the market is better before they put it up for sale. The actual lighthouse doesn't work anymore, but the house is really nice, and the view is amazing."

When I was trying to make my plan earlier, I considered a few options. First, I thought I'd just book a hotel room in Boston for the night. Then, I thought we could go find somewhere to park by the water and set out some blankets. But neither of those ideas felt right for Grace's first time. When I looked out of the corner of my eye and spotted the lighthouse key sitting on the shelf in our kitchen, I knew it would be the perfect place to bring her. My parents wouldn't even notice it was gone and we can be sure nobody will come in and ruin the night. Plus, I won't have to risk breaking both legs sneaking out a window in the morning.

"I've always wanted to see the inside of this place," she says, opening the door and hopping out. I laugh at her eagerness, watching as she skips to the door and waits for me to catch up. I pull the key from my pocket, putting it into the lock and turning the knob. I don't even get a chance to open the door before Grace pushes through, flipping the light switch and looking around the main living area.

When my parents bought the place, it was outdated and unkept. The original lighthouse keeper lived here until he was physically unable to care for the house or himself, and when he passed away, his kids didn't want to go through the hassle of preparing it to be sold. Since my parents knew them personally, they offered them a fair price and took it off their hands. It's weird because, as real estate agents, they normally only buy and sell commercial properties. But they said after they got this place fixed up, they could make some good money off of it.

"What do you think?" I say, watching Grace as her eyes ping-pong around the room like she's not sure what to look at first.

"It's way prettier than I expected," she says, sitting in the plush armchair and immediately standing and skipping across the room before flopping onto the couch like she couldn't wait to test everything out. "Your parents did such a good job."

I chuckle, putting my hands into the pockets of my sweat-pants. "I think my mom secretly loves interior design. She doesn't get to do a lot, so when my dad gives her free rein to bring a vision to life, she goes all out." The whole place is bright and airy, with hints of tan and blue. The old, unfinished maple flooring was ripped out and replaced with European white oak. All of the outdated furniture and lighting fixtures were upgraded, and brand-new stainless-steel appliances were installed. It's modern, but still has a beachy vibe, which is perfect for where we are in New England.

"Well, she's really good at it," she says, kicking off her shoes and putting her feet up on the coffee table. "I've been here five minutes, and it already feels like home." She looks at me, eyes twinkling, and my heart squeezes in my chest. She's so fucking beautiful, and making her happy has always been one of my favorite things to do. The feeling of being rewarded by her sweet smile is reason enough to want to give her the world. I just hope whoever gets to own her heart forever knows what he has and never takes it for granted.

I'm pulled back to reality when the doorbell rings, making Grace's eyes widen in panic.

"It's just a food delivery," I tell her, easing her worries that we're about to be busted again. "I didn't have time to pick up dinner and snacks earlier, so I made an order." She relaxes as I make my way to the door, grabbing the food and giving the driver an extra tip for going to three different places for everything. I wanted to be able to stay here as long as we could, so I got dinner for tonight, snacks for later, and ingredients to make breakfast in the morning.

She stands, following me to the kitchen as I unpack the bags, putting the contents into the cupboards and refrigerator. "What smells good?" she asks, looking at the black bag I set aside on the island as she hoists herself up onto one of the barstools.

I smirk. "I thought you'd like to try something besides Sour Patch Kids tonight. So, I ordered from that new Italian place in Boston. I got you the Shrimp Carbonara and a cannoli." I played it safe, ordering things I've seen her eat before, but I've heard Donatello's blows every other restaurant out of the water. "And if that doesn't hit the spot," I say, reaching into the bag from the grocery store and tossing the small pack of Sour Patch Kids into her lap, "I brought backup."

She tilts her head, biting the inside of her cheek to hide her smile. "Why are you so good to me?"

The sincerity in her eyes prompts me to round the counter, cupping her face in my palm before pressing a gentle kiss to her lips. I know I'm blurring the lines with this whole thing, but when she looks at me like I hung the moon just for her, I can't fucking help it. I have the opportunity to have Grace Valentine for the summer, and I'm going to enjoy it until our time comes to an end and we both head off to school.

It starts innocent. I had every intention of keeping it quick so we could eat dinner, but now that I can taste her on my lips, I quickly turn feral, taking her hair in my fist and holding her to me. As soon as she opens, I deepen the kiss. I lick along the inside of her sweet mouth, swallowing every moan and gasp that comes out of her as I flex my fingers in her golden waves.

She's fucking perfection and I'm gone. Completely gone for her.

"Tanner," she breathes against my lips, "I want you. Right now. I don't want to wait anymore."

As much as I should stop this so we can have our food while it's still warm, I can't even think straight. Fuck dinner. I just need to be inside her. I grab her hips, lifting her off the stool and into my arms. Her legs wrap around my waist and I move my hands to her ass, squeezing firmly as I walk us to the bedroom. My cock is as hard as steel, pressed between us. We never break the kiss. I follow her, our mouths fused together as I lower her onto the bed, dropping my weight on top of her and grinding myself between her parted legs. The friction has me seeing fucking stars, and we're both still fully clothed.

"I have to taste you," I say, wasting no time kissing down her neck, stopping to lick at the cleavage that's peeking out of the top of her sundress. I can't even be bothered to take it off of her before I'm poised between her legs, inhaling the scent of her arousal that's literally filling the entire room.

I pull her panties to the side and lick along her cunt, gathering the wetness and savoring the taste. She moans as I explore, flicking my tongue along her sensitive skin, teasing every part of her. And when I can't take the way I'm torturing us both any longer, I suck her swollen clit between my teeth. She gasps as her hips begin bucking, pushing down hard into my face. We're both losing control and it feels so fucking good to finally let go with her. I can't imagine ever wanting anything more than I want this girl right now.

Yanking her panties down her legs and tossing them somewhere behind me, I return to her dripping pussy, licking and sucking like a man on a mission. "Mmmm," I hum. "You taste so fucking good, baby. You gonna come on my tongue so I can fuck you?"

For a minute, she's so lost in what I'm doing to her that she doesn't answer. But when I push one thick finger inside her, she lets out the sexiest little gasp. "F-fuck me," she stutters. "Tanner, I'm so c-close. I need to—" She doesn't even finish her sentence before I feel her grip me, her muscles fluttering against me as I continue to thrust in and out.

"Good girl, Bunny," I praise. "Make that tight little pussy nice and wet for me. Keep coming." I don't stop. I don't slow down. I just continue fucking her with my finger and my mouth as she shakes and writhes against the mattress.

Eventually, she begins to whimper from the overstimulation, so I pull my finger from her and press one last, soft kiss to her clit. I crawl back up, dragging my tongue over every part of exposed skin that I pass, tasting the saltiness of the sweat that's glistening on her body. I'm so goddamn addicted to her already; I don't know how I'll ever get enough. That should raise every possible red flag, but I can't find a single fuck to give while she's lying sated underneath me.

When we're face to face, she slowly opens her eyes, and when they connect with mine, the emotion is almost too much to take. I definitely don't want to sort through everything I'm feeling right now, because I'm starting to think it's possible that this won't be as simple as I initially thought it would be. Right now, though? I need to focus on Grace and making this a special moment for her.

I reach to the bottom of her dress, pulling it up her body and over her head before tossing it to the floor. Using one hand behind my neck, I pull my shirt off just in time to watch her arch her back, making my mouth water as she unclasps her bra and slides it down her arms.

Fuck. I've never wanted anything more in my whole life.

Barely able to see straight through the lust I'm feeling, I quickly remove my sweats and boxers, that are both soaked in the front with a mixture of us both from when we were grinding against one another. I'm still dripping precum as I lower back down, pressing our bodies tightly together.

Leaning down, I kiss her gently. "Are you still sure?" I ask. "We can wait. If you're hungry, we can—"

"I told you," she says softly, cutting me off before I have a chance to let myself spiral. "I want this. With you. Right now."

"Okay," I say on a shaky exhale. "It's going to hurt at first, so we have to go slow. Promise you'll tell me if it's too much and I'll stop."

She gently grabs hold of my biceps and swallows roughly. "I promise I'll tell you, but I need you to keep going unless I say so."

I line myself up at her entrance, pressing my forehead to hers. I hate that I have to hurt her like this, but hopefully I can be gentle enough to make it bearable. As conflicted as I am about everything that's swirling in my head, I'm still completely sure I'm the only one who will take care of her the way she deserves right now.

We're both trembling as I press my lips to hers and gently thrust inside. She whines in pain, and I pause, waiting for her to tell me whether or not to continue. When she doesn't say anything, I push forward a little bit more, feeling myself break through her barrier. She sucks in a gasp, and I push my tongue into her mouth to swallow her scream. I hold off for just a few seconds before I take another inch. I have to grit my teeth together because she's so warm and wet, I feel like I could come right here. But this isn't about me. It's about her.

"I'm so sorry, baby," I whisper. "You're doing such a good job. I'm almost all the way in."

"Tanner," she whimpers as a tear slips from the corner of her eye. I bring my thumb up to brush it away, wishing I could take away all the pain she's going through right now.

"Do you want the rest of me? Or do you want me to stop?" I ask, on the fence about what I want her to say. Of course I don't want to hurt her, but I also don't want to leave her warmth either.

"More," she whispers, her voice shaking. "I need all of you."

"Okay," I choke out. "Open those big blue eyes and look at me when I make you mine." As soon as she does, we connect in every possible way and it's almost overwhelming. So much so, that I can't stop myself from pushing the rest of the way in. It doesn't seem to cause her any more pain than she's already been through, so I pause when I'm buried to the hilt, giving her a moment to catch her breath and get used to having me inside her.

"Such a good girl," I say, hoping the praise will distract her a little bit. She seemed to really like it when I did it before, so that's what I'll give her. "You're taking my cock so well. So tight." I'm not lying. Her pussy feels like heaven wrapped around me.

"Tanner," she gasps, "can you move a little bit?"

I give her a small smile. "Are you aching, beautiful?"

"Mhmm," she whimpers, so I pull out slowly and carefully push back in. Her gasps and whines turn to moans as I continue, and I can tell it's starting to feel better for her. I pick up my speed until I've set a pace that feels so good, white light starts to dance across the edge of my vision.

"Are you okay?" I ask, hoping the sting and pain have subsided.

"Yeah," she whispers. "It feels…like…maybe I could…"

Oh, thank fuck. Even though she's speaking in breathy,

broken sentences, I know what she's trying to say. And it sets me on a mission to make it happen.

"Can you come for me, baby?" I ask, continuing to pump in and out of her. She squeezes her eyes shut, nodding. "Here, this'll help." I reach between us, using my thumb to stroke her clit from side to side. I can feel her hips push up into me as she whimpers, both of us doing everything we can to coax her release from her body. I want nothing more than for this to be an experience she'll look back on as a good one, and there's definitely a part of me that hopes she compares other guys to me in the future.

The thought of her doing this with anyone else pisses me off, and it's not the first time. Every time I think about what we are versus what she's going to have with boyfriends after she leaves for school, it has me wishing I could hide her away in this lighthouse forever. Keep her for myself, where she's safe, cared for, and respected. God only knows how those assholes will use her, mistreat her, and break her heart.

Fuck. That.

I pick up speed, fully fucking her at this point. She's panting and moaning in pleasure as her hips continue meeting mine with every thrust.

"Yes, Tan," she gasps. "I'm coming!"

I inwardly breathe a sigh of relief as her walls squeeze around me. I feel her getting even wetter as she comes, and I have to close my eyes because the sight of her face while she orgasms has me ready to bust before she's even finished.

"Good girl, baby," I praise as she shakes below me, still somehow in the midst of her orgasm. "You're gripping me so tight. You're gonna make me come."

"P-please," she stutters on a gasp. "Inside me. Just this once. *Please.*"

Not only can I not deny her whatever she asks for, but even if I could, the sound of her begging for it does me in. It all happens so fast; I don't stand a chance of sticking to my rule of pulling out. All in a matter of seconds, my balls draw up painfully tight. White explodes behind my eyes as a euphoric electricity shoots up my spine and through my limbs. My body stiffens and I shoot ropes into her, over and over, filling her so much that I can feel my cum being pushed out and running all over our joined bodies.

I feel like it goes on forever. It's easily the most intense orgasm I've ever had, and if I didn't already know it before, I do now. Sex with Grace Valentine is life changing.

Finally, my muscles start to relax. We're both breathing heavy, trying to recover from…*whatever the fuck that was* as I drop my forehead to hers, inhaling her vanilla scent while I continue to come back down to earth.

"That was," she begins, "*not* what I expected."

My brows pull inward, concerned that maybe I was reading things wrong, and she didn't actually enjoy it. She came. I *felt it*. "What do you mean?"

She shrugs. "My friends all told me that when they lost their virginity, it hurt really bad, and then it just kind of sucked after that. They said it took until the third or fourth time before it started to feel good. But that…was amazing," she says, a shy smile tipping up the corners of her mouth. "Thank you, Tanner."

My heart squeezes again at her words. I lean down, kissing the tip of her nose, making her giggle. "No, thank *you*, Bunny. That was the best sex I've ever had."

Her cheeks turn the cutest shade of pink as her smile grows bigger and she wiggles her brows. "When can we do it again?"

This fucking girl.

"I'm still inside you, Grace," I say on a laugh. "Let's get you cleaned up, eat our dinner, and see if you're still singing the same tune once those endorphins wear off and you realize how sore you are."

She pouts as I pull out, watching as my cum leaks out of

her. There's a small amount of pink mixed in from her blood, and as fucked up as it probably is, I feel an unexpected twinge of possessiveness at the sight. All I can think about is filling her up as many times as I can this summer.

I have a feeling this is the first of many rules I'll be breaking in the next few months.

Fuck.

TWELVE
GRACE

"SAY I WAS RIGHT," Tanner laughs, throwing a piece of popcorn into the air and catching it in his mouth.

"No," I say, shaking my head. I take a step toward where he's lounging on the couch, trying to hide my wince as I walk.

He was right. I'm sore. But I don't want to tell him that because I know he won't touch me again if he thinks it might hurt me. I could see the reluctance in his eyes when he initially pushed into me. It was excruciating. I felt like I was being torn in half, but when I opened my eyes and looked at him, it all faded away. The burn eventually subsided, and it was the most intoxicating thing I've ever felt. I didn't want it to end. The fact that I was actually able to orgasm was just the cherry on top.

There's absolutely nothing like coming while being so full of his cock. I've gotten myself off hundreds of times, but it's never even been close to the way it felt when my inner muscles squeezed against him. It's like finally being complete after years of not knowing you had a missing piece.

We laid together for a few minutes after he pulled out of me, then he helped me up and walked me into the bathroom, where he immediately drew me a bath. He sat on the floor and fed me my dinner as I soaked my sore body in the hot water. He insisted on drying me off and dressing me in his giant Harvard Football hoodie before we headed to the couch to hang out and watch TV.

"You're a bad liar," he says, grabbing my hand as soon as I'm within reach and pulling me down on top of him. He tucks me under his arm and I snuggle into him, enjoying the comfort he's been giving me since we started this arrangement. I'll definitely miss this when I go off to California, because I'm convinced that Tanner Lake could win awards for his cuddling skills. He's so firm, warm, and strong. I've never felt safer and more cared for than I do with him, right now.

I know I'm supposed to be keeping my emotions out of this, but it's definitely hard with the way he's been treating me. Not only was he so gentle and encouraging while we were having sex, but the way he looked at me...I could've sworn his eyes were telling me that he was feeling the same thing I was.

I know it's normal to develop some type of a connection to the person who takes your virginity, so I'm hoping that's all this is. That the more we do it, the more the novelty of my first time being so special will wear off. Maybe once we get into exploring the kinkier stuff, things won't feel as emotionally charged.

At least, I hope so. The last thing I need is to lose Tanner's friendship because I let my heart get involved after we agreed this was only a physical arrangement. Besides, it's not like he'd want to be with me anyway, considering he's about to be drafted into the NFL where the women will be offering themselves to him on silver platters. He's hot as fuck, so I know he'll have his pick of singers, actresses, and supermodels. Why would he settle for a young, inexperienced college student that could potentially cost him his relationship with his best friend?

We're adults. We can enjoy this summer for what it is; me

trying all the new things I'm dying to try so I don't end up making big mistakes with the wrong people once I leave Hope Harbor. I'm thankful to Tanner for doing this. The least I can do is not make him feel bad that I caught feelings when we're done here.

"Okayyyyyy," I say, looking up at him. "Let's say, hypothetically, I was a little bit sore. Like, the tiniest bit. What would be the chances of you fucking me again tonight if that were true?"

He raises a brow. "Have I created a monster already, Gracie girl? Is my stroke game that good that I turned you into a little nympho after only being inside you one time?"

I roll my eyes. "Are you *making fun of me*? Because I thought this was a safe space, Tanner. That's almost as disappointing as the orgasm I faked earlier."

His eyes go wide. "You're lying! I…I *felt* it. You weren't faking! Right?"

I give him a sympathetic look, pushing out my bottom lip in a fake pout. "You poor, poor thing. Did I injure your fragile manhood?"

He's speechless, staring at me like he has no idea what's happening. When I finally break and bark out a loud laugh, his face immediately goes from shocked to annoyed. I'm in hysterics, tears filling my eyes as he digs his fingers into my sides, tickling me in the most torturous way.

"You know what?" he says as he continues his assault, making me kick my feet in an attempt to escape. "I'm not going to fuck you again, you little liar. But I'm definitely going to make you regret being such a brat."

"Finally," I mumble, making him laugh.

"You know, it's not really a punishment if you're going to enjoy it, Bunny."

I roll my eyes, but he's not wrong. The more I think about Tanner being rough with me, the more excited I get to do it. This isn't even something I've been curious about before, but that movie woke something up inside me that craves to know what it's like to be dominated. Would I honestly just have found a random guy at school to do it with? Probably not. Tanner was right when he said that would be dangerous.

But now that I know it's him, I'm dying to get started. I want him to do whatever he wants to me…and to make me do whatever he wants, to him. I want him to spank me and restrain me. I want to be blindfolded, gagged, and choked.

I want it all. Only with him.

Tanner has had my unwavering trust since before I can even remember. When I first started high school, I had a lot of issues as far as wanting to tell some of the girls in my class things about myself. It only takes one time of someone blabbing a secret for the whole world to hear before you learn your lesson. Tanner was always the person I confided in when I was holding something in that I needed to get off my chest. Of course, I couldn't talk about boys or sex with him because I knew how hard he and Riggs worked to keep every guy in the greater Boston area away from me. I knew if I had any hope of dating, I would have to keep them out of it. But, other than that, Tanner knows a lot about me that nobody else does.

A lot of good that did me anyway, considering that up until about an hour ago, I was an eighteen-year-old virgin. Although now I'm kind of glad that I waited. I don't think I would've had the same experience that I had with Tanner, with anyone else.

We start the movie, sharing snacks and drinks as we lie beside one another. This lighthouse is practically in the middle of nowhere, and I feel like we're in our own little bubble here. Nobody knows what's going on, and we can just be completely open with our affection toward one another.

Every once in a while, Tanner leans down to kiss the top of my head, and butterflies take flight in my stomach at the feel of his lips pressed against me. None of this is really new. He's always been open about hugging or putting his arm around me. We've even held hands before when we were out at parties and he didn't want to lose me in the crowd. But now, it all feels different. Even though we're supposed to be keeping this strictly physical, I'm not so naïve that I can't see how we've pushed our relationship beyond the lines of friendship. It's going to be a fine line to walk, keeping myself from falling for him in a way that I can't take back. But I want to learn and explore with him. Nothing has ever felt better than having his hands on me, and I don't want to risk ruining it by catching feelings that he doesn't want me to have. If he can do this and stick to our original plan, so can I.

Because what other choice do I have?

THIRTEEN
TANNER

"BUNNY! WHERE ARE YOU?" I yell, stepping through the door and taking off my shoes. The sun is just about to go down, so Grace and I decided to put together a little campfire and hang out outside. I just got done chopping wood and setting up a sitting area. She was in here getting together the ingredients for s'mores, but I can see straight through to the kitchen, and she's nowhere to be found.

I check the bedroom, but that's also empty. Making my way further down the hall, I stop when movement catches my eye in the bathroom. Because of the angle of the sink, she hasn't noticed me yet, and I watch as she stares at herself in the mirror. Her fingertips go up to her lips, where she touches them gently like she's never seen them before. She slowly glides down her chin, fingers wrapping loosely around her throat. And when she looks back up at herself, I don't think I've ever seen her so content.

Is that from me? Did I put that look on her face?

I can't take my eyes off of her as her hand continues its descent, running between her tits over her tank top, and down to her stomach, where she stops. I'm instantly hit with the memory of how her pussy looked as it leaked my cum, and as scared as that should make me, it just doesn't. I've never had sex without a condom before, always too worried that I would accidentally knock someone up and my football career would end before it even began. That thought didn't even cross my mind with Grace. I just wanted to mark her in some way. I wanted to make her mine, even though I know she'll never truly be.

At least I was her first. Her virginity will always belong to me.

"Oh, hey," she says, breaking me from my thoughts. "Did you need to get in here?"

I stare at her for a moment because I swear she gets prettier every single time I look at her, before I get my shit together enough to answer her question. "The, uhh—" I stutter, tripping over my words "Everything is ready outside."

"Oh, yay!" she says, hopping over to me and kissing my cheek. "Let's go before we miss the sunset." She takes my hand, yanking me from the room and down the hallway, like she always does when she wants to get somewhere fast and one of us is not as excited as she is. Only this time, I can't ignore the warm feeling that travels through my fingers, up my arm, and right to my chest as her hand squeezes mine.

I am so royally fucked.

I push all the messy feelings aside for now, remembering why we're here in the first place. I'm playing the long game here. Not for myself, but for Grace. We had sex. Now I'm going to give her the full princess treatment for the rest of our time together, because whether I like it or not, there's going to be a guy after me. Possibly many, and she shouldn't accept anything less than what she deserves after letting someone inside her body. Plus, I really fucking like hanging out with her. Holding her and kissing her whenever I want is pretty damn nice.

She plops down in one of the Adirondack chairs that I brought from the porch, and I start preparing the wood for our campfire. The sun will be setting in just a few minutes, and the cool New England air is nipping at our skin. The fact that we're on the water makes it even chillier, so I want to make sure I keep Grace warm while we're out here.

It takes me a few minutes to get the fire going, but when I do, I walk over and pull her up from the chair. She scowls, making me chuckle as I sit down where she was and pull her into my lap. She's so small that when she brings her legs up and curls herself into my body, she fits perfectly. I'm immediately warm all over, and I don't think it has as much to do with the fire as it has to do with the beautiful girl that's pressed up against me.

"Thank you for bringing me here," she says quietly as the sun begins to lower at the edge of the water. "Have you ever seen anything prettier than this?" I can see the look of awe in her eyes as she watches what's going on in the distance, but I'm having trouble tearing mine off of her.

"Never," I reply. It's the truth. I've realized in the last few days that I'm spending the summer with a girl who is beyond gorgeous, inside and out. A girl that I've known her whole life, yet I feel as though I'm meeting her all over again through brand new eyes.

She looks over at me, realizing that I'm not even kind of interested in the sunset, and gives me an annoyed look, but it's fake. Her cheeks pinken as she tries to hold back her smile, but I think she might be as smitten as I am because it eventually breaks through, morphing into the cutest little giggle as she cuddles into me. I tighten my arms around her, and we sit in a comfortable silence as the sun sinks down below the water's surface. When it's finally gone and the show is over, I use my pointer finger to hook below Grace's chin and press my lips to hers. She sighs contentedly as we make out, her fists gripping my thick, cotton hoodie as my hands ghost up and down her back.

Seconds turn into minutes, and although my body is

begging me to carry her inside and tear off all her clothes, I don't. We just continue kissing and holding onto each other as we listen to the sounds of the fire crackling and the water lapping against the dock. My heart pounds against my ribcage with every moan that flows out of her and into me while we feed off of one another. This is the biggest rush I've ever experienced, and all we're doing is sitting in a chair together, hidden away where nobody can find us.

This is one of those moments in life that, even while you're still in it, you know you'll never forget how it felt. A moment that, as it happens, starts burrowing itself into every fiber of your being, latching on and becoming a part of who you are. Whether I want this memory to invade my thoughts years from now or not, I know it will. As much as I've been focusing on the fact that I want Grace to compare future boyfriends to me and the way I've been treating her, it's hitting me that I don't think I'll ever have another set of lips on mine that I won't wish were hers.

I move my hand into her hair, flexing my fingers and holding her in place while I devour her mouth, wishing I could make this kiss last forever. But I know I can't. I have to remember what the original plan was and focus on that so we can both go off to school in the fall and follow our dreams.

So, the best thing I can do is give these next few months everything I have until it's all over, and all I have left are the memories of what it felt like when she was mine.

FOURTEEN
GRACE

"BAD FUCKING BUNNY," Tanner says, slapping my clit with his fingers while lying between my parted legs. "You know better than to act like a brat in public when I can't punish you for it, don't you?"

I whimper into the gag in my mouth, nodding my head in affirmation. He's had me tied to the bed for nearly an hour, edging me almost to the point of tears. I can barely even think anymore with how badly I need to come, but I know I deserve every bit of the torture I'm getting right now.

It all started this morning when Tanner picked me up from my house. Our plan was to go to the grocery store for food before we headed out on his dad's boat for the day. His parents are back from Nantucket, and we had to start spending our nights at home so nobody would suspect that something is going on between us. Although it wouldn't be out of the realm of possibility for us to hang out alone every now and then, being together as much as I want to be right now would definitely raise a couple of red flags.

We got away with spending three nights together here at the lighthouse, and they were nothing short of amazing. When we weren't lounging around or goofing off, Tanner was carefully easing me into having sex and doing all the other things that come along with it. After the initial soreness wore off, he stopped being so gentle with my body, fucking me in all kinds of different positions and pushing me to new limits every time. He restrained me with his hands above my head a few times and made me hold off on orgasming until I made it clear that I was uncomfortable. We christened every available surface this place had to offer as he introduced me to some of the kinkier things, not even bothering to get dressed sometimes because we knew there wasn't a point when our clothes would be coming right back off again anyway.

You haven't *lived* until Tanner Lake has served you breakfast completely naked.

Unfortunately, we haven't seen each other as much as I wish we could've since then. We've texted some, but we're trying our best not to tip anyone off to what we're doing. I honestly doubt our parents would care, but I know it might put a rift between him and my brother if he found out. That would be the very last thing I'd want. I know Riggs wouldn't be too keen on his best friend teaching his little sister how to be submissive and railing her into the headboard at every possible moment.

It's Monday, so everybody is at work, leaving us to spend the day on the boat by ourselves. We decided to get stuff from the store, bring it to the lighthouse to pack into a cooler, and then we're going to launch the boat from the dock. But I thought it would be funny to push his buttons a little bit while he was busy reaching to the top shelf in the very *not* empty aisle we were shopping in. If I knew that reaching around to rub his dick would result in this type of suffering, I probably wouldn't have done it. And I *definitely* wouldn't have done it a second time in the checkout line after he specifically told me not to, but I did…and I'm having regrets.

"You made my cock hard in front of a store full of people," he says, leaning down and flicking his tongue roughly on my swollen clit. Clearly, Tanner is done taking it easy on me and we've moved on to the next phase of our arrangement. "Tell me you're sorry."

I inhale through my nose, trying hard to focus on what he's saying as he sucks so hard, I see stars. "Fowwwyyyy," I mumble unintelligibly into the gag, which is really just the belt to the robe that hangs on the back of the bathroom door. My arms are secured above my head, tied to one of the wooden rungs of the headboard with my panties, and each leg has been restrained with a separate piece of rope that I assume Tanner found lying around the lighthouse. I'm spread wide as he brings me to the edge repeatedly, but never lets me fall over. I'm sweating bullets and my body is shaking uncontrollably while he licks and sucks at my skin, stopping every once in a while to slap or pinch my aching bundle of nerves.

"Do you think you deserve to come, you greedy little cock whore?" he asks. "Or should I edge you a few more times."

I whine into the fabric as tears begin to well in my eyes. As painful as this is, I've never felt so alive.

Just like I thought I would, I love being dominated. Having his strong hands holding me down as he punishes me with his tongue and fingers is so fucking hot, there's no way I'd ever ask him to stop. It's by far the most delicious pain I've ever experienced.

I feel my release getting closer than it has since we started, and I try not to let on that I'm going to orgasm because I'm afraid if I do, he'll take it away again.

"Don't do it, Grace," he warns, thrusting two fingers inside and curling them to hit the spot deep inside me that makes my eyes roll back. He reaches up with his free hand, pulling the gag down so it's no longer in my mouth. "Don't you fucking come without my permission."

"Tan," I gasp, "I can't…I *have to.*"

He picks up his speed, finger fucking me roughly as my

toes curl and my legs pull against the ropes. "Are you going to be bad again?"

"No!" I cry out. "No, sir!"

Those must be the magic words, because the next thing out of his mouth is like music to my horny ears. "Okay, baby. Come for me," he says with a hot-as-fuck, deviant smirk lifting one corner of his mouth. He continues fucking me as I let go, exploding around his fingers the second he tells me I can. My back bows off the bed and my body convulses with an orgasm so intense, I black out. And when I come to, he's already got my ankles freed from the rope and is kissing along the red marks from me pulling at them.

He moves up to where I'm lying, untying the panties from my wrists and checking them for any redness. There isn't, but he kisses them for good measure before pushing the sweat soaked hair from my face and dropping his lips to my warm cheeks.

"You did such a good job," he says as I close my eyes and savor the feeling of his kisses moving across my face. "I'm so proud of you. I thought for sure you would give up, but you took it like a boss."

I hum contentedly. "You underestimate me, *sir*," I say, peeking one eye open and giving him a subtle tip of my lips.

"You're fucking perfect, you know that?" he says, giving me a quick peck on the lips before standing up from the bed. I'm still pretty dazed as he walks down the hall, and I hear the bathroom faucet running for a minute before he returns to the room. My eyes are closed again, so my legs jerk together in surprise when I feel him press a warm washcloth between them.

"Sorry," I say, slowly letting them fall back open. "What are you doing? You didn't even come inside me." He's washed me a couple of times after we had sex, to clean the cum from between my legs, but all he did was eat me out and finger me this time, so I'm a bit confused.

"You, uhhh…made a little bit of a mess," he replies.

I jackknife upward, fearing the worst as I lift my butt cheek and look underneath me. There's a wet spot bigger than my entire ass soaking into the sheets, and I immediately freak out. "What is that?" I scream like an absolute maniac. "Did I—" I pause, covering my mouth with my hand. My eyes probably look like dinner plates, which tracks since I've never been so scared in my whole eighteen years on this earth. "Did I pee on you?"

I jump off the bed, running around the room like my hair is on fire, imagining actually urinating in this man's mouth. I will *never* recover from this. I'm never having sex again. As a matter of fact, does anyone have the number to the nunnery? I'm giving my life over to God. There's no place for me in the world of intimate relations.

I panic for another minute, stopping only when I realize that Tanner is lying on the bed, holding his stomach in a full fit of laughter. I freeze, squinting my eyes in annoyance. "Is this funny to you?" I say. "Are there no *limits* to the ways you'll laugh at my expense?"

He sits up, wiping the tears from his eyes—yes, he's actually crying—before he finally takes a relaxed inhale. "Calm down, Bunny. You didn't pee. You squirted."

My eyes return to their large, shocked state. "I did *what?* And why are you saying it like that would be less embarrassing?"

He shrugs. "Because it is."

I pop out my hip, crossing my arms over my chest and scowling deeper. "Oh, really? Please do tell how I shouldn't be considering a move to another planet right now."

He stands, slowly closing the space between us and gripping my waist. I try to turn away like a bratty child, but he holds me in place. I avert my eyes, refusing to look straight at him. "Well, first of all," he begins, "I edged you for over an hour. You came so hard, you actually passed out.

Squirting is completely normal when you're overstimulated like that."

I sneak a peek in his direction and our eyes meet. Even though I should be mortified, which I still kind of am, the look on his face calms me a little.

"Also," he continues, pausing to bring his lips just inches from mine, "it was fucking hot. You are so goddamn sexy, Grace. Even when you don't mean to be. Fuck, baby. I can't get enough of you."

I loosen my arms and lean forward, pressing onto my toes to kiss him. Just like that, all the embarrassment I was feeling melts away. His hands slide up my body and tangle loosely in my hair, eliciting a contented sigh from my mouth into his as we lazily make out. There's no rush, no urgency to move further. It's just us, savoring one another in this moment.

This should alarm me. I know our time together will end when the warm, summer weather fades into fall. As much as I try to remind myself of that every day, it's getting harder and harder to imagine what my life will be like when Tanner Lake stops being mine. How will it feel when I see him and know he's just my brother's best friend again? Will I be okay when he finds someone to spend his future with, knowing that there was a time when he was everything I ever wanted? Or will it tear me apart to sit in the crowd at his wedding, wishing it could be me up there vowing to love him until my last breath?

These weren't feelings I anticipated having to work through when we started doing this. I just wanted to cross losing my virginity off my to-do list before I left for college, and maybe learn a few tricks to take to California with me. But now, the thought of moving across the country and away from Tanner if the Blizzard ends up drafting him makes me sad. It makes me second guess everything I thought I wanted.

I know how crazy that sounds. I'm only eighteen and was accepted into one of the most prestigious fashion design programs in the country. But if I'm completely honest, I never thought I'd get in when I applied. I just didn't want to spend my life wondering *what if*, so I filled out the paperwork and sent it off, thinking I'd get a small envelope in the mail containing a rejection letter a month or so later. When my mom handed me a thick mailer with all the acceptance materials from CCA, I was truly stunned. After the initial shock wore off, I started questioning if I could really just pick up my life and move three-thousand miles away from everyone I love.

I love fashion design. Nothing makes me feel as peaceful as sitting at my sewing machine, creating custom pieces that are unlike anything anyone has ever seen. But half the fun is trying them on for friends and family, hearing their thoughts on my hard work. I know I'll create new relationships wherever I end up, but it won't be the same. It won't be them. And it definitely won't be *him.*

I'm not going to make any hasty decisions right now, but this isn't the first time doubt has crept in about the future. Maybe I'll go to California for a year, hate it, and come home. Or maybe I'll love it and never want to return to New England, although I really don't see that happening since I love it here. I know I'll have to think about it all when my head is a little clearer, but for now, I want to enjoy every single moment I have left with Tanner.

Because, before I know it, he'll be gone and all I'll have left is a heart that needs to be put back together again after I stupidly fell in love with a boy I could never have.

FIFTEEN
TANNER

"TANNER!" Bill says, shaking my hand and pulling me into a quick bro-hug. "How are those two-a-days treating you? Your dad told me they've got you as their starter right now. Congratulations!"

I give him a tight nod. "Yes, sir. We've got a good QB room this year, but they wanted experience under center, so they gave me the nod."

I'm trying to be humble, but I'm fucking relieved that a month into practice, I've secured the starting position. Honestly, I don't think there was really much competition, but it's still nerve-racking to know that one or two bad days could've cost me my entire future. That's football for you, though. You could be on top one day and plummeting to the ground the next. Being in a position to be drafted in the first round by my dream team isn't something I'll take for granted. I know I need to keep my focus on that until they call me up to that podium in April.

It's early evening and I got home from practice about an hour ago. I haven't seen Grace all week because my schedule has been jam packed, but it's Friday and I have two whole days to spend with her. If I can find a way to get her alone, that is.

Tonight, our families are cooking out in the Valentines' back yard. It's never easy being near Grace and not being able to kiss or touch her, but we usually meet up earlier in the day to be alone and curb our urges to be close to one another. Unfortunately, we couldn't make it work today. I had practice from eight to eleven this morning, then again from two to four this afternoon. By the time I made the forty-five minute drive from campus back to Hope Harbor and showered, it was time to walk over here for dinner.

"Well, I'm proud of you, son," Bill says, patting me on the shoulder. "You'll have to excuse me," he says. "I haven't laid eyes on my beautiful wife in hours and I'm itching to see my girl."

Same, bro.

I give him a quiet chuckle as he slips past me and into the kitchen to find Libby. My parents have already started moving around the house, helping bring food out to the patio, which leaves me alone in the entryway to scheme. I know it's risky, but I can't wait any longer to kiss Grace. Quietly making my way up the stairs, I pray I'm still going unnoticed as I hit the landing, turning down the hall toward her bedroom. I knock softly, but when she doesn't answer, I twist the knob to find it unlocked. At first, I push it open just enough to peek my head in. She sits at her sewing table, and even though her hair is falling down over her shoulders, I know she has her earbuds in. Whatever she's listening to must have a good beat, because she bobs her head back-and-forth as she pushes the white fabric through the machine. I watch her as she works, clearly lost in whatever genius piece of art she's creating.

I push the door open all the way, leaning onto the frame and crossing my arms in front of my chest. She looks so beautiful and happy. I'll stand here all day and wait for her to notice me if I have to. Fuck our parents. If they catch me in her room watching her with hearts in my eyes, so be it. It's not like Riggs is here to have to explain all of this to since his team is still in the playoffs, which I'm thankful for. I don't know what Grace and I are anymore, but I can tell you that this thing went beyond friends a long time ago.

The past couple of months have been the best, most exciting ones of my life. And it's not just the sex, although it is by far, the best I've ever had. There's so much more to what we have that makes me count down the minutes until I'm with her again. Sometimes, it's chasing her around the lighthouse while she screams and laughs, trying to escape me. And sometimes it's the way we banter back-and-forth, always knowing what buttons to push to get the other going. But my favorite times are the ones where we're not talking at all. Where we're just holding one another, with nothing to do and nowhere to be besides right there in each other's arms.

I know we have our whole lives ahead of us, and that we have to stay focused on school and everything that comes after, but I can't say there isn't a part of me that secretly wishes we could just say fuck it all and be together. That thought almost knocks me on my ass because, even though it was fleeting, there was a moment there where football was the last thing on my mind.

"There," she says quietly, cutting the thread and holding the piece up in front of her. It's a jersey that she's clearly pulled apart and put back together as a dress. It's cut up the sides and held together with crimson ribbon, tied into little bows. It isn't until she turns it around that I realize whose jersey it is. Across the back is a giant block number 6 and my last name in big twill letters. My mind races as I think about seeing her in it, and being able to pull on every single bow, slowly and carefully unwrapping her like the gift she is.

I'm so gone for this girl, it's unreal.

She turns around, jumping in surprise when she sees me.

"Oh my God, you scared me!" she whisper-shouts, yanking her earbuds out with one hand while clutching the jersey against her chest with the other. "I almost peed!"

"Again?" I say with a laugh. It took me about a week after her little squirting incident to convince her it was nothing to be embarrassed about, but I can't help myself sometimes. Giving her shit for it is so much fun.

She rolls her eyes. "You're such an asshole. Just for that, I'm not showing you what I made."

She has no idea I already got a good look at it, and she won't either, because I'm going to play dumb. I want to see her light up when she reveals the piece to me and tells me all about how she made it. She's so passionate about designing custom clothing, and it radiates from her when she talks about it.

I close the door, but leave it unlatched so nobody downstairs hears, before stalking over to her. "C'mon, baby," I coo. "Be a good girl and show me." I know the last thing I should be doing is kissing her in the house with our parents here, but I can't help it when she looks up at me and a smile blooms across her face.

I weave my hand into her blonde waves and press my lips to hers. As much as I wish I could savor the way she tastes, I know I won't be able to stop myself from taking her right here if I deepen the kiss, so I pull back. She sighs contentedly, leaning into my palm before creating a small amount of space between us and holding up the dress.

I do my best to act completely surprised, widening my eyes and letting my jaw hang open. "Is that my jersey, Bunny?" I ask.

"Mhmm," she hums, clearly very proud of herself. "I thought I could come to a game this season and show it off. If that's okay with you," she nervously adds. "I mean, if you don't want other girls seeing me in it, I understand. I jus—"

"Grace," I say, cutting her off, "the *only* girl I care about seeing with my name and number across her back is you."

She gives me a shy smile, tucking a strand of her hair behind one ear. "Oh. Okay, cool."

God, she's so fucking pretty.

I go to sneak one last kiss, but just as I lean forward, the door swings open loudly.

"Hey, loser! Miss m—" Riggs says, stopping when he sees me. My body stiffens for a few seconds, then I jump away from Grace like she's got the goddamn Bubonic Plague.

"What are you two doing in here?" he asks. "With the door closed."

I stand there, looking guilty as fuck, trying to think of what to say that isn't *'I was just considering fucking your sister into the mattress really quick. Would you mind giving us about fifteen minutes?'* but I'm frozen. Thankfully, Grace has managed to keep her head on straight.

"What are you doing here?" she says, trying to turn her shock into excitement.

"We lost in the last round of playoffs, so I'm free for the rest of the summer," he says, eyebrows raising like he's still looking for the answer to his question. I'm still standing there like a statue as Grace speaks again.

"I was just showing Tanner this jersey dress I made for him. He," she pauses, swallowing roughly, "wants to give it to this girl he likes."

Riggs' face relaxes and he gives me a sly smile. "You fucking dog. Did you bag yourself one of those Harvard bookworms? I bet you they're freaky as fuck in the sack. I guess you'd already know that, though, since you've been doing the ol' pump and dump all over campus for the past three years."

I cringe, because the last thing I want to do is talk about fucking other women with Grace around. Not even to save face in front of my best friend. "Something like that," is what

I settle on. "Uhh, thanks for making it for me, Bunny," I say, turning to her and taking the piece from her hand.

"No problem," she says quietly, turning back toward her table. I want to reach out for her. Hold her. Tell her I love the jersey and can't wait to see her in it. But I can't do any of that. Not in front of Riggs.

"C'mon, man. Let's go get some grub then call a few girls to hang out with later. Earmuffs, baby sis," he says to Grace, and without turning back to us, she loosely puts her hands over her ears. "I haven't gotten my dick wet in three weeks. I hope you saved some pussy for me while I was gone."

I choke on a cough, because he'd fucking murder me right here if he knew that the only pussy I've been inside recently was attached to his sister. "There's plenty left for you," I croak.

"Nice," he says, reaching up for a high-five, which I'm able to play cool long enough to return. I follow him out of the room, hoping to catch her eye as I go, but she keeps them glued to the table, not moving until we're out of sight.

Fuck.

SIXTEEN
GRACE

I SIT on the edge of the dock, kicking my bare feet as I look out over the water. After Riggs interrupted Tanner and me last night, I pulled myself together long enough to go downstairs and eat dinner with our families. I sat quietly, pushing the food around my plate as I listened to my brother blather on about all the college girls that were home for the summer and wanted to hang out with them. We exchanged a few secret glances, but other than that, we didn't speak at all. When I couldn't take being around him and not feeling his body near mine any longer, I quietly slipped away to my room and tossed and turned all night, barely getting a wink of sleep because every bad scenario of what he could be doing played on a loop in my head.

I'll admit, I was jealous. The thought of Tanner spending time with anyone but me made me irrationally upset, considering we agreed that this was just going to be a physical thing for the summer. But that's not where I'm at anymore. As much as I tried to stick to the plan, I think it was inevitable. There was no way I could've stopped it.

I fell in love with Tanner Lake, and I want him to be mine and mine alone. I don't care what I have to do or who we have to piss off to make it happen. Nothing else matters to me right now. Just us. I know he's feeling it, too. I can tell by the way he kisses me. The way he takes care of me. The way he makes love to me. He doesn't have to say the words out loud because I can feel it.

At the beginning of the summer, when we first started this, I had everything planned out. Then life happened. *He happened.* What was important to me then, seems absolutely trivial now that I'm considering a future that may include Tanner and me actually being together for real.

That's why I'm considering alternative options for what I'm going to do in a month when it's time to leave for school. I know it's crazy, and I shouldn't derail all of my plans just because I fell in love, but I don't care. I've waited my whole life to get Tanner to see me as more than his best friend's little sister, and now that he does, I can't just pack up and leave him behind.

I've had my apprehensions about going to CCA since the day I got accepted, but I wanted to give it a try. I wanted a change from the boring life I was living here in Hope Harbor. I wanted to hang out with friends and go on dates with guys who didn't know their arms and legs were in danger of being ripped off their bodies if they touched me. I wanted something new.

But all of that has changed now that I've fallen for Tanner. Do I still want to be a fashion designer? Yes. I can't imagine waking up one day and not wanting to make clothes. Nothing makes me happier than losing myself in the feel of different fabrics, and finding ways to make them into unique pieces that make whoever wears them feel beautiful and confident. I'd never give that up, but staying closer to home doesn't mean I'd have to. I got into schools in Boston and New York, but chose California because I didn't have a reason not to. Now, I might.

I'm not saying I'm going to just throw it all away and

follow Tanner wherever he goes, but if he's willing to give this thing between us a real shot, I'm okay with rearranging some of my initial plans to make it work. In the end, I'll still be designing clothes, so how I get there doesn't really matter to me.

I hear the gravel behind me crunch under the tires of Tanner's car as he pulls down the driveway to the lighthouse, and my stomach does little flips of excitement. I'm kind of nervous to have a talk about our future with him, but we need to do it so I can think carefully about my next move. I know he'll look for me here, so I try to calm my nerves as I continue dipping my toes into the cool water, watching as it ripples away from me in large circles.

"Bunny," he says, walking toward the dock. I stand, wiping the dirt from the back of my shorts as he approaches quickly. He doesn't slow down, crashing into me and digging his hands into my hair before taking my mouth in a searing kiss. I'm caught off guard, stiffening at first, but it isn't long before I'm melting into him, pleading without words for him to keep going. Unfortunately, he pulls back, but slides his arms around my waist and leans his forehead to mine. "Thank God you're here. You didn't answer my text. I was afraid you wouldn't show up."

"I was with my mom when it came through, so I just read it quickly then shoved it in my pocket. I guess I forgot to reply. I'm sorry," I tell him. The truth is, by the time I got to my car to drive here, my mind was racing in so many different directions, I didn't even think about it.

"It's okay, baby," he says. "I'm just glad you're not pissed at me. I swear I didn't talk to any girls last night. I didn't even drink. I just waited until Riggs was occupied, then I snuck out and went home. I didn't want to wake you by calling or texting, so I waited until today."

I can't say I'm not relieved to hear him say that, because part of me was a little worried that maybe I'd been reading him wrong and that he doesn't feel the same way I do. But the other part of me, the part that is completely connected to his mind, body, and soul, is telling me that there's no way he doesn't love me the way I love him.

He leans down, ghosting his lips over the delicate skin of my neck. I tilt my head, giving him full access as I grip onto the fabric of his t-shirt.

"I want to fuck you all night long," he mumbles before licking a hot line across my throat. "I want to be so deep in your pussy, you'll feel me there forever."

Forever.

The word echoes in my head, warming me all over as it flows through me. I want forever with him so badly; I don't give a single fuck what I have to do to get it. I don't care that I'm only eighteen or that my brother is going to be mad that we went behind his back. I don't care that it's reckless to change my college plans to be closer to him while we start building our life together. I can still achieve all of my goals right here in Massachusetts with Tanner by my side.

"I have—" I stutter as he sucks at the sensitive skin under my ear. "I have something I want to tell you."

"Okay," he mumbles as his lips move across my shoulder like he can't decide where he wants to taste me the most. "Can it wait until after? Or should I stop?" He brings his hand up my body, stopping at my breast to pinch my nipple through my shirt, and all of a sudden, nothing else matters right now. I can tell him my plans later.

"It can wait," I whimper. "Please take me inside."

TANNER

I don't know what my deal is tonight, but I'm feeling like I can't get close enough to Grace. My hands aren't touching her body as fast as I want them to. My kisses aren't hard enough to make her lips swell. I'm so goddamn needy for her, and everything feels like it's happening in slow motion.

Maybe it's the way I felt at that party, wanting desperately to get away from all the girls that begged Riggs to bring me along so they could try to hook up with me. Maybe it was having to leave Grace at her parents' house, knowing she might've been worrying about whether or not I would be with someone else. Or maybe it was because she didn't respond when I texted her and I was terrified that she was going to be so mad that she'd call this whole thing off.

Whatever it is, it's got me all the way fucked up.

"Lie the fuck down," I say, shoving her backward onto the bed. She lands on the mattress with a soft *thud*, looking up at me as though I'm the only man in this world that knows what she needs. It makes the beast inside me rip at the bars of his cage, begging to be released. Because I *want to* be the only one. I want her to need me the way I need her right now. I'm desperate for it.

I waste no time tearing her clothes from her body, forgoing all of the pleasantries that I usually take. Normally, I spend a while kissing her body and getting her ready for me, but I can't even see straight right now with the need to get inside her as fast as I can. Her breathing is shallow and ragged, and I know seeing me like this is doing something to her, too.

"Tan, baby," she whines, making me pause for just a split second because that's the first time she's ever called me that. I fucking love it. I want to be her baby tonight. I want to be her everything. "I need you so fucking bad. Please."

I pull my shorts and boxers down in one go, reaching behind my neck and pulling my t-shirt off with one hand. I give my cock a few tentative strokes, but I don't need it. I've been rock hard since before we even made it to the bedroom. It feels so good to touch myself while Grace looks up at me from below, that I have to squeeze my tip because I could blow all over her body without even being inside it.

I practically face plant into her cunt, inhaling deeply before shoving her thighs as far apart as they'll go. I'm sure her muscles are burning, but I want to taste every part of her. Every inch of her skin needs to be touched, and I'm not leaving this room until I'm sure it has been.

I flick my tongue on her swollen clit, earning beautiful gasps and moans. Saliva is gathering in my mouth because of how good she tastes, and I let it roll down and drip onto her hot pussy. I don't even bother trying to swallow because I want to make her as messy as I feel right now. Sucking her sensitive bud between my teeth, I give her everything I have. Her back bows off the mattress and she reaches down, gripping my hair roughly and pushing me into her.

"Dirty girl," I mumble without so much as removing my mouth from her. "Fuck my face." She does, reaching her other hand into my hair and slamming down, groaning loudly when I push my tongue into her. We're rough and frantic, and it's making me feel free of the heart-twisting thoughts that were going on in my head a minute ago.

My cock has never been this reactive to another woman before. I feel feral, humping against the mattress, surely rubbing the precum that's leaking from my slit into the sheets below me. But it's not enough. Not even close.

"You want to be my little slut tonight, Grace?" I ask, looking up at her. "Let me use that body."

"It's yours," she says, barely able to catch her breath. "I'm yours. Do whatever you want to me."

Hearing her say that out loud while the taste of her is still on my tongue snaps the last of my self-control. I don't say a word as I grab roughly at her hips and flip her over onto her stomach. She gasps when I yank her back, pulling her ass up in the air and positioning myself on my knees behind her. Without any warning, I thrust inside until my pelvis is pressed tightly to her ass. I can't think of anything other than being buried so deeply inside her, she'll feel me long after I'm gone. I can hear the breath whoosh loudly from her lungs as she fights to adjust to my intrusion, but I can't stop myself from brutally fucking into her.

I know I should slow down, or at least check in to make sure she's okay, but it's like I'm not even myself right now. It's as though I'm outside of my body, watching like a voyeur as the last of Grace Valentine's innocence is greedily taken from her. She's moaning and screaming in ecstasy, gripping the sheets so tightly that the corners pop up from where they'd been tucked under the mattress. At least I have the where-withal to read her body language and sounds enough to know it feels good to her, too.

I focus on the way her body bounces with each of my thrusts, noticing how perfect her ass looks as I slam into her. I can't stop myself, rearing my hand back and landing my open palm roughly on her creamy skin. A red handprint blooms to life in front of my eyes as she moans loudly.

My Bunny likes to be spanked.

"Feel good, baby?" I say, rubbing my hand over where I struck her in an attempt to soothe the sting.

"So, so good," she replies, prompting me to do it again. And again, each time harder than the last. Her moans turn to whimpers as her body begins to shake. She's practically vibrating with the way she's trembling as she nears the summit.

"Come for me, Grace," I order, picking up my speed. "Squeeze me. Milk me dry. I want to fill you so deep, you'll taste it on the back of your tongue."

She comes on a loud scream, every muscle in her body tightening as she does. I slap her ass again because I can't fucking help it as I get impossibly hard, feeling my balls draw up tight. Fire licks up my spine and spreads throughout my body, and I bust inside her, convulsing wildly as I thrust one, two, three more times until I'm completely spent.

I can't speak. I can barely keep my eyes open as I wrap my arm around her waist and roll us onto our sides without pulling out of her warmth. I know I need to check on her and clean her up, but I can't even move. I just hold her tightly to me, feeling her deep breaths slowly even out before we both fade away from exhaustion.

SEVENTEEN
TANNER

I OPEN MY EYES, seeing the early morning sun peeking through the window. Memories from last night gradually come back to me as I wake. Grace telling me she was mine. Feeling completely out of control as I fucked her until it felt like I couldn't possibly get any deeper. The way she sounded as I took her in a way that was so rough, I almost forgot about her pleasure because all I could focus on was my own.

My cock begins to harden at the thought, and it's then that I realize I'm still inside her. It's been hours since we fell asleep, but I'm still nestled between her thighs, my now semi-hard dick hugged between her silky pussy lips. Without meaning to, my hips thrust forward just slightly, making her whimper in her sleep.

We didn't even pull up the blankets because we were both too weak and drained to move, so I have a clear view of her body as I look down. But as soon as I do, I wish I hadn't.

The first things I notice are the small bruises on her hip. My eyes widen in horror as they move lower, seeing another large, angry bruise in the shape of a hand across her ass. And when I pull myself out of her, eliciting another pained whine from her sleeping body, I realize what I've done.

I hurt Grace.

I was supposed to protect her, and I fucking *hurt her*.

I scramble off the bed, standing over her with my hands gripping my hair. I'm so fucking pissed at myself for losing control and not being more careful. I'm no better than any of the other guys I was worried about her being with, and that's very evident by the marks that are marring her beautiful body right now. Marks that *I put there.* I told her she'd be safe with me. Clearly, she isn't.

Fuck. I hate myself.

She stirs, turning onto her back and I can see the moment the pain hits her because her brows pull in and her eyes flutter open. I should be comforting her and apologizing profusely, but all I can do is take a step backward, away from the bed.

"I lost control," I choke out, gripping the back of my neck. "I'm sorry."

She sits up, lifting her butt off the bed to see the damage I've done. Her hand trails down, gently rubbing over the marks before she looks up at me. "I'm okay. It doesn't hurt that bad."

I shake my head in disbelief, because there's no way she's telling the truth. The bruises are a deep purple with shades of red and blue around the edges, and the sight makes me want to fucking puke. The more I look at them, the worse they get.

I reach down to the floor, pick up my clothes, and quickly get dressed. Grace must be able to see the panic on my face because she shoots up to her knees, crawls across the mattress, and stands up in front of me.

"Tan, seriously. I'm fine. I wanted it. I *liked it*." She reaches for my hand, and I let her because I'm spiraling and I need the connection. Her touch grounds me even though I know I don't deserve it. She should be so pissed at me right now.

I feel tears prick at the backs of my eyes, but I blink them away because this isn't about me. It should've never been about me. I sink down to my knees next to her, gently ghosting my lips along the marks. "I'm so sorry, baby. I'm so sorry," I whisper between kisses. She runs her hands through my hair, massaging my scalp as if she knows I need comforting right now, too.

"Look at me," she says softly. I obey, bringing my eyes up to hers. "I'm okay. Please don't treat me differently because of this, Tanner. I've loved everything you've done to me. I don't regret a single thing." She cradles my face in her hands, looking down at me with one hundred percent sincerity, but I still have a nagging voice in the back of my head telling me I fucked up by losing control with her. Maybe I just need a minute to clear my head, so I don't feel so messed up over it.

I grab her underwear and shorts from the floor, lifting each of her ankles and helping her step into them. I very carefully pull them up her legs, covering the bruises on her body so they're out of sight. I stand, helping her into her bra and tank top before weaving my fingers gently through her hair and dropping my lips to hers. The kiss clears my racing thoughts just enough so that I can take a deep breath, inhaling her scent and recentering myself.

In an attempt to distract myself even more, I remember our conversation from the dock. "You wanted to tell me something before I interrupted you last night. What was it?"

She looks confused for a few seconds, then the imaginary light bulb blinks above her head and she hits me with the most adorable smile. "Oh, yeah," she says. "So, I've been thinking about California,"

I groan. "I was hoping if we ignored its existence, it would just go away."

She giggles. "Well, I very much doubt you could make an entire state disappear, but what if I told you we could just pretend like it isn't there…ever?"

"What do you mean?" I say, genuinely confused.

"I mean, I don't think I want to go anymore. I want to stay here. With you."

I freeze.

Fuck.

This is exactly what I *didn't* want to happen when Grace and I started this arrangement. I was acting on impulse when I proposed it, and my only concern was keeping her away from anyone who could hurt her. But after last night, I realize I can't even be trusted not to.

I've known for weeks that she was falling for me, but I didn't do a single thing to stop it. Why? Because I'm a selfish motherfucker and I didn't want to let her go. I wanted to keep her until the very last minute we had together.

Because I'm falling for her, too.

But I can't let her give up CCA to follow me around to wherever I get drafted. I'd love to play for the Boston Blizzard. It's my dream to never have to leave home. But what happens if I end up somewhere else? What if I get drafted to some team down south and she ends up spending half the year alone, wondering if I'm staying faithful? I'd never even think of looking at another woman, but I know how rough life can be for the significant others of pro athletes, and I can't do that to Grace. She'd live in a constant state of worry, then end up resenting me because I was the reason she didn't chase her dreams in LA. She's better than that. The world deserves to see her talent and wear her clothing. She *has* to go.

"You can't just give up your dream and stay here because of me," I say.

She gives me a hopeful smile, and my fucking heart begins to crack in my chest. "I wouldn't. I'd just take some time off to figure out which school I'd go to here. I declined my acceptances from MCA and the New York Fashion Institute, but I'm sure I can call and get waitlisted for next semester. I want to be with you. Like, for real."

I take a step back, because hearing those words from her

lips is simultaneously the most beautiful and heartbreaking experience of my life, and all I want to do is pull her into my arms and never let go. But I can't. I have to give her a chance to live her life without being held back.

On top of that, I'm not even confident in my ability to keep her safe anymore. She trusted me with her body and now she's covered in marks because I was selfish and took what I wanted without making sure she was okay. Who's to say that it won't happen again? I was so afraid she'd put herself in danger with some random guy in LA, but then I turned around and did it on my own. She's better off with them. Away from me.

I have to make her go.

"Grace," I say, swallowing thickly. "That's not what this is." Her face falls and I feel like I'm going to vomit, but I keep going. Focusing on the wall behind her, because I'm a fucking coward and can't look her in the eye as I rip her heart out, I continue. "We were just having fun for the summer," I choke out, silently begging the burning at the backs of my eyes to go away.

"You're lying," she whispers, tears welling up before they fall down her sun kissed cheeks. "I feel what you feel every time you kiss me. You love me. And I love you, too."

I clear my throat, praying that I can get my next words out without my voice giving everything away. Because she's fucking right. I love her. But she'll never know it because I have no choice but to end this in a way that's so hurtful, she won't think twice about leaving here and going after the future she's wanted since her parents bought her her first sewing machine for her eighth birthday.

"I don't love you," I say, doing my best to harden my voice so she believes me. My throat dries as if it's trying to fight the lie as I force it out, but I continue. "I'm about to be drafted into the NFL. The best I can offer is a quick fuck when

I'm in town, but other than that, I don't have room for anything else. Go live your life. I'll go live mine."

When she doesn't say anything, I bring my eyes back to her face and that's when I feel it. My heart shatters in my chest as I take in the sight in front of me. The woman I love is standing there, her face crumpled as a stream of tears falls from her eyes, rolling down her cheeks and soaking into her shirt. Her arms are wrapped tightly around her stomach, as if she's trying to shield herself from the pain. Her whole body shakes and her bottom lip quivers while she holds back her sobs, but she says nothing.

Every instinct in me is telling me to take it all back. To comfort her and protect her from this heartbreak, even though I'm the one that's causing it. Watching her as she stands there, frozen in place as I make her feel like she means nothing to me is the hardest thing I've ever done, and I hate myself so much for it. But I'm doing this for her…so she can have everything she's ever wanted out of life. And so she can find someone who will love her and keep her safe in ways that I clearly can't.

"Tanner, please," she pleads so quietly, I barely hear her. But she may as well be screaming with the agony it makes me feel. I can't fucking take this. I have to go.

"Goodbye, Grace. Good luck in California," I say, giving in and letting a single tear fall before I turn and walk out of the lighthouse as fast as I can, hearing her bare feet slapping against the hardwood as she chases after me. It's not until I get to my car and open the door that I turn to see her running toward me.

"Tanner! Don't go! Please! *Please,*" she cries as she blows through the door. She winces and stumbles when the sharp gravel digs into the skin on the bottom of her feet, but she doesn't slow down. Tears flow freely down her face as she stretches out her arm for me, and I have to fight back my sobs at the sight. I almost cave and rush toward her so I can put us both out of this misery, but I don't. Instead, I drop down into the driver's seat and slam the door, turning on the engine and reversing as quickly as I can. Whipping the car around, I speed off, finally allowing myself to break down as soon as I'm sure she can't see me. Unable to stop myself, I glance up at the rearview mirror and watch as the love of my life breaks into a million shattered pieces outside the very lighthouse where she gave me everything.

EIGHTEEN
TANNER
PRESENT DAY

I CAN'T STOP my hands from shaking as I grip the wheel of my Tesla. A ride that would normally take me forty-five minutes is now closing in on the two-hour mark because I keep passing by my destination instead of just growing a set of balls and parking the car. Just being back in town for the first time after so long is making me anxious enough, especially knowing that I may have to face the consequences of my mistake. But it's time. I can't avoid it forever and it's been long enough.

I'm not even completely positive Grace will be here. It is her parents' fortieth anniversary party and I know how close they are, but she would've graduated from CCA last year, so I'm guessing she's well into her career at this point. She may not have the time off to travel back home for the weekend. Not everyone has months of freedom from their job like I do each year.

I was drafted late in the first round by the Boston Blizzard four years ago. That day should've been the best day of my life, but there was a dark cloud hanging over me. I smiled and graciously thanked the commissioner and the Blizzard organization for making my dream come true, but when I laid my head on my pillow that night, I felt empty. Like something was missing.

We won the Super Bowl last month, and I was named Most Valuable Player. We fought our asses off all season long, and the victory was well-earned for my guys. This was yet another huge career milestone for me that was tainted by the realization that I was incomplete, and that I only had myself to blame for it. It's weird how even when you have millions of fans screaming your name and cheering for you, you can feel completely and utterly alone.

Making my way around the corner and turning onto Journey Lane for about the fifteenth time today, I take a deep breath and pull to the side of the road, parking my car. There are vehicles lining both sides of the street, which doesn't really surprise me considering the amount of people that love and adore Bill and Libby. They were always like a second set of parents to me. Until I broke their daughter and left her alone to put herself back together. I turn off the car, looking at the two houses that I basically grew up in. One of which, I fell in love in. And she might be in there.

I've been trying to prepare myself for what I might find when I walk through those doors. The likeliness of her not being here is slim, so I'm expecting to see her at some point today. Will she be alone? Will she be here with a boyfriend? A husband? Children? Call me a masochist, and maybe I am, but I can't even begin to tell you how many times I've imagined her holding a baby that belongs to the person I wasn't man enough to be five years ago. I wonder all the time where we'd be if I would've just turned back around after leaving her behind and told her the truth. I was head over heels for her, and my fear of losing control, paired with being scared that she might someday resent me for being the reason she didn't live out her dreams, stopped me from giving us both the one thing we wanted more than anything.

I never stopped wanting her. I've loved her every day since I left Hope Harbor, and the wound I created when I cut her out of my life is still hemorrhaging. I'm afraid that once I go in there and see her with someone else, it might actually kill me.

But I did this. If that's where she ended up, I deserve to see it. I deserve whatever kind of pain it brings when I realize that she really isn't my girl anymore. Who knows? Maybe once I do, I can get the closure I need and move on with my life. I've come to grips with the fact that I will never love anyone again, but maybe knowing that she's safe and taken care of by someone who gives her everything I didn't will make it easier for me to find happiness in my life and career. Or at the very least, be able to celebrate my successes without feeling like they don't mean anything.

I turn off the ignition, wiping my sweaty hands on the front of my pants before getting out of the car. As nervous as I am, I just want to rip the Band-Aid off. It has to be done. My mind is going in a million different directions as my feet carry me to the door, ringing the doorbell and waiting for what seems like hours until it swings open in front of me.

As soon as our eyes connect, all the breath is sucked from my lungs. The smile that was plastered across her face just moments ago turns to complete horror as she looks back at me like she's seen a ghost.

"Hi," is all I can manage. She's fucking beautiful. I don't know how it's possible, but she hasn't changed, yet looks so much different all at the same time. Her hair that used to fall in waves over her shoulders is cut a little bit shorter, framing her heart shaped face perfectly. Her lips are still plump and pink, and I'm instantly taken back to the days when I could kiss them for hours. But the thing that catches me off guard the most is her eyes. They're the same bright blue they were last time I saw her, but there's a hardness behind them. Even as shocked as she is right now, I can tell that this is not the same girl I left behind five years ago.

She doesn't say a word. She just blows right past me, flying off the porch and down the steps toward the driveway.

"Grace, wait," I say, turning and running to catch up with her. Instinctively, I reach out and grab her arm to stop her. The heat that travels through me elicits a hundred different memories all at once, pulling every single time I've ever touched this woman from the depths of my mind right to the forefront as if they happened just yesterday.

She stops at my touch, stiffening but not turning to face me.

"Grace," I whisper, my voice trembling from the adrenaline coursing through me, "can we please talk?"

She turns around, and the look on her face hits me like a pass rusher straight to the chest. It's blank; completely devoid of any emotion whatsoever. Any hopes I had of being forgiven for what I did go down the drain, because the sweet, innocent, carefree girl I remember is no longer there. Left in her place is a woman who is hard and closed off. At least to me.

I did that.

"No, we can't talk," she says flatly. "You can get your hand off of me and leave me alone."

We both look down to where I'm holding firmly to her forearm, and I let go as if she's on fire. The white mark my fingers left behind is visible, and as it fades back to its normal color, I breathe a sigh of relief that I didn't accidentally hurt her.

Again.

I close my eyes and shake the memory of the bruises I left on her away just as she turns to walk down the driveway.

"Please," I beg. She freezes again, and I think maybe she's giving in to my request, but she whips back around and storms in my direction, stopping when our toes are practically touching. Her vanilla scent hits my nose and I try not to let it consume me, which is pretty easy when her hand reaches out and slaps me across the face. I push my tongue into my cheek, looking down at the ground, because while it wasn't physically painful, I've never been hurt so badly by a single strike.

"Five years!" she cries out. "You go away for *five years* without so much as a text or call. I poured my heart out, and you left me crying in the middle of the road. Now you want to talk? Fuck you, Tanner! Fuck. Y—"

"Babe, is everything okay?" a masculine voice says from behind me, prompting us both to look back. "I heard you yelling. You g—oh, hey Lake. What's up? Haven't seen you in a while."

I swallow, trying to speak, but the words come out choked. "Hey, Cash," I say as he moves past me, standing next to Grace. I watch in absolute horror as he reaches out, pulling her into his body with an arm around her waist and she leans into him for comfort.

Cash Hadley.

My high school backup quarterback.

The last guy to touch her before I did.

And by the looks of the diamond ring that slowly glides up his body before pressing against his chest, Grace's fiancé. My heart plummets in my chest as it glints in the light, and I have to look away as bile rises in my throat. I've had nightmares about this very moment, but none of them could've prepared me for the reality of it.

"Yeah, I'm fine. Just not feeling well," she says, giving him her best fake-as-fuck smile. I know it's fake because I know her inside and out, but he clearly doesn't, because he lets go of her and smiles back, nodding.

"Okay. Well, I was in the middle of talking to your dad about the housing project. Go home and lie down. I'll be back when I'm done here."

She nods her head, prompting him to press a quick kiss to her cheek before turning to me. "I assume I'll see you inside?" he asks. I just nod in response because I can't fucking talk with the image of him putting his lips on her playing on repeat in my head. "We'll catch up," he says, and I can't think of anything I'd rather do less.

I shouldn't have come here. I knew there was a chance that she would be with somebody when I decided to make the trip back to Hope Harbor, but I think part of me was hoping that she had waited or that she would be alone. Which is ridiculous, since I gave her absolutely no indication that I was ever coming back for her. I only have myself to blame for the pain I'm feeling right now.

We watch as Cash hustles back into the house, clearly consumed by the conversation he was having with Bill before he heard Grace screaming at me.

"You should go in," she says quietly. "My parents will be happy to see you. Goodbye, Tanner."

And with that, she turns and walks away, leaving me to curse myself for ever putting us in this position in the first place. I stare, watching as she crosses the street, walks three houses down and disappears into the garage. It looks like she's living in the old Robinson house now, not in California like I had originally thought she might be. As kids, we used to use their driveway as a turnaround with our bikes because our parents didn't want us going close to the main roads. The aging couple was always so nice and would even bring out popsicles for us on especially hot days. I have a million memories with her in front of that house, and now she lives there with another man. The man that stepped up when I threw her out like she was nothing.

But the truth is, I loved that girl more than I've ever loved anything in my entire life. More than football, or winning, or any of the other accomplishments I've ever made. None of them even come close to making me feel the way I felt about Grace Valentine.

I thought I was doing the right thing to keep her safe and happy all those years ago, but I know now that I was wrong. Seeing her today made me realize that the closure I was hoping for will never come, and now my punishment for breaking us both is to watch her love someone else.

NINETEEN

GRACE

"WE CAN MOVE this rack over by the front windows to make it visible to customers walking by. We have to try pushing it out before the new summer lines get here," I say to Claire. She owns Praya, the luxury boutique I work at. After I graduated from Hope Harbor Community College two years ago, she was kind enough to hire me as a sales associate. She and my mom have been friends since my family's company built the building, and she took a chance on a business major who hoped to work her way up the ladder. Six months ago, her head fashion buyer passed away, and she transitioned me into the position.

I know what you're thinking. What a tragedy to lose a co-worker so unexpectedly. And while we were very saddened by Gladys' death, it wasn't exactly a shock since she was eighty-five years old. Four years to the day older than Claire. Six years older than our sales manager, Etta. Other than me, there's only one other employee here that doesn't qualify for Medicare.

"What's up, sluts? Party's here!" Monroe announces, busting through the door like she's about to dance on some tables instead of head a marketing meeting. I shake my head, chuckling quietly as the two elderly women roll their eyes and go back to what they were doing before I interrupted them with plans for our new season launch.

"How do you still have a job here?" I ask, taking a sip of my coffee.

She rolls her eyes. "Please. These bitches love me. Also, I'm a goddamn marketing genius."

She's not wrong. At twenty-five years old, she has the knowledge of someone who has been in the industry for decades. Why she chooses to work at a small upscale boutique near the Boston Harbor is beyond me. She could be in some big city heading a marketing team wherever she wants, but I'm glad she's here, because I don't know what I would do without her. She moved into town after a bad breakup about a year ago, so we haven't known each other for long, but I swear we were meant to be friends. Right from our first real conversation, I've felt like she understands and encourages me in a way no other girlfriend ever has.

When I first started working here, I was still at a point where I had no direction in my life. After that summer, I decided against going to California and put myself on the waitlist at both MCA and the New York Fashion Institute. Eventually, I was accepted to both, but something was holding me back. I haven't designed an original piece in years, and every time I try, I end up hating the result. That's why, when I was given the opportunity to work here, I decided it was the right move for me.

I love fashion. My goal has always been to have my own line and maybe sell it in a shop of my own, but that's just not where I am right now. I keep waiting for my creativity to magically return so I can start designing again, but for now, I'm happy doing what I do. Filling this place with the latest trends and seeing customers come from all over to get them gives me a sense of accomplishment that I didn't think I'd find when I decided to go to HHCC and get a business degree. At the time, it was just a placeholder. I had every intention of going to fashion school, but I wanted to make sure I was in a good place to do it. Unfortunately, I never got there.

I'm okay with it, though. It took me a while to start rebuilding my life after Tanner left me to pick myself back up alone, but I was finally starting to feel like everything was back on track.

Until two days ago when he showed up at my parents' door and asked if we could talk.

I've tried so hard to avoid seeing him since that day. I know he was drafted by the Boston Blizzard, and he probably lives within an hour from me, but I make it a point to avoid the city and anything that has to do with the football team. He's a pretty big deal around here and everyone adores him, so it's impossible not to see him on billboards and commercials, but I do what I can. Even though it's been five years, it still kills me to see his face. As soon as anyone around me brings him up in conversation, I exit stage right because I'm afraid to know what his personal life is like these days.

Does he date? Does he have a girlfriend? I assume he isn't married because I feel like my parents or his would be broadcasting that rather loudly, but I'm sure one day I'll get that invitation and it'll break me all over again.

Not that I have any room to talk. Although Cash and I got off to a rough start when I was in high school, our paths ended up crossing again at a friend's birthday party right after I graduated college. I even helped him get a job working for my dad at the construction company when he mentioned that was his dream career. About a year and a half ago, he finally asked me on a date, and I accepted. I wasn't expecting to have much fun, but we really hit it off the second time around, and things have been pretty great ever since.

Like any couple, we have some things that we aren't in one hundred percent agreement about, but those are things

I'm willing to compromise on because I love him. I've learned that I don't always need to feel that rush of adrenaline when I'm with someone. Knowing that he loves me back and that he isn't going to just pick up and leave is good enough to keep me happy. So, when he proposed six months ago, I accepted. Even though we have small differences, he makes me feel safe and secure, which is something I struggled with for a long time after Tanner.

Currently, Cash is in charge of a huge project with my dad that will supply affordable housing to single moms and their children. He's been putting so much time and work into it, spending late nights at the office and on-site, making sure everything is perfect and that it'll be done by the deadline so we can move the families in as soon as possible. I'm so proud of him for everything that he's doing.

"Sooooo," I say to Monroe, catching her attention. "He showed up Saturday."

Her eyes go wide. "*He?* As in, the guy who threw you away like a piece of trash and disappeared from your life forever? That *he*?"

Wow. Next time just punch me in the face.

"Yeah," I say with a wince.

"Oh my God. Did you rip his nutsack off? Is it in your purse? Can I see it?" she replies, making me roll my eyes.

"I ran as fast as I could out of the house."

She put her hands together like she's praying. "Please at least tell me he chased you."

"He chased me," I tell her. "He asked me if we could talk, and I told him no. Then, Cash came out because I started yelling and that was kind of it."

She blows out a breath. "Whoa. So, he knows you're engaged."

I shrug. I didn't come out and tell Tanner that I'm getting married, but I didn't miss the way his eyes locked in on my ring when I put my hand against Cash's chest. I thought it would feel good for him to see that I had moved on despite the way he broke me, but if I'm being completely honest, it kind of sucked. The way his face dropped took me back to that summer all over again.

I know he wasn't completely honest with me that day at the lighthouse. Maybe I shouldn't have told him about my plans to stay in Massachusetts instead of going across the country for college, but I was pretty sure at that point that it wasn't really what I wanted. Being closer to home, and to him, felt like the right thing for me, and his reaction certainly wasn't the one I had hoped for. But the look in his eyes when he told me he didn't love me? To this day, I'm not completely sure I believe it. Not that it matters, because I've moved on and I'm happy. I'm marrying Cash, and we're going to have a long, fulfilling life together. The last thing I need is for Tanner Lake to walk back into my life and make me second-guess everything I've worked so hard for.

"So, what now?" she asks. "Do you think he'll start coming back around now that the ice has been broken?"

"I don't see why he would," I reply. "I'm sure he has a lot going on in Boston that keeps him from visiting home. I know his parents go down there to watch him play and to spend holidays with him, so I don't see a reason for him to start coming around again."

Part of me hopes that that's true. Seeing him brought back so many memories of all the years of friendship we shared. Not to mention, when he grabbed my arm, it was like no time had passed at all since the last time he touched me. It felt so familiar, yet at the same time, it was like I was looking at a complete stranger. I wasn't expecting the overabundance of emotions that hit me at the contact. Everything from being angry that he thought he had the right, to sadness that it's been so long since I've felt his skin on mine…to irritation with myself for feeling that way when it's the last thing I should be wanting.

Then there's the other part of me. The part that wishes I could coexist with him and not think about the past. I know I'm not strong enough to forgive him or be his friend. I guess I'm still too angry for that, but it would be nice to not feel like I had the weight of the world on my shoulders with the amount of effort I put into avoiding him.

I get invited to Blizzard games often, and I always decline because I'm afraid he'll somehow see me in the crowd. I know how impossible that is, but it's always at the back of my mind. I'm terrified that if he really looks at me and sees that there's still so much hurt and anger left over from the day he tore my heart out, it'll put me right back where I started. I refuse to go through that again. That's why I feel safe in my relationship with Cash. We may not have the explosive sexual chemistry that I had with Tanner, but a lot of good that did me anyway. I'd rather know where I stand in my relationship and not have to worry that it'll randomly just end abruptly when I least expect it.

"Well," she says, taking my coffee from my hand and taking a sip before walking toward the meeting room, prompting me to follow, "let's get this marketing meeting over with, Drama Llama. These hoes are going to be needing their morning nap soon." I roll my eyes just as Etta yawns loudly, making us both fight not to laugh.

It's not exactly what I expected my life to look like at twenty-three, but I worked hard to get here, and I know from experience that it could be a hell of a lot worse.

TWENTY
TANNER

"HONEY, you know we have landscapers, right?" my mom says, handing me a glass of lemonade. I stand, wiping the dirt from my hands before I take it, savoring the first sip. It's hot as balls outside and I've been working for hours.

"Yeah, and they do a shitty job," I reply. "The bark is starting to rot on this tree because they put too much mulch around it. And they did the same thing to the shrubbery around the porch. That's why it looks the way it does."

She looks back toward the house. "Jesus. Don't hold back, Tanner," she mumbles, making me huff a laugh.

It's been two months since the Valentines' anniversary party, and even though Grace's message that she's moved on was heard loud and clear, I can't seem to stay away from Hope Harbor. This is the fifth time I've been back since then, always finding a way to stay busy in my parents' front yard, hoping maybe I'll get a glimpse of her outside of her house. So far, I haven't, but the lawn is looking great with all the time I've been spending out here.

I started by tearing up the entire floor of their front porch last month when I noticed one loose board. My dad offered to help, but I told him I was bored with it being the offseason and that I was trying to stay busy. Then, I built my mom some new flower beds, even though there wasn't a damn thing wrong with the old ones. I had to really sell the idea by telling her she didn't have enough pollinator plants, thus guilting her into thinking she was part of the bee endangerment problem in New England. I'm not really proud of that, but it got her to stop asking questions.

Now, it's onto the mulch issue.

It's funny how I stayed away for so long, always finding an excuse to avoid being here. But now that I've broken the dam and seen Grace again, I have an overwhelming urge to be close. I know she hates me and that she probably doesn't want to see me, but I just have this nagging feeling that I need to be here.

"You know," my mom says, "you do have a little place of your own that could probably use some attention if you're so insistent on doing work. I was thinking maybe we could make some updates to—"

"No," I say, probably more firmly than I should. She just wants to help. "I'm not going there. I'm fine right here, doing your yardwork for no pay." I smirk, trying to lighten the mood, and I'm thankful when she smiles back.

"Oh, my poor, sweet child," she mocks. "Is that two-hundred-million-dollar contract extension not covering your bills? Does mommy need to start giving you an allowance for doing your chores again?"

"For fuck's sake, woman," I mumble. "You better watch it or I'll pay off your mortgage when you're not looking."

My parents have refused to take a dime from me since I signed my new contract with the Blizzard. They're very successful and really don't need my help, but it seems ridiculous that they won't let me pay some of their bills when they sacrificed so much to get me where I am today. Not to mention, my contract is a hell of a lot more than I could ever need in this lifetime. I'm a single guy who lives alone. I give almost half of my salary to charity every year and still have more than enough to last me long after I retire.

"You don't scare me, Tanner Patrick," she says smugly before taking the empty glass from my hand and turning back toward the house. She gets halfway to the door before facing me again. "You know, you may get better results on the... *yardwork* if you do it after about a quarter to six on week-days." Her eyes very briefly slide to the other side of the street before she heads back into the house while I stand there completely dumbfounded.

I shake my head, wondering how the fuck my mom knows why I'm out here. She couldn't possibly know the details. That I fell in love with the neighbor and broke her heart, and that's why I've spent years away from home. I may be her son, but if she really knew, she'd probably kick my ass. She'd have to get in line behind Riggs because that mother-fucker would have me eating through a straw if he found out what went down that summer. I'd allow it, too. I deserve that and more for what I did to Grace, although knowing she's going to marry Cash fucking Hadley hurts worse than anything they could do to me.

I can't help but wonder if I pushed her right into his arms. She told me back then that when he touched her, it didn't feel right. Did I leave her so vulnerable that he swooped in and took advantage of her? Or did she just genuinely fall for him? I have so many questions, but what would having answers really get me? More regret? Probably.

I try to distract myself by removing some of the mulch mountains from around the trees in the yard, hoping I can save them before the roots rot completely. Before I know it, the summer sun has cooled off and I look up just in time to see a white SUV turn the corner, pulling into the driveway at the old Robinson house. The light glares off the window at the worst possible angle, preventing me from seeing her completely, but I know it's her by the golden hair framing her face. My shoulders sag as the garage door opens and she pulls inside and out of my view.

I work for a little while longer, praying to God that she comes out to get the mail or something, but give up when the darkness starts to settle in and I hear crickets chirping in the distance. I notice that Cash still hasn't arrived home, and I wonder if Grace ate dinner alone. Is this normal for him to work well into the evening? The thought makes me angry because she deserves better than that. She deserves someone who rushes to be with her at the end of every workday. Someone who counts the hours until he can look into those beautiful blue eyes again.

I could've been that guy. Instead, I'm standing here like a fucking creep hoping she isn't sitting by the door waiting for him to come home.

I pack up the yard tools, returning them to the garage and trying to figure out when I can come back again. I just want another glimpse of her. I want to know that she really is happy and loved the way she should be.

Training camp starts in a few days, so it's going to be harder to make trips out here during the week, but I'll have to figure it out. Because no matter how badly it hurts knowing she's right down the street in a house that she shares with another man, I can't help it. Being in close proximity to Grace again feels like a missing piece has been returned to my otherwise empty existence.

TWENTY-ONE
GRACE

"THAT'S...NOT RIGHT," I whisper to myself, looking at the monstrosity draped across the dress form in front of me. I was so excited when I had a random moment of inspiration earlier while I was looking at the new clothes that were delivered to the boutique. The pieces were amazing, but I thought of a few things that I could do that might make them even better. I decided to come home and put my own twist on some of this season's trending looks, but I guess I'm not quite there yet. What I was seeing in my head is not what I ended up with at all.

I'm not going to get completely discouraged, though. I've been begging my brain to feel something for so long, that I'll take any crumbs of inspiration I get when it comes to making clothes. I think I just need to blow the dust off of my sewing skills, to be honest. My seams are crooked and the entire dress looks kind of lopsided. On top of that, I was a little scared to think outside the box with this one like I would've when I was younger. The result is a plain, boring piece that looks like it would be sold at any old shop. But progress is progress.

I hate to say it, but one of the things I lost the day Tanner left was my motivation to design clothes. I don't think it happened all at once, but as soon as I knew I truly didn't want to go to the California College of the Arts, I decided to take a couple of months off. I was younger and a lot weaker than I am now, but when he walked away, I felt like my world had ended. Before him, I was happy and full of hope for the future. After him, I felt like every day was a struggle to even get out of bed. I mourned the loss of not only my first love, but one of my closest friends. The problem was that it felt so good to lie in bed and cry all day, that it was hard to stop. It took me a long time to move from that stage of emptiness and depression to the one where I was so angry, that I couldn't even see his face on a billboard without wanting to scream at it. Eventually, that anger turned to resentment, which is where I've been for years. Seeing him at my parents' anniversary party stirred up so many different emotions that it was hard to decide which one to let out. At first, it was shock. My parents have sent him an invitation to every event they've had for the past five years, but he's never shown up. He sends flowers or champagne, but has never actually come to celebrate. So, seeing his face when I swung the door open that day knocked me off-kilter for a minute. By the time he chased me down in the driveway, indifference had settled in. It wasn't until he touched me, and I felt the spark of electricity that I thought my body had forgotten, that I realized how angry I still am with him.

I ended up pulling myself together about a year after he left, realizing he was never coming back for me, and signed up for the business management program at our local community college. I figured it would be a good way to ease back into school and gain some knowledge about running a business. I knew my creativity had taken a huge hit, so I didn't want to waste time attempting to design clothes when I wasn't fully myself yet. Before I knew it, two years had gone by, and I had an associate's degree. When Claire offered me a job at her boutique, it seemed like another step in the right direction.

My goal was always to eventually start doing original designs again. I never wanted to give that up, and it never even crossed my mind that I wouldn't be able to do it again in the future. Every now and then, I'll sit down at my sewing machine and give it a try, but I'm just never happy with what I come up with. Sadly, this dress is the closest I've come to being proud of my work in a long time. It's just missing that extra something that used to set my pieces apart from everyone else's.

Just as I'm considering wrapping it up and giving it to my mom for her next birthday, because she loves boring dresses, I hear the garage door open. I check my phone to see that it's almost ten at night, and Cash is just getting home. Now that we're well into the summer, he's been staying late to work on the housing project almost every night. They've broken ground already, but they're still finalizing everything for the inside of the complex. I'm proud of him for being such a hands-on leader with this, but I can't say I don't get a little frustrated sometimes when he's gone.

I turn off the lights and close the spare bedroom door, heading down the stairs and meeting him in the kitchen just as he comes through the door. I can tell right away that he's been drinking, which is not uncommon since the team sometimes goes out after they work overtime.

"Hey, babe," I say, sauntering up to him and wrapping my arms around his waist. "I missed you." I burrow my head into his neck, but he just plants a quick kiss to my temple before pulling away.

"I stink," he says, already making his way toward the hallway. "I'm going to go hop in the shower and get in bed. It was a long day."

I deflate a little, because it seems like it's been weeks since we've spent any real time together, and I'm getting kind of lonely. I spend a lot of extra time with Monroe and visit my parents as often as I can without feeling like I'm intruding on their kid-free life, but sometimes I just want to be with my fiancé.

"Okay," I say quietly, giving him an understanding smile. "I'll get ready in the other bathroom and meet you in bed."

"Sounds good, babe," he says, taking off out of sight. I go into the downstairs bathroom, wash my face, brush my teeth, and fluff my hair a little. When I get to the bedroom, I think I'll have time to change into something a little sexier, so I can hopefully catch his attention, but he's already fast asleep. He must have taken a two-minute shower and barely even dried off before the exhaustion took him out.

I sigh, deciding that it would be okay to take care of myself since he's so tired. Quietly, I tiptoe into the en suite bathroom, locking the door before rooting around under the sink until I find what I'm looking for. I reach into the shower, turning on the tap to muffle any noises that may escape the room.

I drop to my knees, spreading my legs as wide as I can before turning on the small vibrator. Its size looks deceiving, but it packs a punch, which is why it's my favorite. As soon as I touch it to my clit through my thin panties, I start to feel the coil of tightness bloom to life in my stomach. I close my eyes, but immediately open them when I realize the face I'm seeing doesn't belong to my fiancé. I pull the vibrator away, tamping down my arousal for a moment. Taking a deep breath, I close my eyes again, hoping that it was just a fluke, but it wasn't. All I see are Tanner Lake's endless, deep blue pools staring into me.

"Fuck," I say breathlessly, turning off the toy and tossing it across the room. I bring my hands to my face and drag them downward, shame filling me for the way my brain is working right now. I should be envisioning Cash. I'm attracted to him.

I love him. I'm marrying him. So why is it not him that I'm seeing when I'm touching myself?

As turned on as I am, I can't finish myself off like this. Instead, I get up, ignoring the throb between my legs, and put the vibrator back under the sink. I turn off the shower and wash my hands before flipping the light switch and sliding into bed next to my fiancé.

But again, it's not his face I see before I drift off to sleep.

TWENTY-TWO
TANNER

"HUDDLE UP!" I yell to the offense. They all gather around, looking to me for the next play. It's the second week of fully padded practices, and Coach Mills is insistent that we play situational football today in order to prepare for the season. So, we're out here with our starting offense playing against our starting defense, simulating a real game. It's not exactly the same, considering we both pull from the same playbook, but it's better than just doing run-throughs with our positions' coaches. Thankfully, even though we're padded, the defense isn't allowed to hit us. Which is really working for me today, considering my o-line is a little rusty from the offseason.

"Thirty-seven draw on three. Got it?" I say, looking at my running back, Dalton Davis, for confirmation.

He stands, crossing his arms over his chest like the child he is. "That's a great play, captain. One of my favorites, actually. But if you don't tell me where you've been running off to for the past four months, I'm gonna drop the handoff and make you look stupid."

I slide my eyes over to my wide receiver, Blaze Beckham,

lifting an eyebrow in hopes that he can somehow get his best friend under control.

"Don't look at me," he says, shaking his head. "You've been MIA for every guys' night we've had this summer. Cough up an explanation and we'll make sure Coach doesn't have your ass running suicides after practice."

I groan, dragging my hands down my face before looking over to our rookie receiver, Finn Bellamy. "Zip right, double panther on three. You good with that?" He nods his head enthusiastically, because he's new and wants to show that he belongs in our starting lineup. "Okay, break!" I yell, all of us clapping once in unison before we take our spots on the line.

"My wife is here, bro," Dalton mumbles from behind me. "How am I supposed to show off for her if you don't give me the ball?"

I take my spot behind our center, Rick Daniels, before turning back to him. "Have you tried staying the fuck out of my business and focusing on football?" I suggest. "I have a funny feeling that might actually work for you."

"C'mon, Lake," he whines. "You missed most of our offseason workouts, and now you're bailing on us almost every weekend. We just want to know what you're up to. You have a secret girlfriend or something?"

I wish I could say yes. I spent the entire offseason basically stalking Grace from my parents' front yard. I saw her come and go several times, and I know she saw me, too. She probably thinks I'm so pathetic right now, but I don't care. I'm going to continue spending time in Hope Harbor because my instincts are telling me I need to. I can't fight the pull anymore.

"No secret girlfriend," I say. "Just visiting home. It's not a big deal."

I see the moment he drops it, his eyes softening with understanding as he gives me a tight nod. Dalton knows more about my situation with Grace than anyone else on the team. He needed advice when he and his wife were going through a rough patch, and I wanted to show him what his future could look like if he didn't fight for the woman he loved. I didn't give him all the details, but he knows enough to cut this conversation off before anyone else gets involved. I'm thankful that the guys care, but I'm nursing a broken heart while simultaneously making it worse by not staying away. I'm not ready to talk about it all yet. I don't know if I ever will be.

I get in my stance behind Danny Boy, as we all call him, and begin the play, tucking Grace into the back of my mind just like I always do. "Blue, seventeen. Blue, seventeen. Hut, hut, hut!" I yell loudly, taking the snap and rolling back. Bellamy takes off, faking right before slanting in toward the middle of the field. My line hits all their blocks while I let the play develop, firing off to the rookie about forty yards away. He jumps up, making a textbook grab and brings the ball down, tucking it tightly in the crook of his arm before blowing past the free safety and into the endzone.

"Holy fuck," our defensive end, Maverick Moran, mumbles, his mouthguard dropping from his open jaw. "That dude is fast. Hey Becks!" he yells to Blaze. "Let me know if you need a ride to the unemployment office when the rook takes your job."

Blaze flips him off. "Shut the fuck up or I'll tell Bella about the time your athlete's foot was so bad, we started a petition to make you ride to away games in the cargo hold with our luggage." That shuts him up immediately, because the big motherfucker is an absolute teddy bear when it comes to his girl.

All three of the guys have found love over the last year, and I'm happy for them. I just wish I hadn't fucked up so royally in my life, so I could experience the wins we've worked so hard to achieve with someone by my side.

It's not like I haven't tried. I've been set up on a handful of dates over the last few years, but it never worked out. They weren't *her*. I realized pretty quickly that Grace Valentine will always be the girl I compare everyone else to, and they'll never be able to match up. It got to a point where I stopped saying yes to going out on dates because I felt like I was leading the women on when I had no intentions of exploring anything further with them. I'd rather be alone than with someone who I would forever wish was someone else.

We finish up practice and head to the showers. My muscles are aching and I'm exhausted, so I should be going home, but I find myself bypassing the exit and heading toward Hope Harbor. It's almost four o'clock, which will give me about an hour before Grace gets home from work and I might get a look at her beautiful face. It's Friday, so I have the next two days off to catch up on rest.

I realize how pathetic all of this is. I've resorted to full-on stalking at this point, just hoping to get a small glimpse of her as she pulls into her driveway after work on the days that I can make it out there. I know she's not mine. That she's marrying another man. But for some reason, I continue feeling this undeniable pull to be near her. It's the only thing that's made me feel like I can take a deep breath in five years, and I'm quickly becoming addicted to it.

It's going to hurt like a motherfucker when I have to let her go again, but she'll always be worth the pain.

TWENTY-THREE
GRACE

"I'M GOING to end up living in your guest room. I'm about to spend my whole paycheck before I even leave work," Monroe grumbles, looking at her reflection in the mirror as she smooths her hands over her hips. It's a slow day at the boutique, so we decided to try on some of the new designs we just got in and take photos for social media. She's an absolute knockout, so I suggested she model a few of the dresses. Who wouldn't buy something if they thought it would make them look as good as she does in it?

"At least then I'd have some company," I say with a laugh, but it's fake at best. Cash's mornings have been getting earlier, his nights later, and even when he is home, he's too tired to do anything together. I'm trying my best to be understanding because this project is about to make life a lot easier for some very well-deserving women and their children, but it's starting to wear on me. I always feel like I'm coming in second place to whatever Cash has going on in his life. It would be nice to be a priority, just once.

Monroe scoffs. "You're too good for that guy," she says bluntly. "First of all, he takes everything you do for granted. Secondly, he's pretty, but not nearly as pretty as you are. You could do better." One thing about my bestie…she doesn't mince words. She's always had a strong dislike for my fiancé and has never been shy about letting me know.

I roll my eyes and chuckle quietly, because there isn't really a point in arguing. I'm too frustrated with him right now to put any energy into defending him. He doesn't exactly deserve it at the moment.

I take a few photos of her, then send them so she can get them posted to the boutique's social media accounts. We seem to see an influx of customers on the weekend when we make a post on Friday about new inventory, so I'm crossing my fingers that tomorrow brings more people through our doors.

"Nice work, girls," Claire says, looking up from her phone. "You've done enough today, and you got here extra early this morning. Why don't you both take off and enjoy the rest of your evening?" The words are like music to my ears because all I can think about is pouring a glass of wine and soaking my body in a hot bubble bath. If I'm lucky, I'll have enough time before Cash comes home to enjoy a little one-on-one time with my vibrator. It's been months since I had actual intercourse, and if I don't get myself off tonight, I'm going to turn into a different person. Nobody wants that.

I don't argue, packing up my things and hightailing it out of the building toward my car. I make the ten-minute drive, pulling into the garage and noticing that Cash is already here. I should be excited that he's home before dark, but I immediately get the feeling that something is off. I hear loud music coming from upstairs, which catches me off guard because if he's up there, he's either in bed or in his office working. But if it's the latter, he wouldn't have the volume so loud. On the few occasions, he's worked from home, he's asked me to keep the noise down because it distracts him. He doesn't even like it when I run the vacuum if he's in his office.

I don't bother announcing myself as I enter the house, because he wouldn't hear me anyway. Making my way up the stairs, I notice that the office is wide open and empty, so I bypass it, heading toward the bedroom. The door is slightly ajar, and just as I go to push it open, I come to a dead stop when movement catches my eye on the bed.

I recognize Cash's back as he lies naked between a woman's parted legs. I'm frozen, watching as he thrusts into her, grunting while her loud moans fill the room over the rock song that plays in the background. His hand goes up to the headboard and she hooks her ankles above his ass, her fingers sliding around his torso and digging into the skin below his shoulder blades. My brain is screaming at my body to move, but it's like my feet are stuck in cement as I watch my fiancé, who hasn't touched me in months, fuck another woman in the bed that we share.

"Fuck, baby," he says, breathing heavily. "I love you."

"I love you, too," she says back, and that seems to snap me from my stupor. Tears well in my eyes as I turn toward the stairs and run as fast as I can out the front door. I don't grab my purse, my keys, or anything else. All I can think about is getting out of the house and away from all of this.

I sprint down the driveway, not really even knowing where I'm going. It's before five o'clock, so my parents aren't home yet, but I run toward their house. If anything, it'll give me a place to hide while I try to figure out what I'm going to do. I'm numb as my feet carry me down the sidewalk, my vision blurring with the tears that are filling my eyes, but I refuse to let them fall.

"Grace, are you okay?" says a familiar voice. I look up to find Tanner running toward me, concern written all over his face as he approaches. I know I should be mad at him right now, but the sight of him comforts me, making me crash right into his body and wrap my arms around him, fisting the back of his t-shirt in my shaking hands. He embraces me, holding so tightly that it forces the breath from both of our lungs. For a split second, I breathe him in, succumbing to my need to feel safe and protected.

I allow myself just a few more moments of it before I pull away. The tears I was holding in have now started running down my cheeks, prompting him to reach up and smooth them away.

"What's going on?" he asks. "Are you hurt?" He looks me over for any signs of injury, but I shake my head rapidly.

"I need," I start, choking on my words. "I need to get out of here. I left all my stuff inside." I look back at my house, terrified at the thought of going back in there. But as if he can read my mind, Tanner wraps a protective arm around me and leads me to his car. I know I shouldn't get in. He's hurt me worse than anyone else ever could, but all I can think about right now is getting away from here before Cash realizes I saw him. He'll know as soon as he sees my bag on the counter and my car in the garage. I just can't face him right now.

He opens the door to his Tesla, ushering me in and reaching across my body to fasten my seatbelt. There's a nanosecond where we make eye contact, but I have to look away because it's almost too much for me right now. After all these years, and all the anger and resentment I still hold toward him, being near Tanner feels like a lost piece of me has been returned. He shuts my door carefully, running around the front of the car and getting into the driver's seat. He doesn't say a word until we're miles away from my street.

"Can you tell me what happened?" he asks softly.

I sniff, trying my best to get myself together so I can speak. "I got out of work early today. I was excited to get home, but thought it was really weird that Cash was already there. He's been working really late for the past six months, so it was strange to see him home before dark. I knew something was wrong as soon as I got inside." I swallow thickly. "He wasn't alone."

I see his hands as they tighten against the steering wheel.

His jaw clenches and I can tell that he's angry. "That stupid motherfucker. I'm going to kill him," he says quietly.

"No, you aren't," I say. "I can't go home right now. I have two days before I have to be back at work. I just need to figure out where I'm going to stay until I can process all of this." Tears well up in my eyes again, but I fight them back. I've survived worse. I'm not letting Cash break me.

He stays silent for a moment, eventually exhaling slowly. "I have somewhere you can stay."

I don't answer. I just give him a tight nod because as much as I don't want his help, I'm kind of desperate right now. Once Cash realizes I caught him in bed with another woman, he'll be looking for me. I doubt he'll call my parents and tell them he can't find me because they'd have questions. He plays the role of doting fiancé in front of them, so he wouldn't be willing to run the risk of them finding out he's been cheating on me. My phone is in my purse on the counter, so I just need to find a way to text my mom and dad that I'm spending the weekend out of town. That should be enough to buy me a couple of days without raising any red flags. Even though I didn't do anything wrong, I don't want to get them involved until I've sorted out my own emotions.

We drive in silence for a few more minutes, but as soon as he turns down the gravel road, my stomach twists. I sit up straight, looking over at him. I'm sure he can see the fear written across my face as he comes to a stop in front of the lighthouse.

"No," I say, shaking my head rapidly. I do everything I can to stop the stinging in the back of my eyes, but it's no use. They fill with tears and spill over immediately as every memory of the last time I was here rushes back into my mind. Him telling me he didn't love me and walking away as I begged him not to. Crying in the middle of this very road for what seemed like hours before finally getting in my car and driving myself home, where I barely made it into my room before I broke down again. Days went by where I was on autopilot, crying myself to sleep, just to wake up the next morning and do it all over again. "I can't."

He kills the ignition, turning in his seat to face me. I look away because I'll be damned if I let him see what being here is doing to me. He doesn't deserve to know that I'm still affected by it. "Nobody will think to look for you here. I'll leave you alone if you want, but you'll be safe, and you can stay as long as you need to."

He takes his key ring in his hand, removing a key and extending it to me. I stare at it as if it's on fire, pressing my back against the door in an attempt to put space between it and me. "Why do you have a key to the lighthouse, Tanner? Your parents said they sold it."

His eyes meet mine. "They did. To me."

I pull my brows together in confusion. I have so many questions, but my emotions are currently all over the place and I don't think I can handle drudging up the past any further than just being here is already doing. I need to process one thing at a time.

"Will you please stay?" he asks. I turn, looking at the beautiful home, noticing how literally nothing has changed. I can see through the windows that the same curtains are hanging inside. The Adirondack chairs that we used to sit in by the fire are pulled up near the dock. Can I even do this? Can I stay here when it's filled with so many memories that ended in me losing so much?

I consider my options, which are basically none. I can't go to the inn here on the harbor because people will recognize me. I don't want to go to my parents' house because I don't know what to tell them. And I'm not going home. I need time to cool off before I tell Cash that we're over. But we are. That's the only thing about this that I'm completely certain of.

"Okay," I say quietly. He breathes a sigh of relief, exiting the car and walking around to open my door. I hesitate, feeling like I could vomit right here, but my body has a mind of its own, lifting off the seat and carrying me to the front door.

Tanner puts the key in the lock, having to put a little force behind it in order to get the rusted knob to turn. He pushes the door open, letting me walk through as he follows behind me.

I stand there, taking everything in for God knows how long. Nothing has been touched. A thin layer of dust covers the furniture, which tells me that nobody has been here in a while. Off to my right is the kitchen, where I sat on his lap as we ate our breakfast. I look left, seeing the entryway to the living room, where we snuggled on the couch and watched movies until we fell asleep in each other's arms. And straight forward is the hallway that I know leads to the bedroom. The bedroom where Tanner gave me everything, and also where he took it all away.

I know I should be focused on Cash and his betrayal, but being here is stirring up emotions that I have had buried inside me for years. Emotions that I thought I had under control, but are quickly bubbling up to the surface as I stand here next to him.

One minute, I'm telling myself that I'm going to be okay. That I can be here and not relive every detail of what was, undeniably, the darkest time in my life.

The next minute, I'm stepping forward and angrily swiping everything that sits on the counter into the wall beside it. A glass vase filled with seashells smashes into a million pieces and litters the floor beside us. Magazines and stacks of paper fly all around me as I let out my rage on every inanimate object within my reach. I lose control, shouting and sobbing as my chest constricts, unable to hold back the hurt that I've been harboring for what seems like a lifetime. My lungs are burning as I wail, letting everything I'm feeling out into the universe. Tears run down my face, falling to the floor at my feet as I erupt violently.

"I fucking hate you!" I yell. "I deserved better! I *am* better! You threw me away like I was worthless! I gave you everything! Everything! And you broke me!"

I continue tearing the place up, not even sure who I'm screaming at, while Tanner stands there completely frozen behind me. He lets me trash his house until I'm exhausted and out of breath. I only stop when I feel his arms wrap around me from behind, making me sag back into him as the adrenaline that was coursing through me starts to wear off and my body gives out. My chest is heaving as I try to breathe, unable to inhale fully through my sobs. I stare at the mess I made, until I'm eventually lifted from my feet and carried down the hall, hearing broken glass crunch under his shoes as he walks. I lean my head on his shoulder, whimpering softly because everything still hurts so badly.

I want to put up a fight as I feel us approaching the bedroom, but I'm so physically drained, that it wouldn't do much if I did. I don't know if I can go in there without more memories finding their way to the front of my mind. But as he enters the room, pulling back the covers and laying me on the mattress, my exhaustion wins, and I drift off to sleep before I even get a chance to feel another thing.

TWENTY-FOUR
GRACE

SUNLIGHT FILTERS through the curtains as I wake. At first, I can't even open my eyes because my head is pounding so hard. After my breakdown yesterday, I was asleep as soon as my head hit the pillow, and I slept all the way through the night.

I look around the room, flashbacks from the past twenty-four hours slowly trickling back in. The way I snapped, breaking Tanner's things in a blind rage as he watched at a distance. The things I said. Did he think those words were for him?

Were they?

I'd like to say my anger was because of Cash. Maybe some of it was, but stepping into the lighthouse triggered memories that were so painful, I felt like I was brought right back to that day. It broke me all over again, and I allowed myself to feel it for the first time in years.

I sit up, stretching my sore muscles and head toward the bathroom. As soon as I walk through the door, I see several brand-new outfits sitting on the counter. I pick them up, one by one, seeing that they're all my size. There's a t-shirt with a pair of cotton shorts, a pink sundress, and a tank top with a pair of jeans. Everything has the tags still on it, except for one item.

I reach out, pick up the familiar gray hoodie and hold it out in front of me. The crimson Harvard Football logo stretches across the chest, and when I hug it to my body, his scent envelops me. For just a moment, I allow myself to let go of my anger and remember the happy times, like watching the sunset by the fire, wrapped up in one another without a care in the world. I loved Tanner Lake with my whole heart, and I don't regret a single thing about falling for him that summer.

I put the hoodie back, undress and jump in the shower. By the time I'm done and dried off, I'm feeling a million times better than I did yesterday. I opt for the t-shirt and shorts, because I have no plans to leave here today. Eventually, I'll need to sort through everything that happened with Cash, but I'm honestly still numb about that.

I'm almost embarrassed that I didn't see the signs. My dad was always saying what a hard worker he was, so I didn't think twice about the late nights and him always being exhausted. To begin with, our sex life was subpar, at best. So, I overlooked his disinterest, thinking maybe we were just going through a bit of a disconnect and that it would get better when we could spend more time together. But I never would've guessed his lack of desire to have sex with me was because he was getting it from someone else.

I make a mental note to get tested as soon as possible, because even though it's been a long time since we were intimate, I want to be sure. Who knows how long he's been sleeping with another woman, and who else she's been with during that time? I exhale, shaking my head at the thought of where my life is right now. Twenty-three and currently hiding from my ex-fiancé in a lighthouse owned by the person responsible for my first heartbreak.

Big yikes.

I find a brush in the drawer and carefully untangle my hair, braiding it loosely with the hair tie I thankfully keep on my wrist. I take a deep breath, looking in the mirror at my still tired reflection before heading out to the main part of the house to clean up the mess I made yesterday. I half-expect to see Tanner when I make my way to the living room, but the house is completely quiet, and it looks like I'm here alone.

Walking into the kitchen, I'm nervous to see the damage I caused yesterday now that I've calmed down. But I'm completely shocked when I enter the room to see that it's spotless. The glass has been swept from the floor. The papers that were scattered around the room are all set neatly into a pile on the table. And in the spot where the vase full of seashells used to sit, is a brand new one holding a fresh bouquet of white roses.

"Fuck him," I mumble halfheartedly as I lean in to smell them before turning toward the living room. All the dust I noticed yesterday has been wiped away, revealing the same beautiful furniture I remember from the last time I was here. I can't believe I slept through him cleaning all of the mess and coming back with new clothes and flowers. I guess I really was exhausted. I kind of still am.

Turning back toward the kitchen, I throw up a silent prayer that he keeps some type of caffeine around here. I'm not above instant coffee at this point, and I don't care how old it is. As long as it wakes me up, I'll choke it down.

I open the cupboard, finding it completely full of what looks to be brand new food. There's a bag of fresh coffee grounds from the café in town, a loaf of bread, and all the other things I would've bought myself if I was spending a weekend away. The refrigerator is also full, with fresh fruits and vegetables, milk, and most importantly, caramel creamer.

I make quick work of getting the coffee maker brewing and tap my foot against the hardwood floor while I wait. I make a mental list of things I need to do, including getting ahold of my mom to let her know that I won't be home for the next couple of days. I'll probably just tell her I'm having a girls' weekend with Monroe, so she doesn't ask any questions. I also need to make an appointment at the clinic to make sure I have a clean bill of health. I have to admit, I'm feeling kind of gross knowing that Cash was with someone else, and I have no idea how long it was going on. Just the thought makes me want to scrub my body with bleach.

I pour myself a cup of coffee, adding just the right amount of creamer before I make my way to the couch. The first sip hits my soul, making the zombie inside me take a hike, and I feel just a little more like a normal human being. It isn't long before I'm returning to the kitchen for a second cup, this time choosing to wander outside while I drink. It's a warm day, pretty typical for the end of summer in New England. The water laps gently against the shore as the sunlight bounces off the surface, making it look like a blanket of glitter as far as I can see.

As fucked up as my life is right now, even with all the buried emotions being here has stirred up, it's still as beautiful and serene as I remember. I sit in one of the chairs, kicking my feet up on the edge of the firepit and closing my eyes as I let the warm morning sun soak into my skin. I almost drift off, but when I hear a repetitive *thud* in the distance, I sit up straight, twisting around to investigate.

"You've *got to be fucking kidding me*," I groan when I find the source of the noise, ducking my head so I'm blocked from his view, but popping back up slightly for another look. Tanner is standing shirtless next to a large chunk of wood, raising an axe above his head. When he swings it down, the log splits right down the middle. Basketball shorts hang low on his hips, the band of his designer boxer briefs peeking out from the waistband. Beads of sweat roll down his abs, taking their time to explore every single dip and valley as they make their descent.

I sit there, staring like a creep, watching as he chops wood like some kind of edible lumberjack. I know I should stop looking. I'm still so angry and resentful toward him for everything that happened in our past, but I can't deny that he looks even better now than he did five years ago. I thought he was a man before, but the way he's become bigger, harder, and more defined makes me realize that the Tanner I was dealing with before has become a whole new person. But I can't let myself forget what he did. I'm appreciative that he brought me somewhere to hide for the weekend, but that doesn't mean I'm just going to forgive him. I've spent so long trying to make sense of every detail of that day, but the fact that he left me with no answers and no real explanation broke me in a way that I'm not sure I'll ever be able to get past.

I'm not saying that one day Tanner and I can't be friends again, but I'm not dumb enough to give him my trust twice just so he can throw it away like he did before. I learned that lesson the hard way the first time around. Then I decided to take a chance on Cash, and he proved to be no better than Tanner.

Fuck men, for real. You know who's never broken my heart? *My vibrator.* And we're about to have a long and happy life together.

Now that I've reeled myself back in and found my inner bad bitch, I face forward, ignoring the twelve-pack of abs thirty yards away and focusing on the shit show my life has turned into within the past day. I wonder if Cash found my stuff on the counter and realized I caught him. I hope he's scared out of his mind right now, worrying about what I'm going to do. Does he care if I'm upset?

I've been waiting for the feeling of being broken to settle in, but it just hasn't. Don't get me wrong. I'm pissed that he cheated. In our bed, nonetheless. I'd be perfectly happy cutting his dick right off and throwing it out the window of a moving vehicle, but that hopelessness and despair that I'm sadly very familiar with? It's not there.

I try not to dwell on why that is, finishing my coffee and standing to go back inside. But as soon as I round the chair, I'm hit by the sight of Tanner carrying an armful of firewood toward me.

"Good morning," he says quietly. "Did you sleep okay?"

I clear my throat, trying my best to avert my eyes from his half-naked form. "Yeah. Thanks." Fuck, this is awkward. This man has been a part of my life since the day I was born. He's seen me at my best and my worst, and he knows me in ways that nobody else in the world does. So, the fact that I can barely even look at him is sobering. This is our reality now, and I hate that he did this to us. "And thanks for cleaning up. Sorry about…yesterday."

He sets the wood down by the firepit, standing back up in front of me. "Don't apologize for that. You had every right to react the way you did. It's my first time back here too, so I get it."

I snap my eyes up to his, anger immediately rising back to the surface. "You get it?" I choke out. "Yeah, I can imagine how hard it must be for you to revisit the place where you tore my heart out and left it bleeding so you could go live your life. You poor thing." I turn to walk away, but he grabs my arm, halting me.

"Bunny, that's not wha—"

"Don't fucking call me that," I seethe, ripping my arm away from him. "We aren't friends, Tanner. I appreciate you giving me a place to stay for the weekend, but I can assure you that after tomorrow, you can go back to your cushy, comfortable life and stop worrying about me. I'll be fine on my own." I hightail it toward the house, slamming the door and going straight to the bedroom, where I stay until I hear his Tesla pull away, leaving me alone to make sense of all the emotions that are battling one another inside me.

TWENTY-FIVE
TANNER

I WALK INTO THE BAR, heavily considering turning around and going back home. But the guys were right. I've been bailing on them all summer long. I know they would understand if I just opened up and told them the truth about Grace, but they all look to me for guidance when they're having problems. I don't want them to know how fucked up my life has been the entire time I've known them.

We've been having our guys' nights here since they were drafted. It started with me wanting to take them under my wing and build relationships that would transfer onto the field, but over time, Blaze, Dalton, and Maverick have become some of my best friends. I know that sounds ridiculous to say, considering there's so much about me they don't know, but the shame I feel about the way I handled things with Grace back then is something I've never been able to shake. It's embarrassing to let the people who look up to you know that in your younger days, you didn't follow the same advice you now give to them.

"Over here!" Dalton yells, standing up and pointing to where they're sitting. It's not a crowded bar, and we have a special section in the back so we can enjoy our night out without being interrupted by fans. I love hanging with them, but guys' night is not the time or place to be signing autographs and shaking hands.

"Holy shit," Maverick says, reaching out for a high five. "It lives."

I roll my eyes, but he's right to be shocked at my appearance tonight. I haven't been prioritizing my friends the way I should because I'm too consumed with being near Grace, that I'm willing to risk every other relationship in my life just for a chance to look at her.

I decided tonight would be a good night to go out because, first of all, I could definitely use a drink. Secondly, I need something to stop me from driving back to the lighthouse and apologizing for how I handled things earlier. I don't know what I was thinking, acting like being there was harder on me than it was on her. I was the one who left. She begged me to stay.

But what she doesn't know is that I left my heart in the middle of the road with her that day. Between her saying she was considering giving up all of her dreams to stay with me, then me leaving bruises all over her body, I panicked. I spent the following months convincing myself that I had done the right thing to keep her happy and safe. By the time I realized how badly I had really fucked up, I didn't want to barge back into her life if she had started to move on.

Could I have looked her up to see if she was with someone? Or just asked Riggs or either of our parents how she was? Probably. But I always had a fear that they would tell me the exact thing I didn't want to hear. That's why I don't run or even have access to my own social media accounts. Living in ignorance has always seemed to be the easiest thing.

But I don't want easy anymore. I want *her*.

I know I can't just swoop in and try to win her back right away. She was just cheated on and is about to end her engagement. She's raw and vulnerable right now. I'll do everything I can to be there for her until she tells me she doesn't want my help, but I need to slow my roll with thinking that I'm going to be able to gain her forgiveness and trust so easily. I'll work for it forever if it means eventually getting a chance to show her that I still love her more than anything in this world.

But I can't do it alone, which is why I need to finally let the guys in on everything.

We order our appetizers and drinks, waiting for the server to set them on the table before we start telling each other what we have going on. Blaze tells us all about Mads getting another promotion at Tailgate Media, now heading the entire Blizzard media team. That girl works harder than anyone I've ever met, so I'm not surprised.

I go to reach for a loaded nacho, but Dalton pulls the plate away quickly. "Sorry, these are for people who don't hide their whereabouts from their friends. Hey Mav," he turns to look at Maverick, "where were you after practice yesterday?"

Maverick looks up from his phone, clearly annoyed. "Had a photoshoot with Bella at our apartment. Something about 'showing the fans how relatable we are' or some shit."

"Here you go, buddy," Dalton says, handing him a chip before looking back to me. "Easy as that."

I pinch the bridge of my nose, taking a deep breath so I don't end up punching this idiot in the face. When I've collected myself, I sit back in my chair, and tell them everything. I start at the beginning, telling them about how Grace and I agreed to keep things just physical, but that we both fell for each other in the process. I go on, giving them as many details as I'm comfortable with, including how I freaked out on that last day and left her crying outside of the lighthouse. They listen intently, letting me go on about how I still love her more than ever, and how seeing her again solidified that I'll never be able to move on. Then, I do something I never thought I would.

I ask for their help.

"Wow," Blaze says, blowing out a breath. I know he probably has more questions than anyone. When he found out that Mads was into BDSM, I knew I had to help him. I've spent a lot of time since I left Hope Harbor learning the correct way to do things. The bruises I left on Grace's body rattled me at the time, and I put all my extra energy into making sure nothing like that would ever happen again. Deep down, I always hoped I'd find my way back to her, and I wanted to be everything she needed if she ever blessed me with a second chance. Preventing Blaze from making the same mistakes I did was honestly not even a question. "What can we do to help you get your girl back?"

I shake my head, pushing away the defeat I'm feeling after what happened earlier at the lighthouse. "Nothing yet. Right now, it's up to me to gain her trust back. I broke us, and I can tell right now it's not an easy fix. But I'm not going to give up. She's technically still engaged, so the best I can hope for is friendship. Once I have that, you guys can help me show her how perfectly she'll fit into my life."

I know that was probably the thing that hurt Grace the most. I was an idiot when I told her I wouldn't have room for her once I got drafted. Other than saying I didn't love her, that was the biggest lie I told her that day. Because there hasn't been a single win or loss that I've experienced where she wasn't the first thought in my head. I wanted to share it all with her, and I made her think there wasn't a place for her by my side. The truth is, I carried her with me through it all. Every touchdown. Every victory. Every time I looked into the camera, hoping she was watching. I haven't done a single thing in my career without thinking of her first.

And now it's time to show her.

TWENTY-SIX
GRACE

"THANK YOU," I say to the taxi driver, closing the door and turning toward the house. It's still light out, so I'm not expecting Cash to be home from work yet, but when I punch in the code to open the garage door, my stomach drops as both of our cars come into view. I spent the weekend at the lighthouse rehearsing this conversation over and over in my head, but now that I'm here, the nerves have kicked in.

My plan is simple. Go in there, tell him to pack his shit, and kick his ass to the curb. I got all the explanation I needed when I heard him tell whoever he was with that he loved her while he fucked her in our bed. The longer I sat with the details, the more my decision to call off the wedding and cut Cash from my life completely made sense. He not only blatantly disrespected me by bringing another woman into our home, but it obviously wasn't just a one-time lapse of judgment since it seemed like they have deeper feelings for each other. Meanwhile, I've been begging for scraps of attention and supporting him through this project, not knowing that the late nights and disinterest had nothing to do with it. I just want to get this shit over with so I can move on with my life.

I walk into the house, seeing my purse and keys right where I left them when I ran out on Friday. I know he saw them. It's been three days. I used Tanner's old laptop he left at the lighthouse to log into my iMessage and texted my mom, Monroe, and Claire to tell her I was taking a sick day today. I was actually surprised it even worked, but I guess life figured I'd already been kicked enough, so it gave me a little break. I had several texts from Cash asking where I was, but it's clear that he wasn't worried enough to reach out to my family or friends to see if they had heard from me.

Because he knows he's busted.

I'm not inside for thirty seconds before he steps into the room, plastering a saccharine smile on his face as soon as he sees me. "There you are, babe," he says in fake relief. "I was worried sick." He starts walking toward me, but I put my hands out in front of me, stopping his approach.

"Save it," I say firmly. "I saw everything."

His expression drops and his face goes completely white. "I don't know what you *think* you saw, but it isn't what it looks like."

I scoff. "So now you're going to gaslight me into thinking I didn't witness you fucking someone else in our bed. Who is she, Cash?" I ask. I thought I could stay calm, but now that I'm looking at him, I'm fuming.

He hangs his head, knowing he can't talk his way out of this. It doesn't matter either way. My mind is made up. We're over. I just want to know if he'll be at least a somewhat decent human being and come clean. "Sophia," he says quietly.

"Wow," is all I can offer. Sophia is his partner on the housing project. She's worked for my dad for about a decade and is definitely that much older than I am. She was assigned to watch over Cash because this was his first solo project and he needed someone to show him the ropes. I guess she went above and beyond the call of duty, didn't she?

"I'm sorry," he offers. "I didn't mean for it to happen. It just...did."

I feel the blood in my body go completely cold. "I gave you everything I had," I begin, raising my voice in anger. "I supported you even when you left me here alone all night. I bragged about all the good you were doing. I begged you to fuck me and spend time with me, but you acted like I was a burden. And you've been fucking someone else since you started this project?"

His eyes go wide, but he tries to recover. It's too late, though. I already fucking saw the guilt as it passed over his face.

"Were there others?" I ask, not really wanting to know the answer. He just stands there, staring at the wall, not saying anything. "You piece of shit," I say, shaking my head because his silence just told me everything I needed to know.

I blow past him, heading up the staircase and straight to our room. I stomp into the closet, taking the biggest suitcase we have from the shelf and returning to toss it on the bed. Opening his dresser drawer, I reach in, grabbing as many articles of clothing as I can and throwing them in.

"What are you doing, Grace?" he says, leaning against the door jamb.

"Packing your shit. We're done. You can go stay with Sophia." I pull my engagement ring from my finger, throwing it straight at his chest before returning to the dresser for more clothes.

"I'm not leaving," he replies, bending down to pick up the meaningless piece of jewelry. "And if you tell your dad about any of this, we'll both get fired and the project will be put on hold because there's nobody else to head it up. Soph and I are the only ones who would be able to. Do you really want to be the reason all those women and children end up homeless?"

Is this motherfucker *kidding me* right now?

"Are you blackmailing me?" I ask in complete disbelief. I

turn to see a smug look melt across his face as the corner of his mouth tips up in a disgusting smirk.

"That's hardly blackmail, babe. I'm just telling you what'll happen if you open that fat fucking mouth of yours."

My jaw drops. Cash hasn't been the best fiancé. He's ignored me and made me feel like I was never a first priority, but I never thought he had it in him to cheat on me or threaten me like this. Then again, it was so easy for him to put a mask on around my family, making them think I was the center of his world. I guess it isn't impossible that he was doing it to me all along, too.

"Who *are you*?" I whisper, shaking my head.

He laughs. "I'm the guy who's put up with your ass for years so I could get in good at your dad's company. Did you know I applied there while I was still in college so I could get a foot in the door, but my resumé was never even pulled? Why do you think I tried to hook up with you back then? You can't possibly think I'd have really wanted *you* when I had my pick of hot college girls at school. I was playing the long game."

I'm frozen, unable to move or speak. All I can do is stand there while he continues.

"Here's what's going to happen. You're going to pack everything you need, and you're going to leave. You're going to tell everyone we're taking a break because you're getting cold feet, but that we still love each other. When the project is over and I have the experience under my belt, Soph and I are starting our own business, and you can go crying to daddy about how I broke your heart."

My mind is reeling with the way this just got flipped upside down, but I can't risk the project not getting finished. I was able to get to know some of the future tenants when my dad did the initial press conference about it. So many women sacrificing everything to give their children the best lives possible, all on their own. Some of them came from abusive situations, and having safe, affordable housing is giving them a brand-new start. I can't let them down.

I know my dad. If he finds out that Cash is cheating on me, especially with another one of his employees on company time, they'll both get fired. So, I'll play nice. But as soon as those families are safe and sound in their new homes, this man and everything he's building will be burned to the ground.

Keeping my eyes boring into his, I reach into the suitcase, removing his clothes piece by piece and dropping them to the floor in a heap. Fuck him. He can pick them up himself. I make sure to walk on them while I go over to my dresser and mindlessly take out random pieces before taking my time to fold each one meticulously and setting them into the now empty luggage. He stands there, arms folded, shifting his weight from foot to foot like my petty antics are annoying him. Good. He hasn't seen anything yet.

Once I've packed everything I can fit into the bags I have, I load up like a pack mule, determined to make one trip out to my car so I don't have to come back into the house. Cash just stands there like the selfish piece of shit he is, never offering to help. Not that I'd let him.

It's not until I'm in the car, turning off of our street that I let myself cry. All I've ever wanted was to be the most important thing in the world to someone. I wanted to build a life and be happy with them, making plans for the future with a family that we created out of love. I thought I had that a long time ago, and then again now, but both times I ended up alone and humiliated. With Cash, it feels like less of a blow, but it still fucking hurts to know that I never really meant anything to him. I was a steppingstone to the career he wanted. All the times he told me he loved me were only lies to reel me in so he could steal my heart. A heart that, by the time he got to it, was already missing so many pieces.

I tried to put myself back together in the months after

Tanner left, and while I did the best I could, there was still a part of me that would always walk around outside my body. A part that was so close in distance but may as well have been on another planet.

I don't remember the exact moment I realized he wasn't coming back, but eventually, I started learning to live knowing that a small piece of me would never be returned. Cash was a Band-Aid covering that hole and making me feel like someday, I might be okay. Now that we're over, that part has become exposed again and I know how dangerous it is being near the person who has always been its rightful owner. I need to be careful and not give Tanner another chance to walk away with more of me. I would never say the words out loud, not even to myself, but I don't think I could survive losing him again.

It's a short drive back to the lighthouse, but these emotions I've been feeling for the past three days have me so exhausted, I just want to curl up in bed and hibernate for a few days. I can't because I have to work and keep up appearances that everything is fine for the next month or so while the housing project is being finished, but I have all of today to pretend like my life isn't a stage five dumpster fire.

It wasn't even a question that I would be staying at the lighthouse, at least until I can find another option. Tanner gave me a key and told me to stay as long as I wanted. As much as this place stirs up all kinds of memories, it's also giving me a feeling of safety and security that I haven't felt in a while.

When Cash and I bought our house, even though I grew up right there, it took a while for me to feel like it was truly my home. Maybe it was because I was used to just riding my bike by it every day, knowing it was owned by someone else, but when it came time to fill it with our own memories, it just never really felt right.

But not here. Even though I've only ever been here with

him, the inside of this lighthouse feels like it's been ingrained into the deepest part of me. I didn't dig into why Tanner ended up buying it, but a part of me is glad that it wasn't sold off to someone who didn't know all of the amazing memories that were made within these walls. I knew it had been sold shortly after he went back to school that summer, but I never would've thought in a million years that he was the new owner.

What made him buy it? Does it hold a place in his heart the way it does mine? Even though he left and never returned to me, or by the looks of it, to this place, does he feel the same security here that I do?

All these questions swirl around in my head, but it doesn't change the fact that I'm still full of so much resentment toward him for doing what he did. Him coming back into my life certainly muddied things, but I still can't forgive or forget right now. I may never be able to. I may never *want to*. All I know is that I need the comfort this house is currently giving me, and I'm going to soak it up until I find somewhere else to go that isn't my old bedroom at my parents', which would raise way too many eyebrows.

I unload my bags from my car, lugging them into the house and dropping them with a *thud* onto the hardwood floors. I pull up the delivery app on my phone, ordering some food to cook because, although I may be staying here, I won't be eating the groceries Tanner bought. Other than the roof over my head, which I plan on paying rent for, I don't want any help from him. He can keep trying to extend olive branches, but I have to keep him at arm's length to protect myself. My trust has been hanging by a thread for years, and it's all but obliterated after my conversation with Cash today. It's going to take a miracle for me to ever give my heart to anyone again.

I busy myself, hanging my work clothes in the closet while I wait for my groceries to arrive. When they do, I make room in the refrigerator and pantry, unloading the bags and kicking them aside. I'll pick them up later. But right now, I'm starving. My nerves were too out of whack earlier, knowing I had to confront Cash, but it's catching up with me and I know I need to eat.

I keep it simple, throwing some pasta in boiling water and some jarred spaghetti sauce in a large pot I found in the cupboard. I complete the meal with enough cheesy garlic bread to feed a small country, because after the day I've had, I deserve it.

I leave my mess for later as I plate the food and plop down in one of the barstools. I notice that the roses Tanner bought are starting to wilt, an ugly brown fading into the petals as they droop off the stems. I tilt my head, slowly chewing my food as I think about how nothing beautiful ever seems to really last in my life. Not security, not love, not even the most exquisite flowers. They all die at some point, and it hurts my heart knowing that I may never find the lasting happiness my parents have shared for the past forty years.

My appetite begins to elude me, so I finish what I can before moving the rest into a container and placing it in the refrigerator. I'll try again later.

I don't bother doing my dishes because I have all night here by myself. I just want to lie down and take a nap so I don't have to think anymore about all the things I've lost and how I'm going to move forward in my life.

It's all so fucked. I'm going through so much and the only person that even knows half of it, besides Cash and Sophia, is the one person I wish I could stay away from. But instead, I'm here in his house by myself, trying to make sense of how I got to this point.

I know not everything was my fault. I didn't ask to be cheated on, and he obviously planned to use me long before we started building what I thought was a genuine connection. The effort I put into us was all wasted, but I can't even find it in myself to care about the time I lost with Cash. I'm too pissed that he was so careless and put me in danger by sleeping with someone else, *or several someone elses*, while he was sleeping with me.

I decide to go online and order an at-home STI test so I don't have to go to the clinic in town. Obviously, the doctors and nurses aren't able to discuss my medical history, but the nosy ass old biddies in this town have nothing better to do than to sleuth until they find out why I showed up there looking like I've been hit by a Mack truck. No thanks to that. I'll just take the test here, send it out, and wait a few days for the results. And if they're positive, please refer back to that time I mentioned cutting Cash's dick off and throwing it out of a moving vehicle.

I climb into bed, not bothering to set an alarm because honestly, I don't care how long I sleep. The less I'm awake, the less time I have to dwell on everything I have going on. I'll need all the rest I can get in order to put on a show at the boutique tomorrow. We have two big deliveries coming in and I need to get them ready for the customers who will surely be ready to see our fall collections. It took me all summer to hand pick each piece and it's something I'm really excited for.

Exhaling a slow breath, I close my eyes and focus on that, pushing everything else from my tired mind. It isn't long before I'm dozing off peacefully in a bed that smells vaguely like the man I used to love, dreaming of an alternate universe where he stayed, and I fall asleep every night with his arms wrapped around me.

TWENTY-SEVEN
TANNER

I USE my spare key to unlock the door of the lighthouse, careful not to make any noise as I slip inside. The sun has just risen over the harbor, and I wanted to come check on everything before I had to be at practice for the day. I saw Grace come back yesterday on the outdoor security camera, but I knew she'd need some space because I'm guessing her talk with Cash didn't go well. I know I'm the last person she'd want to talk to about that. I've got my work cut out for me fixing the trust that I broke, but I'm not giving up. I'll show her slowly that I'll do whatever it takes to get her back into my life in any capacity.

Which is why I'm here.

I set the new, fresh flowers on the counter, removing the old ones from the vase and tossing them in the trash. I went with yellow roses this time, because they symbolize friendship, and right now, I'd give anything for that with Grace.

After I'm done arranging them and making sure they have enough water, I look around, taking in the mess. I chuckle to myself because some things never change.

Libby always had a rule in the Valentine house. You pick up your own messes, no matter what. But that didn't stop

Grace from leaving her shit everywhere, then when we were asked about it, she'd deny it so she wouldn't get in trouble. Most of the time, I'd take the blame because I knew the consequences would be less severe. I have zero regrets about creating the monster that turned my kitchen into what I'm looking at right now. There are a few pieces of dried-up pasta clumped together in a strainer in the sink. A pot sits on the stove, the bottom caked with red sauce, dots of it splattered all over the cooktop. Grocery bags litter the floor, and I'm a little upset that she wasted money on food when I made sure to fill the kitchen with everything she'd need, but I also understand why she doesn't want any more of my help than necessary.

I make quick work of cleaning up, washing the dishes and wiping everything down. I'm happy to do it because this mess means that she's here, making herself as comfortable as she can possibly be, considering the history that lies within these rooms. As I make my way to the bathroom to toss the kitchen rags into the hamper, I notice the bedroom door is wide open. There isn't a lot of light coming through the curtains, but I can see Grace snuggled up under the covers. My heart cracks in my chest as I look at her face, taking in the way her brows are pulled in, even as she sleeps. She has the weight of the world on her shoulders right now, and what I wouldn't do to bear all of it for her. She used to be so carefree, but I can tell just by what I've seen in the months I've been watching her, that the girl she used to be is now buried deep under the layers of hardness she's developed since I left her.

I have a desperate need to help her find that girl again.

As much as I'd love to stare at her all day, I return to the kitchen, putting a filter in the coffee maker and scooping some fresh grounds into it so it's ready when she gets up. I don't know what time she has to work, but assuming it's a regular nine-to-five, she'll be getting up soon to get ready.

I make my way to the door, turning one last time to look at

the place. When I bought it, I couldn't bring myself to change anything, even though my mom had offered several times to give it a more modern makeover. As much as it hurt me to know everything was here, just the way I left it the day I drove away, I felt like I would be losing the last piece of Grace that I had if I altered it in any way. There were several times over the last few years that I wanted to come here, but I just couldn't. On those nights when I missed her the most, I went back-and-forth on just getting in my car and driving so I could feel closer to her. I promised myself I wouldn't return to Hope Harbor, but the pull was so strong some nights, that I had to get shitty drunk just to stop the memories from playing on a loop in my head.

But now that I'm here, and she's back in my life, regard-less of the circumstances, I'm glad I kept it exactly the way it was. For one whole summer, this place meant everything to us. It's where we truly began and also where we ended. I don't know what it'll take to earn another chance with Grace, but none of that matters, because I'd rather die than know I didn't do everything I could to show her how sorry I am for tearing us apart.

"Have a good day, Bunny. I love you," I whisper into the empty room before walking out the door and reluctantly driving back to Boston, counting down the minutes until I can find an excuse to see her again.

GRACE

I wake with a start, realizing it's morning, and that once again, I slept completely through the night. That's the second time this has happened since I started sleeping at the lighthouse. It's not that I had insomnia or anything, I just never felt fully relaxed enough to stay asleep when I was lying next to Cash. He didn't give me any reason to think I couldn't rest, so I can't really explain it, but it isn't lost on me that being here has allowed me to sleep better than I have in a long time. That would normally be a great thing...if I didn't have to work.

I jackknife up, grabbing my phone off the nightstand and checking the time. I'm supposed to be at work in a half hour, but it's going to take me longer than that to get ready. I left a huge mess in the kitchen last night, thinking I would be awake at some point to clean it up. I can't leave it the way it is in case Tanner drops by, so I need to take care of it before I leave. I didn't even tell him I was coming back because I don't have his phone number, so he might come here to make sure everything was locked up properly.

I get up, rushing to the kitchen, but stop in my tracks when I see that my disaster from yesterday is completely clean. The burnt sauce I let splatter all over the stove has been wiped away and is now gleaming. The noodles that wouldn't fit into the container I put in the fridge have been emptied from the sink. And sitting on the counter are two dozen yellow roses, replacing the white ones that had wilted.

My heart skips. I should be mad that he snuck in here while I was asleep, but of all the emotions I'm experiencing right now, anger isn't one of them. This is his house, after all, and I never told him I would be here today. I want to kick myself for the warm feeling in my chest at knowing we were inside these walls together again, even though I was completely unaware of it. I shouldn't allow myself to have these butterflies in my stomach after everything he did to me. But I don't have long to dwell on all of that. Even without having to clean up, I'm still going to be cutting it close making it on time to the boutique.

Fifteen minutes later, I look somewhat presentable. Thankfully, yesterday's eyeliner easily transitioned in today's smoky eye, so I didn't have much to do as far as make up. My hair is slicked back into a bun on top of my head, and I'm wearing a cotton maxi dress with a knot tied in the bottom to keep it from getting caught under my shoes. I top the look with a denim jacket and rush out the door, remembering to lock it behind me.

The drive to work takes only about ten minutes, so I shove through the door with five minutes to spare before we open. I'm out of breath, and pieces of my blonde hair have escaped my hair tie, sticking up all over like I put my finger in a light socket. But I'm here. That's all that matters.

"Somebody got rode hard and put away wet," Monroe says, raising a brow at me. "Did that useless fiancé of yours finally do something right this morning?"

Ugh.

With everything that happened after work Friday, and needing time to process it all over the weekend, I didn't even have time to fill her in on what went down. Part of me is afraid to actually give her the details, because she is loyal to a fault and has a hell of a right hook. She had a fling with a boxing instructor last year, and he taught her how to throw a proper punch. I've only seen her use it on a heavy bag, but I have no doubt in my mind that if she really wanted to, she could knock Cash the fuck out.

Actually, that's not a terrible idea.

"I don't have a fiancé, and I don't want to talk about it here," I tell her quietly. Her eyes go wide with surprise, but she reins it in just as Claire steps out of her office.

"Fine," she whisper-shouts. "But I'm taking you to lunch later and you're giving me every single detail, so I can decide his fate."

I give her a weak smile, making my way to the back room, where the new deliveries have already been dropped off. The three of us work to unpack everything, hanging it all on a rack to be steamed before it goes onto the floor. Like always, I inspect every piece, thinking of all the ways I would have put my own spin on them to make them even more unique. These thoughts run rampant in my mind all the time, but as soon as I sit down at the sewing machine, I blank. Maybe this new start I'm about to embark on will change things for me.

We're like a well-oiled machine. Claire does the steaming, I bring everything out to where it belongs, and Monroe takes the photos, posting them to social media. I decide on a long-sleeved, off-the-shoulder bodycon dress to be the center of our picture window in the front of the store. The style is blowing up in Paris right now, and it's perfect for a night out in the city.

I can't even imagine having a date or other event to wear something like this to. The amount of charity functions that go on in Boston every weekend ensures that these types of dresses will fly off the racks. There are several affluent families that live right here in Hope Harbor, and the women are always trying to outdo each other. I have a feeling that this little number won't last long.

Before I know it, we have the first line on display and people are already funneling in to check it out. I'm proud of the inventory I've built since I took over as the fashion buyer here. Claire has been so easygoing, letting me try new styles every season, which has definitely paid off for us all.

"Alright. Enough of this shit," Monroe says, tossing my purse into my lap as I sit on the floor, putting shoes on the last mannequin of the morning. "Do you want real food, or are we just walking over to the café?"

As if it has ears of its own, my stomach growls loudly as I stand, brushing the nonexistent dirt off my butt before pulling the crossbody strap of my small bag over my head. She shakes her head on a laugh, wordlessly leading me out the door and to her car. I plop down in the passenger seat,

and she doesn't even have her door closed before the inquisition begins.

"Tell me everything," she says, putting on her blinker and
checking her mirror before she pulls onto the road. There are
only a couple of restaurants that serve good lunch in town, so
I'll let her have the liberty of choosing which one we end
up at.

Now that we're alone, I don't hesitate. I tell her the whole
story. I start with Cash pulling away physically and emotionally months ago, and me thinking it was just work stuff. Then
I tell her what happened on Friday, and how I walked in on
him with a woman, who I found out later was Sophia, in
our bed.

"The old lady with the huge fake tits from your parents'
barbecue last summer?" she asks, nose scrunched in disgust.
"She reminded me of Stifler's mom, if Stifler's mom spent the
better part of her youth crisping herself to death in a tanning
bed."

I laugh at that, because she's right. I never noticed it
before now, but her skin is definitely on the crepey side. She's
a pretty lady and was always nice to me, but you could tell
she tried just a little too hard at keeping up her appearance.

"That's the one," I say quietly. Even though I know it's not
my fault, it's still so embarrassing, saying it all out loud.

She demands more details, so I go on, telling her how I ran
out of the house like a whirling dervish, right into Tanner's
arms. Her head whips toward me as she slams on the brakes,
causing the car behind us to honk at her. My seatbelt locks as
I pitch forward, and I cough in response as the air whooshes
from my lungs.

"Fuck off! Why was he there?" she asks as she accelerates
again.

I blow out a breath, rubbing my chest. "I've seen him a
few times this summer, working on his parents' lawn. I guess
he just got bored during the offseason. But it's a good thing

he was there, because he owns the big lighthouse now and let me stay there while I was hiding from Cash."

She tilts her head, a look of mischief melting over her face. "Did he stay with you?"

"No!" I reply. "I wouldn't have even gone in the first place if I wasn't desperate. The last thing I want is for him to watch this all play out. How pathetic am I that I couldn't keep him, and five years later, I'm still proving that men just don't want to build a life with me?"

She pulls into a parking spot outside of Chowders, turning off the car before looking at me. "Nope," she says, shaking her head rapidly. "We're not going to do that. I'm not going to let you go through this all again. I didn't know you when Tanner left, but I know how badly he hurt you. None of that was your fault, despite the way you beat yourself up for it over the years. Maybe he was worth some of your tears—probably not—but you know who definitely isn't?"

My face falls, but I allow myself a small smile. "Yeah. I know."

"I always told you that you were too good for him. Now you can find the person you're really supposed to be with. But in the meantime, go on and have yourself a little hoe phase. You deserve it."

I snort a laugh, thankful that I can always depend on Monroe to lighten the heavy situations. We get out of the car, entering the restaurant and are thankfully seated immediately. We order our food and continue talking about my future plans as we wait. She asks what my parents said when I told them, and I tell her I'm waiting until the housing project is complete to avoid any drama. She buys it, thankfully. I also decide to keep the details about Cash threatening me to myself, because I know they won't fly with her. She's feisty, and I don't doubt that she'll act on her rage if I let her in on all of that.

"So, are you just going to stay at the lighthouse for now?" she asks.

"I don't want to," I say, balling up the wrapper of my straw before flattening it back out again on the table. Just the thought of being in Tanner's house makes me restless and fidgety. "I realized when I first stepped through the door that I wasn't really over everything that happened between us. I know I can't trust him, and I need to keep a safe distance, but that'll be almost impossible if I don't get out of there and find a place of my own."

She exhales slowly, her expression softening. "Do you think maybe it might be good for the two of you to talk about it? I mean, from what you said, you really cared about each other."

I shake my head. "I don't know, but I'm not ready for that right now. I'm still too raw from everything that's happened. First, he comes back to Hope Harbor for the first time in five years and it seems like every time I turn around, he's there. Then, all of this stuff with Cash. Even though I'm more pissed and embarrassed than anything, it's still a lot. I need some time to sit with it all before I stir up any more old emotions."

We're broken from our conversation as the server approaches the table with our food, and I'm thankful for the reprieve. My mind has been moving at warp speed for days and the silence is welcome as we eat our lunch. I don't know what the future holds for me, or a possible friendship with Tanner, but I can't think about all of that right now. I need to take things one step at a time and heal my heart before I make any big decisions about what happens next.

TWENTY-EIGHT
TANNER

I BRING the ax over my head, swinging it down and splitting the log in front of me. Grace has used approximately zero of the firewood I cut for her over the weekend, but here I am again, trying to look busy so I can be near her. We have the day off today, and it's pretty early, so I'm expecting her to be out the door to go to work any second. I'm not proud of the time I've spent stalking my own security camera, but it's given me a great idea of her daily schedule. She obviously knows I've been here this week, but we have yet to speak again. I'm just dying for any crumbs she'll give me.

My phone buzzes in my pocket with a motion detection notification from my security app, and I look up just in time to see Grace step outside with a coffee cup in her hand. I'm expecting her to be dressed for work, but she isn't. Instead, she's wearing a cropped t-shirt that hangs off one shoulder and a pair of denim shorts so short that if she opened her legs, I'd be able to see the heaven I've been dreaming of for the last five years. She pulls her sunglasses down over her eyes before stomping over to me.

Oh, shit.

"Here," she says, shoving a wad of cash into my chest. Her hip is popped out to one side, and I can tell she's pissed.

"What's that for?" I ask, looking down to where her hand is pressed to me, but not wrapping my fingers around the clump of money. The longer she holds it there, the more I can feel sparks of heat firing off under my skin. My breathing quickens and I know I need to get myself under control before she reads me like a fucking book.

"Rent money for letting me stay here," she says, and I want to put her over my knee and turn her ass red for the tone she's using with me right now. I shake the mental image from my head, looking back up at her.

"I'm not taking your money," I tell her, raising a brow, daring her to defy me. "I told you that you could stay here as long as you wanted." I prop the ax against the log before taking a step into her. I don't miss the quiet gasp that comes out of her as she moves back just a little bit.

She raises her chin, clearly ready to act like a brat. "Yeah? Well, you also told me you'd leave me alone if I wanted you to, so I guess we're both breaking the rules, aren't we?"

I know I should honor that. She hates me right now, and I did tell her that I wouldn't come here if she stayed. I just wanted her to be safe. But now that we're here, this close to each other, and she has fire in her eyes? I don't know if I can stick to my word.

My brain tells me to back off, but my feet carry me forward another step. Our chests are nearly touching as I tower over her. She tries to steel her expression, but her tits are heaving as her breaths get heavier. The beast inside me that's been sleeping for so long cracks one eye open, assessing the situation. And when he sees who's standing in front of us, it's game on. I know better than to push. I hurt her, and I deserve whatever reactions I get. So I'm not sure what possesses me to reach out, wrapping my hand around her throat, the corner of my mouth curling into a devious smirk.

Her eyes widen, which spurs me on, even though I should be on my knees, begging for her forgiveness.

"I own this lighthouse, Grace. And you're my guest. If I want to come here and make sure you have everything you need so you don't have to lift a finger, I will. Do you understand?"

She clenches the bills tightly in her fist as she swallows, nodding her head slowly in response.

"Good girl," I say, dropping my hand and backing away from her before picking up the ax. She stands there, dumbfounded for a moment, before huffing in frustration and stomping back into the house. As soon as the door shuts behind her, I exhale, reaching up to massage the ache in my chest.

Fuck, that felt good.

GRACE

"Who does this motherfucker think he is?" I mumble angrily as I pace the living room. After I practically ran back inside, it took me several minutes to get my breathing regulated, and now I'm fuming.

How dare he step into my personal space like that and tell *me* what's going to happen? And putting his hand on my throat? What even *was* *that*? I'm glad it's my day off today, because I'm going to need several cold showers to recover from it.

I can't even deny the reaction my body had when I looked up at him as he towered over me. The dominance in his eyes had me shrinking into myself and submitting so fast, it almost made my head spin. I'm so fucking turned on right now, I can't even think straight.

"No," I say to myself. "He hurt you. You're a bad bitch, Grace Valentine. You don't need to fall at his feet just because he's tall and hot...and squeezes your throat in the most delicious way, making you all fuzzy in the head."

I'm going crazy. There's no other explanation for the raging emotions I'm feeling right now. I despise him for leaving me here for so long and never coming back. And even more for returning after five years and making it impossible not to be in his orbit. For months, everywhere I've looked, I've either seen some type of reminder of him, or he's been there himself. It's all making the resolve I've spent years building up feel like a house of cards, ready to be blown over at any moment. I'm fighting hard to stay strong and remember everything that happened with us. So, why are the butterflies in my stomach fluttering around like lovesick assholes now that he's so close again?

Every day, this shit gets more confusing. At the beginning, I was perfectly happy staying pissed at Tanner forever. But now I don't know anymore. I'm going through a lot at the moment, and the only person who knows how bad it is, besides Monroe, is him. He's not using my vulnerability against me. Everything he's done has been to help, even though I've been pushing back every chance I get. It's not like he's holding the fact that I'm staying here over my head. He sneaks in in the mornings before I'm awake, makes sure I don't need anything, and replaces the flowers on the counter when they start to wilt. Even though I don't need it, he chops wood and cleans up, making it so that when I'm here, I can truly relax and enjoy the peace and quiet.

He's trying to mend what's broken between us, and it's making me feel too many things all at once.

I know I should stand my ground. What he did back then changed who I am as a person. He took a piece of me that I can never get back, and that's almost impossible to forgive. I was a shell of a person for so long, that I gave up on my dreams and had to reroute my entire path. I'm happy with my job, but it wasn't what I wanted when I was eighteen. I still want more, and had Tanner not broken me, I'd have had a better chance at the life I'd imagined when I was a kid.

I know that's ridiculous. I let a man hurt me so badly, that I gave up, but I was young. He was my first love, and I never could've prepared myself for the damage that was done by him walking away and not giving me any semblance of closure. For so long, I thought it was my fault. That I should've never told him that I wanted to be with him for real. I should've just sucked it up and gone to California after the summer was over, ending our arrangement like we had planned. At least that way, I wouldn't have lost him completely. Yeah, I'd have had to watch him move on and fall in love with someone else. I'd have had to witness his children growing up, wondering what my life would be like if he loved me the way I loved him, and I was the one he chose. But, I'd have had him in my life in some way.

I walk over to the window, looking out to where he's carrying more firewood to the stack that's now almost as tall as I am. I haven't used the firepit once since I've been here, so I don't know why he keeps chopping it. As he walks, I notice the tattoo on his calf. I can't make out what it is from here, but it makes me realize how much we've changed since the last time I saw him. There are parts of his body that I knew like the back of my hand before, but now they're different. He's bigger. Stronger. And his demeanor isn't the same. He used to be loud and obnoxious; always looking for a good time. But now, he seems so reserved. So *controlled*.

My thighs clench as he bends over, the globes of his firm ass straining against the fabric of his basketball shorts as he picks up pieces of fallen bark from the bricks underneath his feet and tosses them into the pit.

God, I miss his body. The way he used to own me and make me feel the way nobody else ever could? I wish I could just give in and take it back, but I know I can't. The risk of having to start over again with another broken heart isn't worth the reward of having him one more time. Because it could never be just sex with him. It never was. We've been there before, and it ended in disaster.

So why am I finding it harder and harder to keep pushing him away?

TWENTY-NINE
GRACE

THUNDER CRASHES right outside the window, jolting me awake. We're having a storm surge right now, and it's been causing the sea levels to rise. It happens here sometimes, so the harbor is always at risk of flooding. But the lighthouse sits on a bit of higher ground, so I thought I'd be okay here tonight. Now that the wind is blowing and the storm is raging, I'm not so sure.

I check the clock, seeing that it's two in the morning. I'm supposed to work at eight, but depending on the conditions, I may not be able to get to the boutique. I'm what you would call a *questionable driver* without high winds and heavy rain, so I'm definitely not chancing it if I don't have to.

I get out of bed, wrapping the comforter around myself because I'm only wearing an oversized t-shirt and a pair of thin panties. I pad out to the living room, flipping the light switch, but nothing happens.

"Fuck," I whine. The power must've been knocked out by the storm. I'm a little bit afraid of the dark, have been since I was a kid, so being here alone is not ideal. But as of right now, I'm safe, so I'm going to try not to panic.

I return to the bedroom, grabbing my phone from where

it's sitting on the absolutely useless charging dock, and make my way to the couch. There's no way I'm going to be able to rest during this shit, so I may as well scroll the internet and start looking at pieces for our winter launches. Those orders will need to be made soon, now that the colder weather is moving in.

I try to busy myself, but every time the wind whips violently, the windows rattle and the foundation groans. I'm getting more anxious by the minute that the tide could reach the house. I don't know what I'd do if it flooded and I was alone.

I decide to turn off my phone because it wasn't fully charged before the power went out and I may need it in an emergency. Instead, I huddle under the blanket, trying to stop my body from trembling with unease.

A loud clap of thunder crashes outside, making me scream into the empty room. I clutch the blanket in my hands so tightly, that they begin to ache. I slam my eyes shut, holding my tears in while I try to think of something calming. Seconds later, the front door swings open, crashing into the wooden table behind it.

"Grace!" Tanner yells, closing the door before running over to me. He sits down, wrapping my shaking body in his arms. I immediately feel safe, melting into him as I cry.

"I'm here. You're okay," he whispers, rocking me gently as I try my hardest to calm down. Adrenaline is still flowing through me while he holds me tightly, burying his face in my hair. "I'm going to carry you out of here, okay?" he asks. "The harbor is flooding, and you can't stay. It's too dangerous."

I just nod because I'm still too panicked to make sense of anything. He wraps the comforter tightly around me, shoving my phone into the pocket of his sweatpants before he lifts me from the couch and walks over to the door. There's water everywhere, and as soon as he steps outside, I can hear how deep it is as his shoes slap against it.

I expect to be lowered into his Tesla, but instead, I'm lifted into the passenger seat of a large pickup truck. I'm still shaking as he pulls the seatbelt over my wrapped body and clicks it into place. He hurries to the driver's side, hopping into the seat and before I know it, we're speeding down the flooded gravel road. It's not until we've left the harbor and are getting on the interstate that I'm able to speak.

"Where are we going?" I ask, looking out the window.

"My house," he replies, making me turn abruptly in my seat, eyes wide as I stare at him.

"No, Tanner," I say, shaking my head. "Just take me back to the inn. I'll stay there."

He continues looking out the windshield, squinting as the wipers go a thousand miles an hour to combat the rain that's pouring down. "You're not going back into town. It's not safe. I'm taking you to my house until the storm passes, then I'll bring you back. I have a full guest suite. You won't even see me."

I consider the alternatives, deciding that he's right and I shouldn't be in Hope Harbor right now. My parents' house is on much higher ground, so they're probably out of the flood zone. But the lighthouse? I'm wondering if it will even make it through this one.

My heart squeezes in my chest at the thought. While I still have so much going on in my head as far as Tanner goes, I don't want to lose the one place in the world where I feel at home right now. I'm still trying to keep as much distance from my parents as possible without raising any suspicions. I have yet to even tell them the fake story Cash concocted because I'm too afraid that they'll be able to read me and figure out that something more is going on. It won't be that much longer before I can tell them everything he did and get back to my normal life. But for now, I have to do what I have to do.

I take my phone from the cup holder between us, opening

the text app and telling Claire that I had to leave and won't be able to get to the boutique tomorrow. I'm sure she won't mind since I can do most of the ordering that needs to get done online. I set the phone back down, closing my eyes, sleep finding me quickly as the adrenaline rush I was having begins to fade away.

TANNER

Grace slept for most of the ride to Boston. I couldn't stop myself from stealing glances, admiring her face as tiny snores came from her exhausted body.

I watched the weather app all night. I knew there was a storm surge, and even though I told myself she would leave the lighthouse if she thought she was in danger, it's like I was being pulled to her. I was already on my way when the security app alerted me that the system had gone into battery backup mode, making me push the gas pedal all the way to the floor so I could get to her faster.

When I found her, trembling on the couch, my instinct was to pull her into my arms. So that's what I did. I know she was terrified, but it gave me a little spark of hope when she didn't push me away. I couldn't leave her there, especially seeing that the land was beginning to flood. Thankfully, she came willingly when I told her we were going to my place. Otherwise, I would have had to kidnap her. Over my dead body would she be staying somewhere she wasn't safe.

I pull up my driveway, seeing the house come into view. We haven't lost power here yet, but the wind and rain certainly aren't taking it any easier on us than they are on the harbor right now. I have my generator ready to go in case of an emergency, but I think we should be able to get through the storm without needing it.

I push the button overhead, watching as the garage door rises. I stay as quiet as possible as I pull in, getting out and rounding the front of the truck to where Grace is still out cold in the passenger seat. Call me a selfish motherfucker, but I don't want to wake her. I just want to be able to hold her close as much as I can. I miss her so fucking much, some nights there's a physical ache in my chest.

I open the door as quietly as I can, noticing that her leg is sticking out from under the blanket, all the way up to her bare thigh. I squeeze my eyes shut, trying to get my bearings, because all I want is to lean down and taste her warm skin. This woman is everything to me, whether she realizes it or not, and the need to claim and own her is stronger than it's ever been with all the time we've spent apart.

I pull the blanket back over her, sliding my arms under her body and pulling her to my chest. She nuzzles her face into my neck immediately, pressing her lips against me while she tries to get comfortable. My cock thickens in my sweatpants because it's been so long since I was last touched like this. Touched *by her*. I only wish she was awake and doing it because she wanted to.

I somehow manage to open the door to my house without waking her. I would give anything to bring her to my bed right now, but I know that's not a possibility, so I continue toward the guest suite. Just as I hit the first stair, she lifts her head, looking straight into my eyes. I expect her to panic immediately, but she doesn't. It's like she's frozen, our lips inches apart, neither of us able to back away.

We just stay there, me holding her at the top of the staircase to my basement. Memories from the past flash behind my eyes and I move in just slightly, giving in to my body's natural pull to the love of my life. I can practically taste her as soft breaths puff against my lips, waiting for her to move the last few centimeters and put me out of my fucking misery.

I feel her stiffen as reality hits her, and I close my eyes, attempting to burn the memory of this moment into my brain before it ends. But I don't get the chance, because she kicks her legs, making me drop them from my grasp. I keep my other arm banded around her back as she slides down my body, only letting go when her feet are firmly planted on the floor and she pulls away.

We stand there for several more seconds, unanswered questions swirling in the air around us before she finally looks away.

"Sorry," she whispers. "I haven't slept well since the rain started."

"I know," I reply. Because I do. Grace isn't afraid of storms, but she's always terrified of the power going out and being left in the dark alone. Unfortunately, I couldn't get to her before that happened tonight, but she's here now, and I plan on leaving every light in the house on for her so she can rest peacefully.

I'm rewarded with a small smile as I put my hand gently on her lower back, leading her down the stairs. We pass the game room, and she peeks inside, taking in the large movie screen and video games lining the walls. As we move further down the hall, we approach the door that I have closed and locked. I don't say anything, trying to ignore it so she doesn't ask what's behind it, but unfortunately, I'm not that lucky.

"What's this room?" She asks quietly. I definitely can't show her, so I wave a dismissive hand, picking up my speed as we walk by.

"Nothing," I rush out. "Just storage."

I hate lying to her, but she's not ready to see anything inside those walls yet. Hopefully, someday she will be. But right now, I'm just trying to do everything I can to gain back her trust and friendship.

She drops it, continuing to walk down the hall until we arrive at the guest suite. I turn the knob, letting her enter before I follow, flipping every light switch on the panel to completely illuminate the entire space. She takes a few slow steps further into the main living area, her eyes ping-ponging around the room, taking it all in.

"Wow," she says. "This is bigger than my whole house."

I clear my throat, trying not to think about the fact that we're alone here. There's not a single soul for miles. "I had it built so my parents had a place to stay when they came to visit. I wanted them to have everything they needed right here."

She looks over her shoulder at me, and I swear I see just a small piece of the old Grace behind her eyes. "Thanks for letting me stay."

You can stay forever.

The thought is as natural as breathing. There hasn't been a single day since I moved in that I haven't wondered what it would feel like having her here. It was always just a fantasy, but now it's real.

And suddenly, it feels like home.

THIRTY
GRACE

I KICK OFF THE COVERS, hopping out of bed because there's no way I'm falling asleep tonight. This place is amazing. It's so big and cozy, but knowing that Tanner is just up the stairs is making me restless.

After he got me settled in, we said a very awkward goodnight before he told me I could lock the door behind him. I know he wants me to feel like I'm being left alone, but at this point, I don't even know if I want to be.

When I woke up in his arms earlier, a part of me that had been buried for so long felt like it was sparking back to life. Being in such close proximity to him made my head spin in a way that I've craved since the last time I touched him. It's getting harder and harder to continue fighting the way I still feel about him.

I shouldn't, but I open the door, heading down the hall and up the stairs. I make my way to the kitchen, where I open the fridge and take out a bottle of water. Every light up here is on and I can't help but wonder if he did it because he knows I'm still afraid of the dark. He knows everything about me, and he's never judged me for any of my weird quirks. Cash just used to laugh and tell me to stop being a child. He never understood me. Not the way Tanner does.

I pull out a chair and sit down at the table, looking around the huge space. This house is way too big for one person, even if he does have more money than God. I wonder if he built this place thinking that one day he'd have a family. I can't stop my mind from wondering that if things hadn't gone down the way they did between us, would I be here with him now? Would we be married? Would we have children? All of those questions remain unanswered because he made the choice long ago to leave me behind so he could live this life.

I'm unable to sit still, standing and walking around the room. I probably shouldn't, but he did tell me that I was welcome to come upstairs and to make myself at home. Since I'm nosy as fuck, I don't fight the urge to open drawers and cupboards, looking around to see what's inside. And when I find a matte black key that looks very similar to the door in the downstairs hallway, my curiosity peaks. He seemed so secretive about what was in that room, and it only made me want to see it for myself even more.

Unable to shake the undeniable pull to that door, I make my way down the staircase and stand in front of it. I hesitate for a moment, trying to convince myself that this is wrong, but the voice in the back of my head telling me to just peek inside wins. I reach out, fitting the key into the lock, and I'm slightly shocked when I twist and hear the faint click of it disengaging. I turn the knob, slowly and quietly pushing my way in. Whatever I was expecting to see when I came in here —this is definitely not it.

The room is shrouded in black and gray. Everything from the carpet to the damask wallpaper is rich and dangerous looking. Off to my left is a large, four post bed with black silk sheets. Next to it on the wall, hangs a wide variety of whips and paddles. And dangling from each post is a black, soft cuff restraint.

I'm completely speechless as I take a few steps forward, looking into the back corner, where a dark wood Saint Andrews cross stands. There are also several other pieces of furniture, including a spanking bench and a large, velvet covered throne in the center of the room. I've watched plenty of BDSM porn, so I know what all of these things are, but I've never seen them in person.

I turn to leave, needing some air because the very last thing I expected when I came in here was to find Tanner's sex room. I want to vomit thinking about all of this equipment and what it's used for. *Who* it's used *with*. But as soon as my feet begin to move, a tall shadow steps into the doorway, then inside the room, sucking all of the oxygen right out of it. He's wearing only a pair of snug-fitting black boxer briefs that are hiked all the way up his muscular thighs. His hair is mussed like he was asleep, but his exhausted eyes tell me he hasn't been able to rest any better than I have tonight.

I stand completely still, unable to rip my eyes away from Tanner's, even though my brain is telling me to get the fuck out of here. To put some distance between us so I can process everything I've seen tonight. But the pull I have to him ever since he came back into my life is too strong for me to fight. Every part of me is at odds right now, and it has me wanting to scream. To cry. To walk over and punch him so hard that he feels even a fraction of the pain I feel when I think about how many women he's had in this room.

"Grace," he says, putting his hands up in surrender. "It's not what you think."

I huff an incredulous laugh. "It doesn't matter what I think, Tanner. You made it clear that your life didn't have room for me in it. So, if you want to bring women to your sex dungeon and—" I stop, because I honestly can't say the words out loud. "You can do whatever you want," is what I settle on. After five years of thinking about him being with other people, I thought I was okay with it. But seeing this room for myself, knowing that he's doing all the things *we* talked about doing together, with other women; I want to crawl out of my own skin. I'm feeling everything and nothing all at once, and it's making me want to scream.

He takes a tentative step toward me, and I instinctively take one back, keeping him at a safe distance. I don't trust myself anymore. One minute, I want him to touch me. To kiss me. *Anything* to feel close to him. But right now, I need to let myself feel the anger. Because when I finally get the strength to let him go again, I'm going to need this moment to fuel my resolve.

"I've never—" he begins, squeezing his eyes shut. "I've never brought anybody in here."

My brows furrow in confusion. "When did you put it in?" I ask, thinking it must be a pretty new addition to his house if it hasn't been used yet. Part of me is relieved, and my body loosens a little, knowing I'm not standing in the middle of a room where he's dominated people who aren't me.

He takes a breath, staring into my eyes. "When I built the house. Four years ago."

To say that I'm shocked would be a massive understatement. We've been apart for half a decade. He's had this house, with this room, almost as long. He's clearly still into kink if he has all of this equipment, so why is he telling me nobody's ever been in here. It doesn't make sense.

"Why?" I blurt. Part of me cringes, because I really don't know if I can go through hearing about him being with anyone else, but the other part of me needs to understand.

"Because I couldn't…be with anyone else."

It takes me a moment to register what he's saying. And maybe I'm not understanding him correctly, but does he mean that he hasn't been with anyone else…at all? I shouldn't dig any deeper, but I need the answer more than I need my next breath.

"At all? Since me?" I ask so quietly, I'm surprised he can even hear me. But when he looks down, giving a small shake of his head, I suck in a quick breath. My hand flies up over my mouth and I do everything I can to stop the tears from welling up in my eyes. I'm feeling so many different things right now, it's hard to settle on one dominant emotion. But for some reason, when I take a second to sift through them, the thing I'm zeroing in on the most is how fucking angry I am.

He's still focusing his attention on the floor, clearly unable to look me in the eye, which makes me even more pissed off.

No. *No.* He left me, alone and broken, begging him to stay, so we could 'live our lives'. And now he's telling me that he never even did it? He never tried to find happiness? Fuck him for doing this to me. To *us.*

"Tanner, look at me," I say through clenched teeth. He does, but I can see the desperation in his eyes. He's hoping I don't bring it all back up, and as much as I don't want to relive that day, I need to know.

I raise my chin, finding all the confidence and bravery I can muster. "Say it. Say it out loud," I order.

"Grace," he replies, and I can hear his voice shake.

"Say it!" I yell. "Tell me you broke us for nothing! Because I didn't go off to California anyway! I was so devastated by you ripping my heart out that I couldn't even bring myself to leave Hope Harbor! I stayed, went to community college, and worked my way to the top at the boutique, all while hoping you'd come back for me, but you never did! I haven't designed a single piece since that day, Tanner," I say, seething at this point because I realize that his choice fucked us both so badly that we were left empty and alone because of it. "It's dumb because I shouldn't have given you an ounce of my life after you walked away, but you didn't just take a piece of me. You took *everything.* And I fucking hate you for it."

I release a shaky exhale, my eyes burning into him as I vibrate with rage. I need to get out of here. I will my feet to move. I beg them to, even. But when Tanner drops to his knees where he stands, I may as well have roots attached to me because there's no way I'm going anywhere. I stand there completely silent, unable to breathe as he looks up at me.

"I'm sorry," he says quietly, bringing his gaze to mine. His shoulders are pulled low, and the regret for what he's done is painted across his expression. "What can I do to make it better? I know I can't fix it overnight, but I'll do anything. I'll give you anything you ask for. Just say it, Grace. *Please.*"

I want to tell him there's nothing that he can do, but the truth is, I don't know anything anymore. I know that I still love him, and that fact makes me even angrier, because I know that if I didn't, it would be a hell of a lot easier to walk out of this room. To leave him here on his knees, begging me for forgiveness. But for some reason, I just can't bring myself to go.

I stand there, staring at him as he puts his hands in his lap and bows his head.

It's his submission. To me.

My mind is going in a thousand directions all at once, but I can't put any solid thoughts together right now. All I know is that I want to punish him. I want to punish him for leaving me alone all these years and not finding the happy life he said he wanted. For making me wait and never coming back. And for making me feel all of these things I thought I was strong enough to let go of, but once again, are proving just how weak I really am.

I am *so sick* of being weak. I just want to take my power back.

"Crawl to me," I say, my voice shaking. I expect him to hesitate or tell me no, but he doesn't. He leans forward onto his hands, and he *fucking crawls*. I back up as he moves, not stopping until I feel the backs of my legs hit the throne behind me. I stay standing, waiting for him to reach me before I sit. This position, me in this big, beautiful chair, and him on all fours in front of me, gives me a feeling of control so intense, that it takes on a life of its own. I feel like a goddess in front of this man, who at this point, would do anything for just an ounce of my forgiveness. But I can't just give it. If I'm ever able to move on from what he did to me, it'll be because he earned it.

I slide my hands up my thighs, lifting the t-shirt that lies over them. I have no idea what I'm doing, but I don't stop myself when my instinct tells me to grab the sides of my panties and slowly bring them down my legs. I lift my feet one at a time, pulling them off until the thin fabric is balled in my fist.

"Open," I order. He sits back on his haunches, and as soon as he obeys, I shove the black lace into his mouth. His eyes slam shut, and he takes a deep inhale through his nose as he whimpers around them. I feel an overwhelming urge to make him pay for what he did to us. Seeing him like this, paired with the amount of power I'm feeling in this position has me so turned on, I can barely see straight. My head is telling me how wrong this is, but my body is saying something completely different.

I open my legs, allowing him to see my pussy, that's probably leaking onto the velvet of the chair already. I wonder if he can tell how hard my clit is throbbing just by looking at it. It's like I'm a completely different person as I bring my hand down and swipe my middle finger down my slit, watching his eyes as they widen.

"Do you miss it?" I ask, using my fingers to spread myself for him.

"Mhmm," he mumbles into the fabric. His breathing is heavy and his face twists in pain when I enter my pussy up to my first knuckle, but he doesn't look away. He just watches me play with myself. I want him to touch me so badly, but I don't know if I'll be able to stop myself from switching places with him, begging him to dominate me like I've craved since the day he left. I'm not sure if I'll ever be ready to do that with him, but right now? I'm too angry. I want him to hurt. I want to humiliate and break him like he did to me.

"Look at you," I mock. "Such a little slut on your knees, begging for the pussy you threw away." I add a second finger, pushing them both inside until my palm is flush with my hot, wet skin. I pump in and out, warmth beginning to coil in the pit of my stomach. "The tables have turned, haven't they?" I breathe. He nods his head, leaning forward slightly, but I put my foot on his chest, pushing him back.

"Uh uh," I scold. "No touching. No smelling. Just sit there like a good boy and suck on my panties while I make myself come."

I've never touched myself in front of anyone. I suggested it to Cash once, but he was always threatened by anything that made me feel good that wasn't him. It's the same reason I was forced to hide my toys in a box under the bathroom sink. It only took one knock-down, drag-out fight about them for me to never acknowledge them again in front of him. He referred to it as a *me problem* that I needed a little extra help getting off during sex with him. He even told me I needed to talk to a therapist when I suggested trying out different types of bondage or impact play. So, I made it easier on us both by faking orgasms, leaving him in bed while I went to the bathroom to shower, and taking care of myself while he unknowingly slept like he didn't have a single fuck to give.

Sometimes it was easy. All I had to do was stroke my clit and think about being tied down and fucked to get myself off. Other times, I'd end up on my knees and elbows, on the floor with a vibrator in one hand and my throat squeezed in the other. In the really desperate situations, I'd close my eyes and bring myself back to the lighthouse, coming almost instantly when I imagined a familiar voice in my head, demanding me to get there. I tried my best to block him out, especially since he was gone and I was with Cash, but I'll admit I don't feel nearly as bad about it knowing that I was more than likely being cheated on for the entirety of our relationship.

Now that I'm looking at the face I desperately tried not to see every time I touched myself, knowing he's really here, on his knees for me, I know it won't take much for me to go over the edge. So, I keep my fingers moving in and out, using my other hand to rub my swollen, sensitive clit.

"Oh my God, yes," I moan, putting on a show. Tanner's teeth are clenched around my panties that are hanging out of his mouth, and I can feel how hard he's breathing as puffs of hot air ricochet off the skin of my thighs. Beads of sweat gather at his temples as he tries his hardest to stay focused on my pussy, barely even blinking while he watches me fuck myself. I can feel my resolve crumbling every time I look at him, and I know I won't be able to go without letting him touch me for much longer. And to be honest, I don't want to.

"You want to feel it?" I ask. His eyebrows pinch in as he nods his head quickly, clearly unashamed at how desperate he looks below me.

"One finger," I tell him, spreading my legs wider. He wastes no time, reaching up and sinking his pointer finger in alongside mine, causing a delicious stretch as I adjust to the new intrusion. I try to hold in my moan, but it's in vain because just knowing a part of him is inside me is so overwhelming, I have to recite the state capitals just so I don't explode right now.

We work together, bringing me to the precipice faster than I've been able to do on my own, probably ever. I'm moaning and grinding into our hands, unabashedly using our fingers to coax my desperate pussy toward release.

"I'm so close," I grit out. "Do you want to feel my cunt suck our fingers in when I come, Tan?"

The corded veins in his neck are visible as he swallows

roughly, trying to reel himself back in so he can reply. "Mhmm," he whines into my panties, making my walls involuntarily tighten against us at the sound. I can hear the angst in his voice and breathing, and even though I'd love to keep him inside me, I also want to make him feel even an ounce of the ache I've felt for him since he walked away.

"Too fucking bad," I say, catching him off guard when I shove him back, knocking him off balance. His finger slips from me just as my orgasm hits, my inner muscles contracting around mine as I come on a loud scream. My eyes are closed, and my body is shaking as I work myself through it, only opening them when I've finally started to float back down to earth. My heart is pounding wildly in my chest as I look at Tanner, who's still kneeling in front of me with my panties hanging from his clenched teeth. His posture is slumped forward and his eyes are glazed over with unshed tears of frustration. He looks so small and defeated, but I can't bring myself out of this power-hungry state long enough to show him even a semblance of mercy. At least, not yet.

I lean forward, gripping onto the soaked lace and carefully pulling it from his mouth. I swipe my fingers, that are still wet with my cum, gently across his top lip, allowing him a small taste of my pleasure. He immediately darts his tongue out, lapping it up like he's dying of thirst and it's the only drop of water for miles. My eyes lock onto the motion, and I have to suppress my moan as the reminder of what his mouth is capable of triggers an aftershock that makes my pussy muscles spasm again.

I stare down at him for several more seconds, breathing heavily as the adrenaline rush from my orgasm begins to ebb away. As if a switch is flipped, I snap back to reality in an instant, shaking my head and blinking rapidly as I try to process what I just did. What *we* just did.

He's still staring at me like he has no clue what the fuck to say or do as I stand from the throne and hightail it out of the room without another word. I run as fast as my feet will carry me, down the hall and into the guest suite, barely even getting through the door before I have it closed and locked behind me. Leaning my back against it, I slide down to the ground, unable to hold myself up anymore with how badly my legs are shaking.

Whatever that was that just happened between Tanner and me, as confusing as it was, was the hottest fucking thing I've ever experienced. But I'm also completely sure I just complicated something that was already fucked up enough to begin with.

Now I have to decide if the way it made me feel was worth having my heart torn from my chest for a second time.

THIRTY-ONE
TANNER

"OKAY, BOYS," I say, leaning into the huddle. "All we need is a first down here, so we're going to keep it simple. Twenty-two hurricane on three. Twenty-two hurricane on three. Got it?" They all nod their heads in understanding. I turn to my wide receiver, Blaze. "Just try to get out of bounds. We'll run it up the middle after that to eat up the rest of the time."

"You got it, Cap," he says, slapping my shoulder.

We clap in unison before taking our positions at the line of scrimmage. It's the last game of the preseason, so all the starters are getting some playing time today. The past two weeks have been solely for the purpose of the rookies and second string getting a chance to see the field in a real game-play situation, but now that the regular season is right around the corner, the starters are all just trying to make sure there's nothing else we need to work on in the next week.

I ready myself behind Danny Boy, kicking my left foot out behind me. Most quarterbacks use that signal to send a player in motion, but not me. My offense knows I do that before every play for a reason I've never been willing to explain.

Bending my knees and positioning my hands between my center's legs, readying myself for the snap. I look up, finding the Mike linebacker quickly and letting my team know where he is. "Ninety-one's the Mike! Ninety-one! Down, set, hut, hut, hut!"

Daniels snaps the ball and I roll back, keeping an eye on the blitz, but my line has it covered. I wait for Blaze to run his route, and when I feel someone rushing my blind side, I fire off the pass. He catches it just short of the first down line, spinning past the defender and running out of bounds. I could have told him to take it to the house, but I don't want to risk him getting hurt. We're safer just running something easy up the middle to win the game.

In the end, we beat the Dallas Sharpshooters seventeen to six. Both sides played great, with the defense not allowing a single first down in the second half. I'm proud of my guys as we head to the locker room, sitting on the benches while Coach goes through the post-game formalities.

I'd like to say I'm listening, but the truth is that I barely got through that game with the amount of time I spent thinking about Grace. What happened in my playroom the other night is on repeat in my head. I don't think I've experienced anything hotter than her telling me to crawl to her. And when she shoved her panties into my mouth, I swear I almost came without even being touched. I'm pretty sure I've been rocking a half chub ever since, which is not ideal when your job requires you to wear a jockstrap.

Even though it was just my finger, sliding back into her body after so long was like a thousand-pound weight had been lifted off of me. I know she was pissed because of what that room represents, but I wasn't lying when I told her that nobody else has been in there. I haven't had sex with anyone since her.

When I first went back to school, I was nursing a heartbreak of my own. I kept a full schedule with classes and football to stop from spiraling, pouring myself into bed after practice every day, thankful for the exhaustion that had set in.

As long as I was working or sleeping, I didn't have time to think about everything that I had given up.

The draft came and went, and that gave me even more of an excuse to go hard with workouts and studying game tape. It was the only thing that stopped me from getting in my car and crashing back into her life.

I can't tell you how many times I drove halfway to Hope Harbor every summer, talking myself out of it and going back to Boston. I think that was more of a selfish move on my part, because had I seen her happy with someone else, I don't know if I could've survived it. Even at the anniversary party, when I saw that she was engaged to Cash, it felt like I wouldn't make it. The only thing that saved me was the sadness in her eyes when I looked into them. Whether it was from me, or the fact that she wasn't content in her relationship, I'd have taken hope from either one. In the end, I think it was a little bit of both.

I know she still feels something. Otherwise, she wouldn't have gotten so upset the other night. The way she lashed out made me want to reach out and hold her, but she deserves to lay into me whenever she feels like she has to. I left her with no real explanation, and nobody to help her through the pain I caused. If she wants to scream at me every day from now until forever, I'll let her. Now that I know the impact my decision really had on her future, I wouldn't blame her if she never forgave me for it.

"Good game, bro," Maverick says, sitting down next to me. I look around to see that most of the guys are already coming out from the showers, and I'm still sitting here thinking about Grace. In my defense, though, who wouldn't have the mental image of her sitting on the throne with her fingers in her cunt, taking her own pleasure? I barely even made it back to my room before I ripped down my boxers and stroked my cock furiously with the taste of her still on my tongue.

"You too, man," I reply. "D looks good this year."

He nods in agreement before hitting me with a questioning look. "I thought we lost you out there a couple times. What's going on?"

That's one thing about this team. We can all read each other so easily. It's great on the field, but not always so great off of it. Although now that I have Grace at my house, maybe it's time to ask for back up. I know we didn't exactly leave on great terms a few nights ago, and the only time I've seen her since was when I went down to make sure she had everything she needed. But she would've found some other place to stay if she didn't want to be there.

The storm went on for two days, ending just yesterday. I haven't had a chance to make it to the lighthouse to see the damage, but I know it's not going to be an easy fix. At the very least, I'm going to need an extraction team to come in for water removal. Worst case scenario would be that I'd need to replace the floors. Either way, Grace can't go back there yet.

Dalton and Blaze make their way back into the room, flanking my sides as I look up at Maverick. "She's at my house," I tell them.

"Is that good or bad?" Blaze asks, seeing that my face is lacking the excitement it would be showing if everything was going well.

"I don't know," I say, pinching the bridge of my nose. "I need to find a way to show her that she has a place in my life. That it's empty without her. I fucked up so badly when I let her go, and it's been a fight to even get her to a point where she isn't raging every time she sees me. We still have a lot of shit to work out, but I want her to know that it's okay to relax around me."

Mav sits forward. "Does she like Bella Simon, by any chance?"

I whip my head up, raising a brow. "Are you suggesting we dangle your world-famous pop star girlfriend in front of

Grace like a piece of meat so she'll realize how well she'd fit in with us?"

He pauses for a moment, pursing his lips as he considers my question. "Yeah. I am."

"You're a fucking genius," I tell him, a wide smile stretching across my face. I look around the group. "You guys busy tonight?"

"Fuck yeah, we are," Dalton says with a cocky grin. "Busy helping you get your girl back."

"WHAT IS THE ROCK OF GIBRALTAR?" I yell at the TV. I've been watching old episodes of Jeopardy to keep myself from turning on the Blizzard game. I've been avoiding Tanner for days now, and I'm dying to see him, even if it's on a screen. But after the other night, and all the emotions battling each other in my head, I'm trying to get myself together.

I've spent three days in here, working on my phone and watching trash television. I even managed to read every single piece of email in my inbox, which should win me some kind of award because it took an entire day. The best one of them all was the result of my STI testing, which was negative across the board, so Cash's dick will remain intact.

Godspeed, Sophia.

"Who is Queen Victoria?" the contestant answers correctly.

"What the fuck?" I mumble to myself. I almost never get the questions right, but I was way off that time.

I set my pint of Ben & Jerry's aside, kicking my pink bunny slippers up onto the coffee table. Since I came here in only a t-shirt and panties, I wasn't surprised to see several bags full of comfy clothes and new undergarments sitting outside the guest suite door the following morning. I was, however, shocked to see a brand new sewing machine with an entire box full of threads and other supplies next to it. I'm ashamed to admit the amount of times I've re-read the note that was attached to the top. I pick it up from beside me, staring at the familiar handwriting and the words that I've all but memorized over the last few days.

> Dear Grace,
> I know this won't give back all the things I've taken from you, but you have a gift that the world deserves to see. I hope this strikes some of the inspiration that's been missing from your life. I believe in you, and I can't wait to see you shine.
> Love always,
> Tanner

The machine is still in the box, sitting just inside the door to the living area of the suite. It's certainly a step up from the old one I have at my house, which makes me a little excited to give it a try the next time I feel like I might be able to design a piece. I know eventually, I will. I just need the right motivation.

As muddied as my emotions are about where Tanner and I stand, I have to give him credit for everything he's done for me in the last few weeks. Not only has he offered me places to stay, but he's been taking care of me nonstop, making sure I have anything I could possibly want or need. He's been gone all day at Blizzard Stadium, so I snuck up to the kitchen to grab stuff to refill the refrigerator down here. He had all my favorites stocked and ready to go, including several pints of Cherry Garcia so I can wallow in self-pity properly.

He gets me. Goddamn his pretty ass for that.

I'm about to guess another wrong answer when there's a knock on the door. I freeze for a moment, but muster up the courage to face him.

I walk over, inching the door open and peeking at him. "Hi," I say quietly.

"Hey," he replies, awkwardly shoving his hands into the pockets of his grey sweatpants. He smells amazing, like he's fresh from the shower, his familiar cologne enveloping the space around us. I almost let my eyes roll back in my head when I inhale, but I fight the urge.

"I have someone upstairs who wants to meet you."

I scrunch my eyebrows, confused as to who could be here for me.

The corner of his lips tip up in a ghost of a smile as he looks down at my mismatched outfit and slippers. "I think you look adorable, but I'd be a terrible person if I didn't suggest changing before you come up."

I hesitate, because after the other night, I don't know how to act around him. When I took off from the sex room and came back to the guest suite, it was more of a defense mechanism than anything. I knew that if I had stayed, I might've done something stupid like kissed him or told him how much I've missed him over the last five years, and I'm still not sure if I think he deserves that right now.

"Okay," I finally say in agreement, turning toward the bedroom while he waits. I don't know what he meant out there, but I opt for black leggings and an off-the-shoulder sweater before checking the mirror to make sure the rest of me is okay. I'm only wearing mascara and lip balm, but it'll do. It's not like some A-list celebrity is up there waiting to meet me.

I return to the living room, grabbing my phone from the end table and walking out the door with Tanner following behind me. Before I even get to the top of the staircase, I hear the commotion.

Several loud voices laugh and talk as rap music plays quietly on the living room speakers. I slow down, wanting to be closer to him because even though I have no idea where we stand, his presence is comforting. He looks down at me with a soft smile, nodding his head at the doorway as if to say *go on in*. I do, and I have to do a triple take because I know I'm not seeing things right.

Sitting on one end of the couch is a tall man with deep dimples in his cheeks. A beautiful woman with black hair sits on his lap, laughing as he plants kisses all over her face.

On the other end of the couch is another man, with a brunette leaning into him. He says something in her ear, and she raises a brow before mouthing what looks to be *'Yes, Daddy.'* But none of that is what has me frozen like a moron in the doorway. Because in the chair across the room is Bella fucking Simon.

"Tanner, what's happening?" I whisper. He just chuckles, putting a hand on my lower back to let me know he's still with me, as my idol stands and starts walking my way. A very large man with quads bigger than my whole body trails behind her, wrapping both arms around her as she stops in front of me.

"Oh my God! You must be Grace. It's so nice to meet you. I'm Bella," she says cheerfully, extending her hand.

My jaw drops, because she knows who I am, as I stick out my hand and place it in hers. "I'm—," I stutter, unable to think. It hasn't registered that she already said my name, but none of that matters because I don't remember it anyway.

"You're happy to meet her," Tanner whispers in my ear, his warm breath against my skin snapping me back to reality.

"Yes, that." I immediately cringe, because I'm fucking this up in the most ridiculous way right now. But Bella just smiles, moving our hands up and down in a shake. I can't believe she's actually standing in front of me. I knew that she was dating one of the Blizzard players, but I had no idea that he was in Tanner's little bro group, and I definitely didn't expect to see her lounging around in his living room.

I've been a huge fan of hers since I can remember. One of my core memories is sitting outside the stadium with my brother and Tanner, listening to her perform because we couldn't get tickets. They've gotten harder and harder to get over the years, so I still haven't been to one of her shows. Although, this is way better than seeing her on a stage with hundreds of thousands of other people in the room.

"Tanner told me about the jersey dress you made when he was in college," she says. The memory jolts me, because that was one of the last days we had together before he left me. It was also the last piece I ever made. Sadness tries to take over, reminding me that I never even got a chance to wear it, but Bella continues, and I quickly push my emotions down. "I'm looking for some cute game day outfits for this season. Would you be interested in making some for me? Everything I've found so far hasn't really been my style."

I shouldn't say yes. I haven't been able to make a single thing in so long, and I don't want to let her down. But the hopeful look in her eyes has me feeling all kinds of inspired. I want to help her. I want to make her such amazing outfits, that she's proud to walk into that stadium every Sunday wearing them.

"I'd love to," I say, exhaling in relief, because this might just be the thing I needed to get my groove back.

"I want cute stuff too," the girl with the black hair whines, her bottom lip pushing out in a pout.

"Grace, I'm going to level with you," the guy she is sitting with says. "I'm financially irresponsible. I have absolutely no budget when it comes to my wife's happiness. If you can make her whatever she wants, I'll pay for it. I don't care how much it costs."

I laugh out loud, covering my mouth with my hand, because this is insane. Not only am I going to try making pieces again, but they're for women who are so high-profile in the area that there's no way they won't be seen all over the Internet.

"Me, too!" shouts the brunette. "I like to call my look *Sideline Chic*, but I'd love to incorporate some more Blizzard colors into the outfits I wear on game days."

I'm still in shock as Tanner goes around the room introducing me to everyone. We fall into easy conversations, and I notice how happy all of the couples look as they show affection to one another. It all seems so easy, and I wish I could have that.

I look across the room to where Tanner is sitting in a chair, our eyes meeting as he gives me a soft smile. I hate the way we left things between us the other night. I've given myself a little bit of time to sort it out, but I really need to decide what's next. Do I want to give him another chance? Can I trust him with my heart? Will I regret not walking away?

All of that remains to be seen, but I know it's getting harder and harder to fight the pull I have to him, whether I want to or not.

THIRTY-THREE
GRACE

I PUT the last of the glassware in the dishwasher, closing it and pressing the start button.

"You didn't have to do that," Tanner says, wiping down the counter before he throws the sponge back into the sink. "I invited them here. I didn't expect you to clean up the mess."

"Why do you have that room?" I blurt, unable to hold in the question any longer. As the night went by, and I spent more time in close proximity to him, the need to have this conversation began to eat away at me. I just want to understand.

He puffs out his cheeks, releasing the breath he was holding in. He motions for me to come sit with him at the barstools, so I abandon the cleaning and follow him. He's facing me, and he gently puts his hands on the outsides of my thighs as leverage to spin my chair toward him. As always, electricity sparks to life under his hands when he touches me, but I do my best to ignore it. "My journey with kink started with you, but it didn't end the day I left." I wince, not expecting those words to hit me as hard as they do, but I sit quietly, so he can continue.

"After I hurt you, I became obsessed with what I did

wrong. I started researching and realized how unsafe we were back then. We never even established a safe word. It's a miracle you weren't injured worse than you were."

"I told you. I liked it. I asked you for everything you did to me."

He nods. "I know, but that doesn't change what happened and how it affected me. When I reached what I felt was the end of the Internet as far as safety during scenes, I still didn't feel like it was enough. In one of the kink forums I was in, people suggested that I visit a BDSM club to see for myself how it should be done. I never expected to be a participant in any of it, but that's exactly what happened."

I shoot out of the barstool, unable to hear him finish this story. But before I can even move my feet, his fingers close around my wrist, holding me in place.

"I need you to listen to me, Grace. This is really important." The desperation and sincerity in his eyes has me pulling myself back up into my seat, even though I'm not sure I can bear whatever it is he's going to tell me.

"I met a married couple that worked there. Their job was to teach men and women how to safely dominate their partners. At first, they just demonstrated everything, but when they saw that I was still scared of losing control, they suggested a more hands-on approach.

"I want you to know that I never intimately touched her. It was strictly for learning purposes, and other than providing aftercare, I never let my hands roam on her body. They were very aware of my limits, and respected the fact that I only belong to one woman."

My breathing quickens, trying to put all of these pieces together. The way he's looking at me, practically begging me to understand, is making it hard to focus. "Were you ever alone with her?" I don't care if it makes me look jealous. I have to know. My heart pounds in my chest and my throat constricts, making it harder to breathe with every second he doesn't answer.

"Once. But it was a demonstration for a friend, who was struggling to understand the lifestyle. He needed my help, and I don't regret it. But I promise you, even then, I never touched her in an intimate way with any part of my body. Her husband watched on a video stream from the next room. Our limits were discussed ahead of time, and none of them were crossed."

I exhale quietly, hoping he doesn't see the relief as it passes through me. I don't know why I think I have a right to even be upset with him for being with someone else. I was engaged to be married up until a few weeks ago. As far as everybody on the outside knows, I still am. But as I sit here next to Tanner, Cash is a distant memory. His betrayal doesn't mean a goddamn thing to me now that the missing piece of my heart is right here beside me. All I'd have to do to get it back is reach out and take it. But could I? Or has too much changed?

I look up at him. "Do you still go there? Do you *want to*?"

He shakes his head rapidly. "I don't need that anymore, Grace. I meant it when I said I never intended to participate. I'm glad I did, because it gave me the confidence I needed to know that I'll never lose control again. But as far as wanting to be there? No. I have everything I need right here, right now."

His words put me at ease, because even though I know I should be doing everything I can to protect myself from being hurt again, I also can't deny that I'm not in the same place I was a few weeks ago. I haven't forgotten what he did to me. I don't think I ever could. But the longer I try to pretend that things haven't changed for us since he came back into my life, the worse it feels knowing that no part of him is mine. I just don't want to stay away anymore. I don't know if I'm able to open my heart to him, and this might end poorly, but my body is exhausted from trying to fight the fact that I want him to touch me so badly. The other night in the sex room wasn't enough.

"Will you take me back into your room?" I ask before I can stop the words from coming out of my mouth. His brows pinch in, like he's having trouble understanding what I mean, so I throw caution to the wind, telling him what I need. "I want you to touch me, Tanner. I want you to dominate me."

"Grace," he breathes. "Are you sure you want to do that?"

"It's the only thing I'm sure about right now." That's the honest truth. My head and my heart are at war right now, but my body is winning the battle. I want him to show me what it's like.

He swallows thickly, hesitating before he finally speaks again. "If we do this, we're doing it the right way. I need to know what your limits are before we even go in there, and I want you to know mine. We'll have a safe word, and you'll use it at the first sign of discomfort. Do you understand me?"

I nod, because I can't find my voice to agree out loud.

"Okay. Tell me your limits, hard and soft."

Confusion washes over me as I try to put meaning behind his words, but I don't really understand them. And since he knows me so well, I don't even have to vocalize that for him to explain further.

"I need to know the things that you absolutely do not want me to do to you. I also need to know the things that are negotiable and what their terms are."

I rack my brain, thinking back to the past experiences we've shared. I never lied to him when I told him I didn't have any regrets about the things we did before. So, I can't imagine that there's anything I wouldn't allow him to try now.

"I don't think I have any," I say quietly. He shakes his head rapidly, letting me know that my answer is unacceptable.

"I refuse to do this with you if you're going in there without any limits. I'm not the same guy I was before. I take this very seriously and I refuse to hurt you or make you uncomfortable in any way."

I try to remember all the BDSM porn I've watched, zeroing in on anything that I wouldn't want to try myself.

"Don't spit on me," I tell him.

I expect him to laugh, but he gives me a tight nod in affirmation. "No spitting. Good. What else?"

I sit up straight, wanting to exude the confidence I feel inside. "There's nothing else, Tanner. Do whatever you want to me. I'll use my safe word if I have to."

He raises a brow. "Slapping? Biting? Breath play? Degradation? All okay?"

I steel my expression, so he knows that I understand what I'm saying. "Yes."

He takes a moment, looking into my eyes for any sign of hesitation. I stand strong, not even blinking until he finally stands up, towering over me. "My only limit is that I can't fuck you," he says firmly. I want to question him, but I have a feeling I already know the answer. He doesn't want to take it from me. He wants me to give it. "You good with that?"

"Yes," I whisper, looking up at him. There's fire in his eyes as he reaches out, encasing my hand in his and leading me down the stairs.

THIRTY-FOUR
TANNER

I'M DOING my best not to let my nerves and anticipation show as I lead Grace into the playroom. Now that we've discussed our limits, I'm ready to show her how it should've been for us all along, and what I've spent our time apart learning.

It's going to be so tempting to fuck her while we do this, but I know we aren't ready for that yet. There's so much left unsaid between us. I know I'm capable of doing this type of play without it ending in sex, because that's all I've done since I started learning, but this is Grace. The love of my fucking life. The only woman I'll ever want to be inside until the day I die.

But this isn't about me. She wants me to dominate her, and that's what I'm going to do. If and when she gives herself to me fully, it'll be because all the broken things between us have finally healed.

I stop, stepping in front of her. There are only a few inches between our bodies and when I inhale her scent, my head spins. Being this close to her, knowing I have her consent to do just about whatever I want to her, is so intoxicating that I start to feel lightheaded.

Grabbing the fabric of my shirt behind my neck with one hand, I remove it before reaching out and grasping the hem of hers. I savor the moment, slowly peeling it over her head, my gaze locking onto her full tits that spill from the top of her white lace bra. I squeeze my eyes shut, repeating to myself that I can do this, before reaching around to unclasp where it's fastened behind her back. Our lips are millimeters apart, and when our eyes connect, she sucks in a quiet gasp. I want nothing more than to kiss her so roughly, she'll taste me forever, but I can't. I need to control myself tonight.

When I undo the clasp, letting her bra fall to the ground at her feet, she arches her back just slightly in an attempt to get me to touch her. And fuck, I want to. I want to suck them. Lick them. Slap them so they turn the beautiful shade of pink I know she's capable of.

But I don't. Instead, I kneel in front of her, curling my fingers under the waistband of her leggings and panties, pulling them both down her legs at the same time. When she lifts her feet to step out of them, the scent of her arousal smacks me in the face so hard, I immediately feel my cock start to weep in my briefs. I have never wanted anything so badly in my entire life. I want to taste her, feel her, and fuck her in the filthiest ways.

Keep control, Tanner. You can do this.

I return to my feet, leading her over to the spanking bench because it'll be more comfortable for her. I plan on keeping her in here as long as I can, and if I cuff her to the cross, I know her arms and legs will get tired quickly. "Lie down here," I order quietly. "On your stomach. One knee on each side."

She obeys, placing one knee on each platform and resting her front half on the bench. I have it angled slightly upward so she can lift her head to see me, because I'll be damned if she doesn't look me in my eyes as I own her.

My cock twitches in my pants as I move behind her, fastening the cuffs at her ankles. Both of her holes are visible to me and I'm in physical pain at this point from how badly I want to feel her from the inside. I haven't fucked a woman in five years, and up until now, I could always quell the urge by thinking about Grace. But that won't work in this situation, so I'm going to have to pull from the depths of my self-restraint to get through tonight.

I walk around the front of the bench, cuffing her wrists. I secure the final set of restraints around the backs of her thighs, so she's completely immobile—mine to do with whatever I please. She turns her head to look over at me, lust completely clouding her expression.

Fuck. Me.

I need a minute to regroup, so I walk over to the wall and take down a paddle, as well as a riding crop with a feather tickler on the other end. I want to make her head spin with so many different sensations, she'll be begging me to let her come.

By the time I return to the bench, Grace's entire body is trembling. Her hands are balled into fists and her forehead is pressed tightly to the cushion in front of her. I'm not sure if she's nervous or excited, but I know we need to communicate here in order to make this work.

"Can you look at me, beautiful?" I say, placing my finger under her chin and gently lifting her head. She looks up at me and I swear I can see into her fucking soul. I don't even need her words, but I ask for them anyway. "Are you okay to keep going?"

"Yes, please," she says on a shaky breath.

"What's your safe word?" I ask. "Pick anything you want."

"Banana," she replies.

"Good girl," I praise, rounding the bench and taking my spot behind her. "If it gets to be too much, or you're uncomfortable in any way, use that word and I'll stop immediately. Understood?"

"Yes, sir."

Fuuuuuuck.

Hearing that phrase from her lips after so long almost does me the fuck in right there. I'm ready to drop to my knees. Eat her. Fuck her. Worship her until every broken piece of us has been put back together. But she asked me to do this, and I'm determined to give her anything she wants.

I start slow, dragging the feather across her creamy skin, watching as she shivers at the contact. Goosebumps raise along her flesh in its wake, and I allow myself one small thing, leaning forward and pressing my lips to her shoulder. It's quick, but it makes me dizzy in the best way. I never thought I'd get the opportunity to do it again, and even just this small gesture heals me a little.

"Do you want mean words or nice words?" I ask. I know she said she was okay with both praise and degradation, but now that she's in the moment, I want to make sure.

"Yes," she says, shaking her head rapidly as if she is having trouble thinking. "I mean, I want both."

"You want to be my beautiful, filthy little slut tonight, Bunny?" I ask. She nods her head and I can see that her breathing is already accelerating. I stand straight, taking in the sight of her. I can already tell she's wet, as a small bead of arousal peeks out from between her pussy lips. "Aww," I mock. "I haven't even touched you yet and your greedy little cunt is already crying for me."

Her hips thrust forward just barely, as if she's desperate to feel something, and it makes me want to drop everything and give her relief. She fucking deserves it after everything she's been through, but I want this to be the most erotic thing she's ever experienced, so I need to remember what I've learned and take my time tonight.

I flip the feather tickler between my fingers so the crop is now facing the floor. I drag it across her ass before rearing it back and slapping it quickly against her plump skin. She yelps in response, but relaxes once the initial sting subsides.

"Are you okay?" I ask after the first strike.

"Yes, sir," she answers, prompting me to give her another on the opposite cheek. I'm not putting a lot of force behind it because she's never done this before. I just want her to get a feel for the toys.

"You're doing so good," I praise. "Do you want the paddle?"

"Please," she says, her voice shaking.

I look down, running my hands gently over the red marks from the crop. They're barely raised, and I've left myself plenty of space to swat other places so they're distributed evenly around her backside. I'm feeling surprisingly in control, probably because I'm so aware of what went wrong the last time we did this, and how I've put so much time into learning to do it correctly.

Picking up the paddle, I gently press it against her ass so she knows what's coming next. She pushes back against it and I move it away. "You're not in charge here, Grace. Press into me one more time and I'm putting you in a forced orgasm belt and leaving you here overnight."

"S-sorry," she says, and I watch as that bead of arousal finally frees itself from her body and slides down toward her clit. My eyes lock onto the little pink bud that's so swollen, I can see it sticking out of the delicate hood that covers it. What I'd give to flatten my tongue against it, licking up the drop of her sweetness before it goes to waste.

"It's okay, beautiful. You're still learning," I reassure her before landing the paddle firmly against the lower part of her ass. She lets out a gorgeous little scream in response. It's everything I imagined and more when I've stroked my cock to this very image. I'm so goddamn hard right now, every muscle in my body hurts, but there's not a single thing that could make me stop as long as Grace wants me to keep going.

I use the paddle two more times before I finally can't take it anymore and need to get my hands on her just a little bit more. If she ends up hating this and I never get to touch her again, I want to keep this moment locked away in my brain for the nights I long to feel her this way.

I use my hands to gently soothe the red marks on her ass, savoring every gasp and moan that escapes her lips as I do. I'm careful to stay away from her pussy, because I know if I feel it against my fingers, I'll take what I'm so desperate for. I've felt the need to own this woman so many times, but it's never been as strong as it is right now. I know I'm still treading a fine line with her and I'm afraid if I overstep, I'll lose her completely.

"Look at that," I say, in awe of the way she looks with my marks on her. "Do you want more?"

"Yes, sir. More. *Please*," she begs. And what my girl wants, she gets.

I smooth my hand over her ass cheek once before landing a hard slap against it. She gasps, dropping her head forward onto the bench. I move to the other cheek, rearing back and swatting her again. I give her two more, alternating sides, watching as her body shakes below me.

As I go to deliver another strike, she sucks in a quick breath.

"Banana!"

Fuck.

THIRTY-FIVE
GRACE

"FUCK, FUCK, FUCK," Tanner says quietly as he undoes the restraints, freeing me from the bench. I'm shaking and my ass is on fire from what we just did, but the pain isn't what caused me to use my safe word.

"Come here, baby," Tanner says, carefully scooping me up and quickly carrying me to the bed. He lays me down, wrapping a soft, cashmere blanket tightly around my trembling body. He slides in beside me and holds me to his chest as I gasp for air. "You're safe. Do you want me to keep holding you or do you want me to let go?"

"Hold me," I whisper, finally setting the tears that are pricking at the backs of my eyes free. Once the first one falls, it's like a dam breaks, and I can't make it stop. Sobs rack my body as he squeezes me firmly in his arms, not letting go for what feels like forever.

"Shhh, shhh," he soothes. "I'm here. You're safe. I'm so sorry. I'm *so sorry*, Grace." He kisses my hair, gently rocking me as I begin to calm down, my muscles finally loosening so I can lean into him.

"Do you feel safe?" he asks, almost whispering against the top of my head. I nod in response, sniffling as more tears slowly roll down my cheeks. He twists his body, still holding me in one arm as he grabs something from the table beside him. "I need you to drink some for me," he says, handing me a bottle of water. I take it, swallowing as much as I can stomach before giving it back. It must be enough because he reaches back over, setting it down, and I hear the crinkle of a plastic package.

"Let's get a little sugar in you, okay?" he says, grabbing my hand and pouring a few Sour Patch Kids into my open palm. I look up at him, shocked that he keeps my favorite candy in here, but he's already turned away to set the bag back on the table. I place one on my tongue as he returns both arms to me. He lets me finish them before he speaks again. "Can you tell me what caused you to use your safe word? Was I too rough?"

I take a deep breath, releasing it on a shaky exhale. I feel like such a mess right now, but I need to be honest with him. He needs to know that I didn't stop him because I didn't like what he was doing. "You weren't too rough. I just…" I pause. "The last time you spanked me," I choke out, "you left."

He squeezes me tighter, bringing his hand to my hair and gripping it gently to hold me against him. I can feel his heart hammering in his chest as I feel more pieces of us slowly slide toward one another before snapping back into place.

He eventually loosens his hold. "Grace, look at me." I do, and when I see the emotion in his expression, it sucks the air right from my lungs. His eyes glisten as they fill with tears, and I blink, letting more of my own spill over because I'm exhausted from being strong for so long. I want us to be raw together. To feel this so we can make our way through it side by side.

He swallows thickly, reaching out with one hand and wiping the tears from my cheeks. "I've regretted that moment every single day since I drove away from you. I've spent years wondering if we'd ever get another chance. Years beating myself up for all the ways I hurt you. At the time, I was so scared that you'd give up everything and end up resenting me for not being enough to keep you safe and happy, and I panicked. I thought you'd be better off without me in your life so you could make your own dreams come true. I should've told you the truth back then. I loved you with every piece of me. I still do, and I'll never, ever leave you again. I've always been yours, Grace. Even when I wasn't there."

"But why didn't you come back?" I ask. "If you loved me and missed me, why did you stay away for so long?" I've both wanted and feared the answer to that question, but right now, I need it if I'm going to move on. I have to know what kept him from coming back and making things right.

He gives me a weak smile. "Because I was selfish. After I got drafted and realized that I'd never feel whole without you, I wanted to find you and beg for forgiveness. But when I ran through all of the what-ifs, I got scared. What if you were happy with someone else? What if me returning fucked up everything you'd built while I was gone and made you hate me even more? What if you didn't love me anymore?" he chokes out as tears spill down his face. "It was hard enough walking away after you confessed how you felt, but if I had to leave again knowing that your heart was truly no longer mine? I wouldn't have survived it, Grace. I would've died."

I don't wait another second. I can't. I'm fucking done being without this man. I smash my lips to his in a desperate, bruising kiss. Fireworks explode around us, and we both breathe a sigh of relief as we finally taste each other again after so long. It's like coming home after being lost at sea, unsure if you'd ever find your way back again. He groans, gripping my hair tightly in his fist as I open my mouth, letting him plunge his tongue inside.

"I love you. I love you so much," he says into my mouth. "Please forgive me, baby. I never stopped loving you and I never will. I'll spend every second of my life proving that I'm worthy of you. Whatever it takes. I'll do it. *Please.*"

"I forgive you," I reply on a shaky whisper, feeling the last of the weight that I've carried on my shoulders all these years fall away. Hearing him say that he loves me for the first time is something I never thought I'd experience, and the sound is like an electric current that jolts my heart back to life in my chest. He exhales in relief as he pulls my hair, tilting my head and deepening our connection.

There's nothing exploratory about the way we're moving against one another. It's like we know each other inside and out as we kiss like two wild animals. Without separating, he grabs my hips, yanking my naked body up so I'm straddling him. A needy whimper slips from my lips as I rock on his erection, angling myself so we're both able to feel the hot friction being created. Something hits my clit just perfectly as I slide forward, that even through his pants and boxers, I feel my orgasm bloom to life deep inside me.

"Wha—" I moan loudly, "what is that?" I can't stop myself from continuing to grind along his length. It feels so good.

He smiles against my lips. "That's a present for you, Bunny."

I pull back, brows furrowing tightly in confusion. "What do you mean?"

"I can't tell you and ruin the surprise. You have to unwrap it first," he says, and I see a hint of the playful Tanner that I love so much. "Take my cock out, baby."

I hesitate for a moment, but obey, curling my fingers into the waistband of his sweats and slowly dragging them down to his thighs. I can see his hard cock straining against his boxer briefs, and my eyes catch on the ridges bumping down it under the material. I look up at him, shock written all over my face as he raises a brow, daring me to continue. I do, pulling his underwear down until his huge dick springs free.

I gasp. Not because it's definitely gotten bigger since the

last time I saw it. Not because of the way it's as hard as steel, slapping up against his stomach as soon as it's been freed from its restraints. All those things, I could've expected. But what I didn't see coming were the five metal bars running up his shaft.

"You're pierced," I whisper.

"I am," he replies, smirking. "They're all yours, baby. Never been used."

I look up, eyes wide as saucers. "You were serious about that? You haven't been with *anyone?*"

He shakes his head. "Not since you."

When he said it the other night, and then again when we were talking in the kitchen, I wasn't sure if I believed him. I know he has no reason to lie about it, but Tanner is a gorgeous guy with an amazing personality, and he spends some of his free time at a sex club. Or, he *did*. I'm sure women throw themselves at him all the time. So, the fact that he's waited all this time for me? It's unreal.

I look straight at him. "I want you now, Tan. I don't want to fight it anymore."

He exhales in relief. "Thank fuck."

TANNER

Holy fucking shit.

Hoooooolyyyyy fucking shit.

I'm about to fuck Grace.

I feel like I'm about to lose my virginity all over again as I turn us over so her back is on the mattress and I'm hovering over her. I lean down, kissing her deeply again, trying to make up for all the time we spent apart, and erasing the memory of any lips that were on hers since mine. She opens her legs and I finish pulling my pants and briefs down my legs, kicking them to the floor beside the bed. When I settle between her thighs, rubbing my Jacob's Ladder piercing against her slick skin, I almost fucking lose it and blow all over her, but the look on her face as each barbell passes over her clit is enough to have me gritting my teeth so I can watch her come undone over and over.

"Tanner, oh my God," she says, panting while her eyes roll back.

"You like them, baby? I can feel how hard and swollen you are for me right now."

"Yes," she moans. "But I need to feel them inside me."

I want nothing more than to sink inside her, but I want to make sure she's ready. "I don't want to move faster than you're ready for, Grace. I'll wait forever if you need me to. Are you completely sure you want to do this with me?"

She nods her head slowly. "My life has been incomplete, Tan. I tried so hard to move on, but I didn't like who I was without you. I love you and I want all of you."

I breathe a sigh of relief, dropping my forehead to hers. I finally got to hear the words I've been dreaming of for what seems like a lifetime. And fuck, it feels better than any victory I could ever experience on the football field.

I kiss her again before sitting back on my heels and pulling her with me. I bunch several pillows behind her head, lifting her bottom half and placing another one under her butt which angles her hips upward.

"Look down, baby. Watch your pretty little cunt swallow every rung," I say, waiting for her undivided attention on where we're joined before lining up and thrusting forward just enough for the first barbell to be pushed past her entrance. My eyes roll back at the feeling of her wrapped around my head, and she clenches when she sees it.

"Don't fucking do that," I grit out. "Unless you want this to be over before I'm all the way in."

"Do what?" she says with a devious smile as she tightens again, making me grunt.

I take a second to get my shit together before reaching up to pinch her nipple roughly. Her eyes slam shut, and she hisses a breath through her teeth as I do. "Don't forget I know all the right ways to punish you now, Bunny. So, unless you want that ass and pussy on fire tomorrow, you better be a good girl and listen to what I say."

"Yes, sir," she says on a breathy moan, and I finally put us both out of our misery, sliding in further. I grab her hair, tilting her head to look back down at where we're joined.

"Watch," I command. Her eyes widen as I thrust the rest of the way in, pressing my pelvis tightly to her body. I see stars as she clenches, this time involuntarily, trying to get used to the new feeling. All the years I've spent celibate, waiting to have her back, are catching up with me as I try not to come inside her before I even get a chance to move. I've obviously fucked my hand a lot since then, but it's nothing compared to Grace's tight pussy strangling me.

"Jesus Christ," I force out. "You're so goddamn tight. You were fucking made for me, baby. Made to take this big cock." I pull out, making sure I'm not going to nut too quickly before thrusting back in. We both moan in unison as pleasure flows through us like we share one body.

When I feel like I can go faster and harder, I do, pounding into her relentlessly as she writhes below me. It may not seem like we're making love with how rough it is, but we are. In every sense of the word. This is us.

"Feels so good," she whines. "Please, sir. Make me come."

"You want to soak me, baby? See if I can make it rain all over these sheets?" I ask. She nods her head rapidly in response. I lean back even further, pulling her hips up off the pillow as I fuck up into her. I use my thumb to rub her clit from side to side, just like she likes, as the head of my cock bumps her g-spot with every thrust.

She's a sloppy, moaning mess as her inner muscles start to flutter around me. I can feel a pressure deep inside her that tells me I have my girl right where I want her. "Atta girl," I praise. "Push it out for me. Let it go." A couple more thrusts and she comes so hard, it forces my cock right out. She soaks the pillow, screaming in ecstasy as her body shakes uncontrollably. I land a couple slaps to her sensitive clit to prolong her orgasm, making her clamp her legs tightly around my hips.

Before she's even had time to recover, I push back inside, earning the sweetest little whimper from her overstimulated body.

"Use your safe word if you need to," I say on an exhale as I pick up my pace, feeling her cunt grip me with how fucking swollen she is right now. She doesn't say anything as I use her, only able to moan and cry out in a mix between pain and pleasure.

"You're my little pain slut, aren't you?" I grit out, fire licking up my spine. I feel like my soul is leaving my body as I slam into her, chasing my sweet release. "Your poor, used little pussy hurts so bad, but I can feel that you're ready to come again."

I lean forward, pressing some of my weight onto her as I fuck her into another goddamn dimension. We're grunting, panting, moaning as we kiss so dirty, my lips feel like they could bruise from the force.

"I'm gonna come," I say into her mouth. "I need another one from you."

She doesn't have to be told twice. Her pussy seizes around me, making my vision go black as I empty everything I have to give into her. I work us through our orgasms, only stopping when we're both completely spent and exhausted.

We lie there, me on top of her, gasping for breath as we calm down. I'm so tired, I could fall asleep right here inside her, but I don't want to even blink. Now that I have her back, I don't want to waste a single second not looking at her beautiful face.

"I love you," I say, kissing her cheek. "I love you," I murmur, kissing the tip of her nose. "I love you," I whisper, kissing her other cheek as she giggles underneath me.

"I love you, too," she replies, and fuck if my whole world hasn't started spinning again.

"YEAH, thanks for taking care of it, Grady," Tanner says into his phone before hanging up and setting it on the kitchen table.

"Is it bad?" I ask, turning away from the stove where I'm cooking breakfast to look at him.

"Yeah," he replies, dragging his hands down his face. "The floors have water trapped under them and it'll turn to mold if we don't have them pulled up and replaced."

I cringe. Since he's had practice every day this week, Tanner hasn't been able to get to the lighthouse to assess the damage. Every handyman in Hope Harbor has been booked solid with all the homes that were affected by the storm. Since it's right on the water, his little place got hit pretty hard. They were able to remove most of the water, but the damage is too bad to make it habitable right now.

"I can find somewhere else to go," I say, knowing it's going to put stress on him that I won't be able to stay there.

He looks up at me, raising a brow. *Fuck, he's hot.* "Did you really think I was letting you leave here anyway?" he asks, making me smile.

I've been driving back-and-forth to work on the days I

have to be at the boutique, and working from here on the days that Claire doesn't need me. I even told my parents I was staying here. They actually bought my story about needing some time away from Cash so I could think long and hard before marrying him, and they honestly weren't too surprised when I told them I had been at the lighthouse. They were thankful that Tanner came to bring me to safety during the storm, and to them, it just looks like two friends reconnecting after years apart. They know all about his guest suite, so I don't think they've given a second thought to me being here.

I've always suspected that my mom knew a little more than she let on about my relationship with Tanner, but thankfully, my dad just wants me to be sure before I get married to Cash. My happiness has always been their number one priority, so they were completely on board with me taking some time to myself. Little do they know, that that cheating, lying sack of shit is about to be out of our lives for good. Now that the housing project is finished and the grand opening is just days away, I've already got a plan as to how he'll be taken care of.

"Are you finally going to give the place a new look?" I ask. He kept the lighthouse exactly the same as it was when we used to go there, but now that he has the chance, I figured he might want to update it to be more modern.

"Fuck no," he says, looking at me like I have an extra head growing out of my shoulder. "It's part of us."

"Is that why you got that?" I ask, pointing my spatula at the tattoo on his leg. I couldn't make out what it was the day he was chopping wood, but since I've spent the last week relearning every inch of his body, I've gotten to take in every detail of the intricate lighthouse portrait inked into his skin. Each line tells the story of love, heartbreak, and healing. It serves as a permanent reminder of where we came from, and the amazing road that still lies ahead.

He stands from the table, walking over to me and pulling me into him. "I got it," he says, pausing to drop a soft kiss to my lips, "because not a second went by while we were apart that I didn't wish I could relive that summer. On the days when I thought I couldn't breathe without you, I'd close my eyes and go back to that lighthouse, remembering what it felt like to hold my whole life in my arms."

"I love you so much," I say, pressing up onto my toes to kiss him again. I never thought we'd make it back to each other. I spent months trying to put myself back together after he left, and I thought I had. But now I know what it feels like to truly be complete. I was a shell of who I used to be without Tanner by my side, and being here with him now makes all the pain and suffering we endured worth it. I'd go through it all over again if it meant getting to love him for the rest of my life.

"You're my lighthouse," he whispers. "My way back home in the storm."

He tightens his arms around me, and we make out like teenagers, breathing each other in until the sizzling behind me forces me to pull away. He doesn't let me go as I flip the bacon, trailing wet kisses along my neck and shoulder. I try to focus on our breakfast as Tanner does everything he can to distract me. And just as I consider abandoning my mission to feed him before he heads to the stadium for tonight's prime-time game, the doorbell rings.

I suck in an excited breath, releasing it on a high-pitched squeal. "She's here!" I yell, jumping on my toes as Tanner chuckles behind me. I shove the spatula into his chest, and he takes over the cooking while I run to the door, skidding to a stop to collect myself before pulling it open.

"Happy game day!" Bella says, doing a cute little shimmy with her shoulders.

"Fuck, babe," Maverick says, making his way up the steps. "Wait for a guy next time."

She rolls her eyes playfully. "Get faster, Mav." He pinches her side, making her bark out a laugh as I step aside so they can come in.

"Tanner's in the kitchen," I tell him. He grabs Bella's face, dropping a chaste kiss to her lips before heading out of the room. I wait until he's gone before I give her the rundown.

"Okay," I say nervously. "I haven't designed anything in a really long time. So if you hate it, tell me. I promise you won't hurt my feelings."

At first, when she asked me to make some game day outfits for her, I wanted to say no. After struggling to create anything for so long, I had almost considered giving up on my dream to become a fashion designer altogether. But as soon as I sat down at my new sewing machine, everything just came together so perfectly. Tears of relief fell from my eyes as I fed the pieces of Maverick's cut up jersey through, making perfect stitches along the seams. When I was done, Tanner held me and told me how proud he was that I kept trying until I succeeded. I'm even considering reapplying to the Massachusetts College of the Arts fashion program. I still have a long way to go with my concepts, but now that I've made one piece, I want to make them all.

We enter the spare bedroom that Tanner allowed me to overtake the day after I met Bella, and I lead her to the dress form that's wearing her outfit for tonight. It's the first game of the regular season, so all eyes will be on her. Being a world-famous pop star means that every time there's a break on the field, the cameras are focused on you. I can't say I'm not nervous that she'll be wearing something I created. The Internet can be a mean place, and if people don't like her outfit, that'll take a little bit of the wind out of my sails.

"Oh my God, Grace," she says, a huge smile blooming across her face. "You seriously *made this*?" She reaches out, running her hand down the jersey dress like she's touching something made of pure gold. It's reminiscent of the Harvard one I made to wear for Tanner the summer we spent together. I loved it so much, and never got a chance to wear it, so I wanted to reinvent it for Bella. I took the jersey she gave me, cutting it up the sides and adding eyelet holes all the way up. I tied it back together with ice blue ribbon, giving it a bunched look on each side. The numbers on the front and back are embellished with crystals, making it sparkle every time the light hits it. And to complete the look, I customized a pair of knee-high boots with a chunky heel to match. Replicas of Maverick's jersey nameplate run up the sides, with a number nine on the back of each heel, so that when she stands still, his full number ninety-nine will be visible. I even had time to add a vinyl Blizzard logo to a clear clutch, so she can carry her essentials without having her bag checked at security.

"Do you like it?" I ask, praying she says yes. It's not every day you get to dress the person you've idolized since you were a teenager.

"I don't like it," she says, and my stomach sinks into my butt. Damn it. I honestly thought I had nailed it with this one. She smiles mischievously. "I love it!"

My eyes go wide, and I exhale a breath of relief as she hops on the balls of her feet, letting out a little squeak of excitement.

"Do you want to put it on?" I ask. Families and friends don't usually arrive at the stadium at the same time as the players, but because of the security risk, Bella always gets there early so they can get her into a luxury suite before anyone sees her.

"Yes!" she says. "But you might need to make some repairs once Mav sees me in this. It's possible he'll want to claw it off of me before we even leave."

I laugh, but I have a feeling she's not kidding. I don't think I've ever seen a guy unable to keep his hands off his girl like Maverick. I don't blame him though. Bella is everything.

Not only is she absolutely gorgeous, but she's also the most down to earth girl I've ever met. I'm so thankful she gave me a chance to do this for her. Even if I'm never able to make another piece, I'll always have this memory.

I help her into the dress, retying all of the ribbons to hug her toned frame. Once her shoes are zipped, and the clutch is in her hand, I take a step back, admiring my creation. This was always in me. I just needed a little inspiration.

She hugs me tightly before we leave the room, rejoining the guys in the kitchen. As soon as Maverick's eyes land on his girlfriend, I'm glad I brought a travel sewing kit with me downstairs. That dress is definitely not making it out of this house unscathed.

"Turn around, Songbird," he practically growls, obviously not caring who hears it. She turns slowly, putting on a show for him as she reveals his name and number stretched across her back.

"I'd like to order ten more of these," he says, making me laugh before he walks over to Bella and spins her, kissing her roughly on the lips.

I give them a little bit of privacy, sauntering over to Tanner, and sitting on his lap at the table. I wrap my arms around his neck, trying to ignore the kissing sounds coming from the other side of the room.

"I'd call that a success," he says, burying his face in my neck and sucking the sensitive skin between his teeth. I try not to moan at the contact, but when he bites down, I can't help myself. "Have I told you how proud I am?"

I giggle. "Only about eighty-five times this morning."

He looks up at me with all the love and affection in the world. "You are so fucking amazing, Bunny. I love you with my entire heart."

"SORRY," Mads says breathlessly as Bella's bodyguard lets her into the suite. "Your husband," she points at Dia, "wouldn't shut the fuck up during his pregame interview about a record he broke last year. That I didn't even *ask him about.*"

"That tracks," she replies. "Nobody loves Dalton Davis more than Dalton Davis, and that says a lot because I love his goofy ass to the moon and back."

I laugh, because this group is so much fun to be around. The way they all joke and banter with one another makes me want to be part of it.

"You look amazing!" Mads says to Bella, who does a spin to show off the dress I designed.

"Right?" she says, bouncing on the balls of her feet. "Grace, I can't believe this is the first thing you've made in a while. I've had designers charge me way more for less quality. You should think about starting your own line. The WAGs would eat it up!"

My eyes go wide. "Really? I never thought about specifi- cally doing game day fashion. I always saw myself as more of a ready-to-wear designer. Do you really think I could do couture?"

"Are you kidding?" Dia says. "This is your *thing*, Grace. You're a natural at it. And the fact that you made it in just a couple of days is even more impressive."

I can't believe what they're saying. I always just assumed that maybe someday, my pieces could be sold in boutiques. I'd make unique designs, but then they'd be mass produced in as many sizes as the distributor ordered and placed on racks next to hundreds of others. But this would be so much different. I'd be able to make exactly what the customer wanted, to their exact measurements. Nobody would be excluded.

"Holy shit," I say on a laugh. "Maybe I will."

Dia chuckles. "I bet Daddy Tanner would invest in your new business."

I furrow my brows in confusion. "Daddy Tanner?"

"Oh my God, Diamond. She's new. You're going to scare her away with your stupid theories," Mads says, rubbing her temples in annoyance.

"What?" Dia asks. "The people want to know. And by people, I mean me."

I look between them. "Want to know *what*?"

Mads blows out a breath. "My best friend here seems to think Tanner is some kind of sex god. That he's into whips and chains, and has a pierced dick."

My eyes go wide and I freeze where I'm sitting. *Oh, shit. What do I say?*

"She literally called him the *final boss of daddy doms*," Bella adds with a giggle.

My palms are sweating and my mouth feels like it's full of cotton balls as I laugh nervously. I'm obviously terrible at hiding things, because they see right through it.

"I told you!" Dia yells, jumping from her seat. "Pay up, bitches!" She walks over to Bella and Mads and they each hand her a hundred-dollar bill before she shoves them into her bag and sits back down.

I don't confirm or deny anything because as I look down onto the field, the lights dim and the fans go wild.

"And now! Your Boston Blizzard!" says the announcer as the team shoots out of the tunnel. My eyes lock on Tanner as he runs to the opposite end zone, hyping up the people in the stands as they scream. They fucking love him. And so do I.

The girls line up next to me, watching their guys as they go through warm-up drills. Maverick points up to the suite and Bella blows him a kiss in return. I look between them, smiling because they're so adorable.

I look back just in time to see Blaze catch an easy pass, patting his hand over his heart. Mads smiles, then walks toward the snack bar in the back of the room.

"My turn," Dia says, sliding in next to me. I'm confused, but I look to the field where Dalton locks his eyes on her, wiggling his left hand. She does the same, her large diamond wedding ring glinting in the light.

"What is that?" I ask.

"Oh!" Bella says. "That's their way of saying they love us from the field. They all have a little signal so we know they see us."

I swoon. "That's the cutest thing I've ever seen!"

It makes me wonder what Tanner's would be if we had one. I look down, smiling as he lines up behind the center and taps his left toe behind him. I remember from watching him in high school that a player should be moving after he does it, but no one does. On the next rep, he does it again. I focus on the movement because he does it before every single play, and it draws my eyes to his tattoo. *Our lighthouse.*

Maybe.

"Mads?" I say, calling her back over because she knows this game better than anyone I've ever met. "Shouldn't a player be in motion when Tanner does that with his foot?"

"Yep," she replies, taking a bite of cheese and setting it down on her plate. "I thought it was the weirdest thing at first because he's done it before every single play, so I asked Blaze and he said it's a personal thing. Nobody knows why he does it."

"Did he do it in college?" I ask. I have to know if it started before or after me.

"I've watched his highlight reels and it looks like he didn't do it a single time before his senior year. Didn't you watch him play back then?"

I never watched him play after he left. My parents made it to some of his home games the following season, and our dads are loyal Blizzard fans, but I couldn't bring myself to watch with them because I knew it would hurt too much. I avoided football at all costs. Of course there were occasions when he'd show up on the news or on the cover of a sports magazine, but I did my best to get away before I really got to see or hear him. I knew if I started, I'd fall down a rabbit hole and it would bring me back into the dark place I had to claw my way out of once I realized he wasn't coming back.

"No," I whisper, looking down as he does it again, this time, looking up toward the suite. I know he can't see the details of my expression, but if he could, he'd know just how much that gesture means to me. He wanted to tell me he loved me, even when he didn't know if I'd see it. Every game that we've been apart, he's spoken to me.

I realize then that Tanner Lake really has always been mine. As much as I say he's kept my heart all these years, I unknowingly had his, too.

The rest of the night is a blur. We laugh, dance, eat and drink while we watch our guys dominate the field, winning with a score of twenty-four to seven. And when they enter the suite after the game, all looking and smelling like snacks from their post-game showers, I fly in his direction, jumping into his open arms. I press my lips to his, making him freeze for a moment because it was unexpected, but he eventually melts into it, bringing a hand to the back of my head to hold me in place while we kiss. But I'm not going anywhere. I'm right where I belong.

"The foot thing," I mumble against his lips. "Was it for me?"

He chuckles. "You saw that? Clever girl." He lowers me to the ground, resting his hands on my hips as he smiles down at me.

"I never saw it. I couldn't bring myself to watch you play after—" I don't finish, because we both know.

"Doesn't matter, baby," he says. "What's important is that you're here now and I can tell you I love you whenever I want."

He leans down, kissing me again. "Thank you for coming. I can't explain how good it felt knowing my whole heart was right here in this stadium. And this?" he says, plucking the hem of his jersey that I'm wearing. I didn't customize it because I worked until the last second on Bella's, so I just grabbed one from his closet and accessorized it as best as I could. "I'm fucking you in this when we get home."

Just like that, heat begins to gather in my core. I'll never know how such simple words can make me so damn horny, but it's certainly a superpower that's exclusive to Tanner.

"Can't wait, *sir*." I whisper so only he can hear me. I turn to make sure no one is watching before sneaking my hand down between us, but he grabs my wrist, halting me.

He raises a brow. "Careful, Bunny," he chides. "I distinctly remember the last time you made me hard in public. So, unless you want to wet the bed again, I'd rethink your next move."

"Oh my God!" I say, slapping his chest before I cover my face with my hands. That is still hands down, one of my most embarrassing moments to date. But of course, he'll never let me live it down.

And I wouldn't have it any other way.

THIRTY-EIGHT
TANNER

"BABY, we're going to be late," I say, fastening my cufflinks as I walk in the door to the bedroom Grace has been using to sew. "You better be—" I'm cut off when I see that she hasn't even started getting ready for the evening. She sits on the floor in a pair of denim overalls, a pink pincushion on her wrist, and a pencil sticking out of her messy bun.

The grand opening for her dad's company's housing project is tonight and she has a whole big scheme planned to let everyone know just what Cash has been up to, how he used his relationship with her to get to the top, and how he plans to start a business of his own with the connections he's made. When she told me the whole story, I was livid. I wanted to get in my car and beat the shit out of him myself, but my girl deserves her retribution. She won't tell me what she's got up her sleeve, but I honestly can't wait to see the fireworks.

She looks up at me sheepishly. "Sorry. Inspiration struck and I promised Dalton I'd have his wife dressed like the queen of the WAGs this Sunday."

I laugh. "Dia could be in a burlap sack and every woman in the place would be terrified of her, while simultaneously wanting to be her best friend." She giggles as she continues cutting the fabric laid out in front of her. I reach out, swiping the scissors from her hand, making her scowl up at me.

"Tan!" she whines. "I need ten more minutes, then I'll get ready. I promise."

I shake my head. "Nope. You can finish this later. Get that fine ass up and ready, or I'll use these," I pause, waving her fabric scissors in the air, "to cut paper."

She sucks in a gasp, her jaw dropping in disgust. "You wouldn't *dare*."

I raise a brow. "Shower. Now. Or I'll spend the night making a paper doll chain a mile long."

She scoffs. "Okay, *Daddy Tanner*," she mumbles, making me chuckle before she hops up and saunters out of the room, swinging her heart shaped ass as she goes.

I pull up to the valet at the event center, tossing the keys to the attendant and rounding the front of the car to open Grace's door. Her parents know she's been staying with me while repairs are being made to the lighthouse, so arriving together won't raise any suspicions, but I'm making it a point not to be outwardly affectionate until she's told them about Cash. When I touch her and kiss her in front of her family, it'll be with their approval. I just hope they don't make me beg for it. I will if I have to, but I have a feeling her parents won't object. Her brother, on the other hand?

Let's just say I'm happy the Fury made it to the postseason, so I have a little more time to figure out how I'm going to break the news to him that I'm fucking his sister.

I'll work on my delivery before then.

I offer my hand, helping her out of the car before putting it gently on her lower back while she walks up the stairs. Since this was such a special project for Bill's company, he chose to make the grand opening into a charity event that'll benefit the families moving in. His goal is to furnish every unit and start college funds for the children. I made an anonymous donation of one million dollars already, but I plan on making another one in the name of the future Mr. and Mrs. Tanner Lake later tonight. We aren't engaged yet, but I don't plan on waiting much longer. I was born to be Grace Valentine's husband.

"I love you," I whisper, quiet enough so only she can hear me as I drop my hand and put a few inches of space between us. I instantly miss her warmth, but I'll make up for it when I have her alone later.

"I love you, too," she whispers back, raising her hand in a wave. I look away from her just in time to see both of our mothers making their way toward us. I swallow thickly, hoping I don't somehow blow our cover. I've never been particularly good at lying, and sweat beads at the back of my neck as I go through the million scenarios where I open my mouth and fuck this all up before my girl has a chance to get the revenge she deserves.

"Look at the two of you," Libby says, giving us each a hug. "Don't you make an adorable couple!"

My eyes go wide, and I look over at Grace, whose expression is mirroring my own. We're so fucked.

"Don't be ridiculous, Lib," my mom chides. "You know they're *just friends*. If it were anything more than that, they'd have made the leap years ago."

I grab a glass of champagne off a tray that's passing by, throwing it back in one go as they all turn to look at me.

"Eh, you're right," Libby replies. "But imagine all the sneaking around they could've done if they had. We'd have never even known."

If I didn't know any better, I'd say there was a mocking

tone in their voices. But they couldn't possibly know my past with Grace, could they? We were so careful that summer, making sure we only hung out where nobody would see us together. If her mom knew, wouldn't she hate me for disappearing at the exact same time her daughter became inexplicably sad and decided not to go off to California for college? Wouldn't my mom have shown up at my dorm and dragged me back to Hope Harbor to make things right?

My head is spinning as they share a look and walk off, laughing amongst themselves.

"What the fuck just happened?" Grace whispers, making me shake my head in confusion.

"I have no idea," I reply.

We don't have long to dwell on it, because Bill takes his spot behind the podium on stage and taps the microphone. "Can I have your attention for a minute?" he addresses the crowd, making every voice in the large room go quiet to hear what he says next.

"I've been in the construction business for twenty-five years. I've always done my best to give back to my community, but it never felt like it was truly enough. You took me from a young man with a small startup, to a CEO who now has the means to make a difference in the lives of those who need a little extra help on their journey. This housing project has given over forty families a fresh start, so they can spend more time focusing on what's really important in life." He pauses for a moment, and I notice that Grace is no longer standing next to me. I look to my left and right, but she's nowhere to be seen as he continues.

"I'd like to take a moment to say thank you to the man who headed up this project. It was his first time working on something of this caliber, and I can't go without giving him the recognition he deserves for it. Cash Hadley, why don't you come up here and say a few words, son."

I grit my teeth together at the term of endearment because

that shithead doesn't deserve an ounce of the respect he's being given, even if Bill doesn't realize what he's done yet. But considering Grace's current absence, I'm willing to bet it won't be long before it's all out in the open.

The crowd claps as Cash rises from his seat and walks toward the stage, stopping to shake Bill's hand before moving behind the podium. My hands tighten into fists at my sides, and it takes every bit of self-restraint in my body not to fly up there and beat the shit out of him for using the Valentines the way he did. But I need to let this play out. This is her moment, not mine.

"Thank you," he says with a fake-as-fuck smile. "I am so grateful to have been a part of this project. Knowing that I was able to oversee the construction of this building that is making such an impact in Hope Harbor, is a very humbling experience. I want to thank the Valentine family for trusting me with this responsibility. Especially my beautiful fiancée, Grace. Come on up, sweetheart."

My heart sinks to my stomach as she emerges from the group and climbs the stairs to the stage. Bill runs out, handing her a second microphone, looking like he couldn't be prouder of his daughter. As he walks away, Cash leans in, dropping a kiss to her cheek. I almost lose it right there, because he doesn't deserve to even breathe the same air as her, let alone fucking touch her. But I can tell by the look on her face that she has everything under control.

She pulls the microphone up to her mouth. "Cash, congratulations on such an amazing accomplishment. The long hours and dedication you've put into this project are truly admirable. To show you how proud I am, I put together a little video to celebrate your journey over the last year."

He looks down at her, confused, but wraps an arm around her waist and pulls her into him. She turns her head as a large projection screen lowers behind them and the lights in the room dim. Everyone watches with bated breath as the video starts rolling. It's obviously security camera footage from the corner of an upstairs hallway. Grace comes into the frame for a moment before disappearing into a room. Cash follows, standing in the doorway, his back still visible on the screen. While we can't see her at all, the sound picks up their conversation perfectly.

"What are you doing, Grace?"

"Packing your shit. We're done. You can go stay with Sophia."

"I'm not leaving, and if you tell your dad about any of this, we'll both get fired and the project will be put on hold because there's nobody else to head it up. Soph and I are the only ones who would be able to. Do you really want to be the reason all those women and children end up homeless?"

"Are you blackmailing me?"

"That's hardly blackmail, babe. I'm just telling you what'll happen if you open that fat fucking mouth of yours."

The crowd gasps and my jaw clenches so tightly, I'm surprised my teeth don't break. He's out of his fucking mind if he thinks he's going to get away with talking to my girl that way. I'll fucking kill him.

I try my best to push my emotions down and stay in the present.

"Who are you?"

"I'm the guy who's put up with your ass for years so I could get in good at your dad's company. Did you know I applied there while I was still in college so I could get a foot in the door, but my resumé was never even pulled? Why do you think I tried to hook up with you back then? You can't possibly think I'd have really wanted you when I had my pick of hot college girls at school. I was playing the long game.

"Here's what's going to happen. You're going to pack everything you need, and you're going to leave. You're going to tell everyone we're taking a break because you're getting cold feet, but that we still love each other. When the project is over and I have the experience under my belt, Soph and I are starting our own busi-

ness, and you can go crying to daddy about how I broke your heart."

The video fades into another clip from the same camera, where Cash can be seen leading a tall blonde down the hallway, stopping to kiss her against the wall before lifting her up and carrying her into the bedroom and out of view.

The screen goes black, and the lights come back on just in time for that same woman, Sophia, presumably, to run through the crowd and out the doors as everyone watches. When they close behind her, all eyes return to the stage, where Cash stands next to Grace, looking like he's seen a ghost.

You can hear a pin drop as everybody whispers to one another, all waiting to see what happens next.

"I...I...," he stutters, unable to come up with a way to talk himself out of the mess he's in.

"Don't say another fucking word," Bill booms as he walks toward them. Grace steps away from Cash as her father lays into him. "How dare you disrespect my family like this? You were nothing but a cocky, immature boy until my daughter brought you in and begged us to give you a shot. You should be thanking her for your very short career, because I can promise you that you'll never work in this industry again. Now, get out of my sight, you piece of shit."

The whole crowd erupts into cheers as Cash backs away, disappearing backstage. I look at Grace, whose expression is completely blank, like she's in utter disbelief of how that all played out. She's my only concern as I run up the stairs and yank her into my arms, not giving a single fuck who sees as I hold her trembling body against me.

"You're okay, baby," I whisper into her hair. "You did such a good job. I'm so fucking proud of you."

She looks up at me, smiling weakly. God, she's so beautiful. *My little badass.*

"I can't believe I did that," she says on a shaky exhale.

"Me either," I laugh. "But it was fucking awesome. Made me a tiny bit hard," I say quietly, holding my thumb and pointer finger a millimeter apart in demonstration.

She looks up, scowling before she playfully slaps at my chest. "You're gross."

I give her a cocky grin. "You love it."

"We called this, you know," Libby says as both sets of our parents walk toward us. "We knew you'd find your way back to one another." My mom leans into her best friend, knocking their shoulders together. My dad just smiles as he shakes his head at them.

"You knew?" Grace chokes out.

My mom gives her a soft smile. "The hardest thing we've ever done is watch both of you go through the pain of heartbreak. But we knew it wouldn't be right of us to meddle in your lives, so we did our best to be there if you needed us, while letting you realize on your own that you were meant for each other."

"Took a little longer than expected, but we made it," Libby says in relief, rolling her eyes playfully as Bill wraps an arm around her waist and kisses the top of her head.

"Wow," I say, my eyes wide with shock. "That's...a lot of information. And you guys are okay with us being together?"

My dad scoffs. "Your mothers have been planning your wedding since Grace was born."

"I just can't wait to see what happens when you tell Riggs," Bill says with a laugh, rubbing his hands together with glee.

I have to admit the thought makes me a little bit sick to my stomach. He's my best friend. Even though we aren't as close as we used to be because of our careers, he's still one of the most important people in my life, and I don't want him to think that I betrayed him in any way. But the truth is, our moms are right. Grace and I were meant to be together, and nothing in this universe could've kept us apart. We may have taken the long road, but in the end, we found our way back to each other.

We all go our separate ways, with Grace and me deciding that we've had enough fun for the night and gathering our things to go back home.

"Oh!" she says as we make our way to the door. "I left my clutch backstage before I hooked up to the video system. I have to go grab it."

I follow, because there's no way I'm leaving her alone. She runs over to an empty chair, plucking her bag from the seat and turning back to me. But before we can make our way out, Cash steps out from where he was hiding in the corner.

"You fucking bitch," he seethes, not giving a fuck that I'm right here. He thinks I won't lay his ass out because we're at a charity event, but if he doesn't watch his mouth, he's going to find out just how wrong he is. "You just couldn't follow instructions, could you? You've never worked for anything a day in your perfect, privileged life, and now you've ruined everything for me. I should've known better than to trust a lying slut like y—"

He's cut off when I grab him by the collar of his dress shirt, squeezing hard enough to make his eyes bug out. "Listen carefully, motherfucker. Because I'm only going to say this once," I grit out. "If you ever speak to my future wife again, you're going to find out just how hard it is to pick your teeth up off the floor with ten broken fingers. Do you understand?"

I tighten my grip, making him wince before leaning in. "Thanks for keeping my side of the bed warm, just like you used to do with the bench in high school. I just have a quick question though."

"What?" he rasps.

I grin. "How's it feel knowing that every time you fucked her, it was my cock she was thinking about?"

His jaw drops and I let him go, slowly stepping away with

my eyes locked on his. I feel Grace grab my hand, her presence calming my raging emotions as I turn to see her smiling
up at me.

"Take me home and show me what a good girl I've been,
sir," she says, loud enough for him to hear. Not that I give a
fuck. As far as I'm concerned, he doesn't exist.

"My pleasure, Bunny."

THIRTY-NINE
TANNER

I ENTER THE PLAYROOM, my cock already starting to harden at the sight in front of me. Grace is on her knees on the floor, just like I told her to be when we walked in the door tonight. Seeing her take Cash down so confidently had me rock hard, my cock begging me to take her to a vacant room and fuck her against a wall. But I knew I needed to get her home in order to do everything I want to do to her.

I take her in as she waits for me, wearing nothing but a white leather thigh harness. Small bows decorate the straps that run down the middle of each ass cheek, and I have to bite my knuckles to stop from groaning out loud. I've never gotten to fully experience a scene like this sexually, and I'm questioning whether or not I'm going to be able to do everything I want to do before the need to be inside her overwhelms me.

I can see her shoulders rising and falling as she takes quick, shallow breaths, and I know the anticipation of what's about to happen is killing her.

Good.

I take my time, rolling up the sleeves of my white button up dress shirt before walking over to the wall and pulling down four bondage cuffs. I return to her, putting my fingers under her chin and tipping it up so her eyes are on mine. "Are you sure about this?" I ask.

"Yes, sir," she replies confidently.

"Is spanking a limit?" After the last time, and the way she reacted, I want to make sure nothing about that has changed. I don't want to cross any lines with her.

"I want you to spank me, sir. Please turn my ass red."

Fuuuuuuckkkkkkk.

I chuckle darkly. "I'll be doing more than that tonight, beautiful," I tell her. "You'll be sleeping on your stomach for a week after I'm done with you."

She releases a shaky exhale as I wrap a cuff around each wrist, double checking that they're tight enough for her not to slip out, but not so tight that they're cutting off her circulation. She's going to be in them for a while.

"Stand," I order. She obeys immediately, and I sink to my knees in front of her, securing the other cuffs around her ankles. I press a soft kiss to her exposed pussy before standing back up.

"I want you on my cross," I say, making her tremble with anticipation. Truthfully, I want her everywhere in this room, but I had the St. Andrew's cross built to her exact height, and I've fantasized a million times about what she'd look like spread out for me on it.

Putting a gentle hand on her lower back, I lead her across the room before spinning her to face me. I bring my mouth to hers, teasing her lips with my tongue until she opens for me. I kiss her roughly, walking her backward until she's pressed against the padding that runs along the wood of the cross. Without breaking away from her lips, I take each wrist and hook them to the rings at the top of each side. She's not stretched to her limit, so she has a little room to move, but it's very minimal. As I run my hands slowly down her arms, I can feel her thighs clench together against me. She's already aching, and we haven't even started.

"Bad girl," I scold, slapping her thigh before kneeling down and extending her leg out, securing the ankle cuff to one of the lower rings, then doing the same to the other. She's spread eagle, splayed wide for me to take whatever I want from her. And that's exactly what I plan to do.

"Such a pretty little slut," I say. "Holes wide open for me. I want them so badly, I can't decide which one to wreck first." Her eyes widen, but I don't miss the heat behind them. She's as turned on as I am right now thinking about the ways I'm going to defile her tonight. "And make no mistake, Grace. You'll be dripping cum from every one of them before you leave this room. I don't care if I have to fill you up after you've passed out. You'll take every fucking drop I have to give, won't you?"

"Mhmm," she squeaks out.

I turn, going to the chest of drawers and opening the top one. I'd be lying if I said I didn't have every detail of this night planned the moment I had this room built for us. There was never a question that Grace would be the only woman to ever set foot in it, so everything is set up for the things I've wanted to do to her.

I reach in, grabbing the three items that await her before closing the drawer and returning to where she's spread out for me. I set two on the side table for later as I step in front of her, looking into her eyes.

"This is going to get intense," I warn. "If it's too much, or if you just want me to stop, use your safe word."

"I will. I promise," she replies, looking at me with all the trust in the world. God, I fucking love this beautiful, perfect girl.

"Deep breath," I say, barely giving her a chance to let my words register before pinching her nipple tightly in the first clamp. She hisses a breath through her teeth, but the moan that comes after it tells me that she's going to like this as much as I am. "Good girl, baby," I praise. "Again." This time, she's ready for it when I clamp the other tight bud. I give the chain hanging between them a light tug, eliciting a loud whimper from her body.

I take a step back, admiring the sight in front of me. She's a goddess with her arms and legs stretched out, the harness hugging her waist and thighs, and her nipples that could cut glass being squeezed so tightly, I bet she could come just from me ghosting my fingers along them.

I step forward, putting my fingertips against her sternum and slowly inching my way down. Her breathing quickens and every muscle in her body tightens as I lower them between her tits, down to her belly button, then stop, resting them right above her mound. She attempts to raise to her tippy toes, desperate for those final few inches, but the restraints on her ankles prevent her from doing so.

"Aww," I mock, pushing my bottom lip into a patronizing pout. "Did you want to feel my fingers, beautiful?"

"Yes, sir. P-please," she stutters, trying to press up again to where I'm hovering over her clit. "Touch me."

I rear back my hand, landing a hard slap to the already swollen bundle of nerves. She cries out, slamming her eyes shut at the contact.

"Not a fucking chance," I tell her. "You'll take what I give, when I give it. And if you beg again, I'll gag you. Do you understand?"

"Yes," she replies on a soft exhale. She's so worked up right now, and I haven't even really touched her yet. The power it gives me is more intoxicating than anything I've ever felt, and I can't stop myself from undoing my pants and pulling them down enough to give my cock room to grow. I'm so hard already, but I know I'm nowhere near where I'll be by the time I push into her. I want to feel as desperate as she does, so I ignore the urge to stroke myself, instead, focusing on her.

"Are you wet right now?" I ask. "Does me telling you what a needy slut you are make your cunt tingle?"

"I'm so wet," she whimpers in response. The sound makes me throb inside my boxer briefs as a bead of precum leaks from my tip. My instincts are telling me to fuck her right now, but I've waited so long for this, I'm going to make it last until I'm physically unable to take the torture anymore.

I reach between her legs, and I don't even have to fully breach her entrance to know that she's dripping. I can tell she's trying so hard to be good when she really wants to grind into me for relief.

I take mercy on her, spearing my middle finger all the way inside her warmth. She moans out loud, clenching so tightly that when I go to retreat, I only get sucked in further. I fight it, pulling out enough to add another finger before pressing back in until I'm cupping her with my palm.

"Is this what you wanted?" I coo. "To be stuffed full of my fingers so your greedy pussy could come?"

"Mhmm," she whines, losing the fight and grinding down, meeting me thrust for thrust. The chain hanging from her nipples swings as her tits bounce from the force, and it makes me double down, fucking her harder.

"Tanner! Yes!" she shouts as blotches of red bloom to life all over her hot skin. Sweat beads at her temples and I can feel her inner walls clamping down as her orgasm barrels toward her. Moans and heavy breaths fill the room, mixing with the sound of my fingers pushing into her dripping heat.

"I'm going to make you come harder than you ever have in your life, but I need you to be a good girl and let it happen, okay?" I ask as she bounces on my hand. She nods her head rapidly, her pussy beginning to seize around me. Just before she falls over the edge, I yank myself from her, but I don't let the build-up ebb.

"Show me what a fucking slut you are, Grace. Come for me." I grit out, reaching up to release both nipples from the clamps at the same time. I watch as blood rushes back to them and oxytocin flows through her body, triggering an intense, hands-free orgasm. Her hips buck wildly, fucking the air while she screams my name, riding it out until she has nothing left to give. It's the most awe-inspiring sight I've ever seen in my whole life, and I'm the lucky bastard that gets to watch her come undone like this.

When I see her muscles starting to go lax, I band an arm around her waist for support, so she doesn't pull on her wrists and shoulders. I kiss her cheek and whisper praises into her ear as she trembles with the aftershocks. She's exhausted, but I've barely even started, so I give her several minutes to recover before reaching up and releasing the wrist cuffs from the cross. When I'm sure that she's steady, I kneel in front of her, undoing her ankles while she uses my shoulders to stay upright. She's wobbly, but still completely coherent.

Not for long, though.

I stand, making sure she's able to bear her own weight, gently running my hands up and down her waist. "You okay?" I ask.

She exhales a soft laugh as she nods her head. And when she looks up at me with that gorgeous, dickmatized smile that I love so much, I break character for just a moment and grin back at her. "Was that funny?" I ask, raising a brow.

"I didn't know nipples could do that," she says, making me bark out a laugh. I fucking love this girl so goddamn much.

"I have a feeling I'm going to show you lots of things you didn't know your body was capable of," I reply. "You did so fucking good. Do you want to be done or are you ready for more?" I honestly would be happy, either way. As much as

I've thought of this moment for the last five years, we have all the time in the world to play.

"I'm so ready for more," she rasps, looking up at me through her long, thick lashes. "I want to make you feel good, sir."

"There's my good fucking girl. Why don't you get on your knees."

She obeys, immediately lowering herself down to the floor, waiting for her next instruction. I make her squirm for a bit, slowly unbuttoning my shirt before shrugging it off my shoulders. I toss it aside, removing my pants and socks next.

"Take it out," I say, towering over her. The heat from before returns to her eyes as she reaches up, pulling my waistband down enough to free my aching cock. "Lick it."

Leaning forward, she braces one hand on my thigh, using the other to grip the base before running her warm, wet tongue over my piercings. I grit my teeth to calm down, because the way she's keeping eye contact as she does it is enough to do me in right here. She's a fucking wet dream on her knees, making sure to cover every inch of me with saliva.

"Look at you," I coo, "so eager to please." She preens under my praise, taking my tip into her mouth.

I land a tight slap to her cheek, causing her to pop off of me. "Did I tell you that you could do that?"

"No, sir," she replies. "I'm sorry. You just taste so good."

I grin down at her. "Okay, you want to suck it so badly? Fine." I pull off my briefs before reaching down and clipping each of the wrist cuffs to the hooks on her waist harness. There's an inch or so of slack, but otherwise, she's completely restrained.

I walk over to the chest, opening another drawer and pulling out a small red ball. When I return, I hold it up in front of her. "If you want to stop, squeeze this." I demonstrate, showing her how it squeaks between my fingers. She can't tap my thighs to tell me she feels unsafe, and she won't be able to speak in a minute.

"Okay," she says, her voice trembling with need as I put the ball in her right hand.

"You ready to get face fucked, Bunny?" I ask, feeling a jolt of power flow through my veins as she nods her assent. "Open."

As soon as her lips part, I shove between them, immediately hitting the back of her throat. It constricts around me as her eyes widen, tears beginning to pool in them almost immediately. I bring my hand to the back of her head as she tries to retreat, preventing her from moving. Taking a few more seconds to enjoy every sensation, I let go and pull out of her mouth. She coughs and sputters as her lungs fill back up, but I don't give her much of a reprieve.

"Deep breath," I tell her. She inhales and I push back in, holding her tightly to me while her throat violently spasms in protest. Her eyes fill again, and her face starts to turn a beautiful shade of pink as I look down at her with a cocky smirk. I give her two light slaps to the cheek as she tries to fight my hand on the back of her head.

"Nope," I say. "You don't need air. You're okay." I give it another few seconds, pulling out again while she struggles to breathe. A string of thick saliva still connects us, her makeup is smudged under her eyes, and I swear, she's never looked more beautiful. And just when I think she can't possibly surprise me any more than she already has with how well she's taking this, she does.

"More."

FORTY
GRACE

"FUCK," Tanner groans, "I love you." He doesn't give me a chance to return the sentiment before he's shoving back into my mouth, this time, thrusting his hips while I try to close my lips around him.

"Uh uh," he says. "Open that mouth like a good little fuck doll while I wreck your throat." My eyes roll back at his words. I'm dripping onto the floor as I look up at him while he dominates me. I'm completely positive I've never been this turned on in my whole life.

His fingers dig into my scalp, pulling tightly on my hair. I'm very aware of the ball in my hand, but I'm feeling like I can take more, so I let him continue. He pushes back further and further with every snap of his hips, causing my throat to constrict violently. My cheeks are covered in tears, snot is running from my nose, and I'm drooling onto my chin more every time he retreats.

"You're leaking from every hole, aren't you, baby?" he mocks, pouting down at me while he continues thrusting. "Poor, messy girl."

He wants to play games? Okay.

I wait until he's buried as far as my body will take him

before making a *gluck gluck* sound at the back of my throat. He pulls out so fast, I'd think his ass was on fire if I didn't know any better.

"Where did you learn that?" he asks, gasping for breath. "Because I know it wasn't from me."

I know I'm a mess, but I look up at him with my most innocent smile. "*Call Her Daddy.*"

"The podcast?" he asks, completely breaking character as I nod. He shakes his head in disbelief before raising a brow. "Cute, Bunny. Real fucking cute. But you're gonna pay for almost making me come before I got a chance to feel your pussy wrapped around me."

That shuts me right up, but it's too late. He reaches down, freeing my wrists from the harness and grabbing my arm, pulling me to stand.

"Back on the cross," he says, putting a hand on my lower back while I wobble over to the corner. I put my back to it like before, but he grabs my hips, spinning me so I'm facing it. He pulls my hands up, one at a time, hooking them to rings that are a little lower than last time. At first, I think he just doesn't want me to have to stretch them so far, but then he pulls my ass toward him, making me bend at the waist. My arms pull tightly, and I lean forward, putting my face on the cross to hold myself up.

"I'm going to leave your legs free right now. I need you to tell me if this is too much, okay?" he says in a soothing tone. My stomach clenches because whatever is causing him to be so caring, *I want it.*

"Okay," I reply, exhaling a shaky breath. I hear a clicking sound before something cold runs between my ass cheeks. He smooths a finger through it, spreading what has to be lube over my puckered hole. I suck in a quick breath in surprise, making him pause.

"Do you want to stop?" he asks.

"No, sir," I reply. "Please keep going."

He leans over my back, turning my face and pressing a soft kiss to my lips just as I feel his fingertip press into me. I clench involuntarily, but as he parts my lips with his tongue, I relax. He doesn't go any further before pulling back out, and when he pushes in again, this time to the second knuckle, I let out a moan so loud, I can't believe it came from my body.

"There you go, beautiful," he says. "You're doing great." His free hand gently roams by back, relaxing me until I've opened enough to take his entire finger. He continues licking into my mouth, our tongues tangling as I feel myself clench again. But this time, it's the most euphoric sensation I've ever experienced.

It doesn't take long before he's able to fit another digit inside me. I'm meeting his thrusts with my hips, feeling like if I just had a little bit more *something*, I could explode. But I don't get a chance because he's gone in an instant, making me cry out in desperation.

I turn my head toward him, watching as he picks something white and fluffy off the table. At first, I think I'm seeing things. But when he holds it up in front of me, revealing a butt plug with a bunny tail, I realize I was right. I look back at him, scrunching my eyebrows together in question, making him chuckle. He flips the cap on the lube, drizzling more between my cheeks before coating the plug. It's small, hardly bigger than two of his fingers, so I'm excited to see how it feels.

"Ready?" he asks. I nod before pressing my forehead back onto the padded wood in front of me.

"Breathe for me," he instructs, and I obey as he slowly slides the cool metal inside my tight hole. I immediate notice how heavy it is as it presses against my inner walls. It's foreign, just like his fingers were, but the longer I stand there, the better it feels.

He groans. "Fuuuuck, Bunny. You're so goddamn sexy." I'm feeling powerful, like a queen in front of her king as I wiggle my hips, making the tail brush against my sensitive skin. He laughs, giving my ass a playful slap before taking it in both hands and pulling my cheeks apart.

"Let's see how well you can climb my ladder with that tight little asshole filled," he rasps, sounding like he could snap at any second.

And fuck if I don't want to be the one who makes him lose control.

TANNER

"Tanner, I need you," she whines, shaking her tail at me again. When I saw this plug online, I had to have it. I couldn't wait to see my Bunny wearing it. I fucked my fist so many times to the thought, but none of that lives up to the reality as I spread her, looking down at where she's clenched tightly around the toy.

I'm as hard as stone, leaking precum everywhere, unable to go another second without sinking inside her. So, I don't. I grab the rubber cock ring from the side table and carefully fit it over my piercings, making sure it's in place. I want this to last as long as Grace can handle it. I've waited too long to have her like this.

I line myself up at her entrance, slowly pushing inside so she can feel every barbell push past her clit as she swallows me. When I'm completely buried, I pause, giving her some time to adjust.

"I'm—," she chokes out, trying again, "I'm so full."

"You're doing so good, baby. You're absolutely stuffed and you're taking it like such a good girl."

She clenches at the praise, making herself impossibly

tighter. I feel like I could bust right now, but fuck that. I'm about to make us both see stars.

I pull out slowly, slamming back in and earning a loud moan from my girl. I repeat the move, over and over, until I'm properly fucking her. Her ass ripples with every thrust and I land a couple of hard spanks before I have to squeeze my eyes shut so I don't come this quickly. She asked me to turn it red, but that's not happening since I'm barely holding on right now. The cock ring is virtually pointless with how tight she feels wearing the plug. I never stood a chance at lasting.

"Tan," she whimpers as her legs start to give out from under her. I wrap an arm around her waist, curling my body over hers as I use the other to rub quick circles on her clit. I feel small flutters against my cock almost immediately, which is good because even that has me clenching my ass to stop myself from coming.

"Can't, can't, can't," she chants, her words almost unintelligible, and I know I need to step it up if I want her to get off soon.

"Hey," I say on a rough exhale, catching what's left of her attention. She lifts her head, turning to look at me, barely able to focus. Then, I go in for the kill.

"I'm close. I need you to do something for me." She nods weakly, her head lolling to the side as she struggles to maintain eye contact. I grab her face, holding it straight at mine as I feel my release barrel toward me.

"Have my baby, Grace."

"Oh my God," she chokes out. I deliver one tight slap to her clit, and that's all it takes for us both to go off, me emptying into her as she convulses with a full-body orgasm. Her loud cries fill the room and I slam my lips to hers, swallowing every single one of them.

It feels never ending as I shoot rope after rope into her. And when we've finally both floated back down to earth, I carefully remove the plug before pressing my hips tightly to her ass, holding my cum inside. I know she's on birth control for her heavy periods, but if there's even a fraction of a chance that she could get pregnant, I'll fill her every day. Call me selfish or reckless, but I love her. We wasted so much time apart and I don't want any more to go by before we start our life together. She's always been it for me.

I pull out, keeping my arm around her for support as I use my free hand to remove the wrist cuffs. I somehow manage to pull the cock ring off without letting her go, using one of my knees to bear her weight as she leans back into me. I scoop her up and she immediately sinks into me, her soft breaths puffing against my neck. I carefully lay her on the bed, sliding in next to her and caressing her hair.

"Thank you," I say, making her hum in acknowledgement. She might not realize it, but she's given me everything I've ever wanted, and more. "Are you okay?" I ask, reaching for the bottle of water I had set out and helping her drink. Even though she can barely open her heavy eyes, she takes a couple sips before curling back into me.

"I'm perfect," she whispers. "Life is perfect."

And I couldn't agree more.

FORTY-ONE
GRACE

"HOLY SHIT!" I say as my phone continues blowing up with notifications from every social media app I have. It's been going off nonstop all week. Ever since people saw Bella's jersey dress, I've been getting requests left and right for custom game day designs. I'm still not to a point where I feel comfortable taking on a lot of them at a time, but I can start small and make them for the girls until I feel like I'm able to branch out.

Now that I've had a chance to really think about what went wrong with my education and career, I realize that the answer is *absolutely nothing*. I've always wanted to create Haute Couture, but I think a part of me never knew what my niche would be. My mind was telling me to go in that direction, but I didn't listen because I didn't think I was good enough. Now that I have a chance to do it all without having to go to college for fashion, I may just ride the wave as long as it lasts. My business degree will come in handy if I decide to actually make a career out of this, so it's not like I'm unprepared. I have Tanner, my family, and my friends who support me in every way I could ever need, and for the first time in a while, my life feels completely full.

"We told you," Dia says, smoothing a hand over the corset I made out of one of Dalton's jerseys. Her white leather pants are laced up the sides, and there's the number thirty-seven on one of the heart-shaped pockets on the butt. I paired it with some silver rhinestone stilettos and found a vintage Blizzard jacket online to finish the look. I also hid a crown brooch on the strap of her stadium bag, because she's every bit of the queen I promised her husband she'd be tonight.

Unfortunately, Mads is still stuck down on the field, so we're getting ready for kickoff without her. After this week, the guys have three away games in a row, and Tanner asked me if I wanted to tag along with the girls and see more of the country. I'm pretty sure he just didn't want to spend a day without me, which I'm definitely not complaining about. Maybe a day will come where I need a little break from him, but today isn't it.

We all hurry to the big window, watching as our guys signal to us in their own ways. I'll never get over the fact that Tanner did it for all those years and I missed it every time. I can promise that I'll see every single one of them from here on out, until he decides it's time to hang up his cleats. Whether it's in person or on TV, I never want to miss another game. Mark my words, Tanner Lake will go down as one of the all-time greats, and I couldn't be prouder to be by his side.

TANNER

I check the defense one last time before getting in my stance behind my center. We're losing by two field goals, so we need a touchdown to tie. With the extra point, we can win this very hard-fought game. It's been a push and pull between us and our division rivals, the Miami Rage, since kickoff. Emotions and tempers have been high all day, and I know it's gotten into the heads of some of the rookies. But we're not here to patty-cake. I need to get the new guys' confidence up, and there's only one way to do it. I glance up at the clock, seeing that we have time for one, *maybe two* plays. But we won't need them both.

I already called the play from the huddle, so now that we're on the line, I'm going to use a dummy cadence to confuse the defense. They've been on my guys all night, and there's no way we're beating them unless we outsmart them. I start stringing together some nonsense, sounding as confident as I can, while the guys wait for my signal.

"Red ninety-six! Coconut! Gator seven! Hut, hike!"

Danny Boy makes the snap into my waiting hands as I turn to Dalton for the fake handoff. He pretends like he's grabbing it, closing his arms in an attempt to make the defense think he has the ball, while I spin out to my blindside and watch as Blaze and Finn run deep routes up the field. They're both lightning fast, and somehow manage to get open at the same time. Knowing I need to lead this team the right way, I take a chance and fire it off to the rookie. The tight end who's supposed to be blocking for him is left in the dust, along with the rest of the team, because Finn Bellamy might be the fastest guy in the league right now. I wouldn't say that to Blaze's face, but it's the truth.

Right when he hits the ten-yard line, the ball drops perfectly into his waiting hands. Less than a second later, he's in the end zone, and we have the six. We all rush over to him, celebrating his first NFL touchdown, the energy in the entire stadium fueling us to put on a show for our fans. The guys do the dance they choreographed earlier this week as I pretend to take pictures like a proud dad.

It's not that far off. I love this group of guys and the relationships we have. It's been a wild year, but at the end of the day, all that matters is that we were there to help each other when we needed it. We've all been through love, loss, heartbreak, and so many different emotions. It's nice to know I've had my brothers by my side through it all.

I remove my helmet and watch as Ramirez kicks the extra point. The ball sails straight down the pipe as always, because that's what Ramirez does. Maverick and the defense take the field as the opposing offense goes for a quick Hail Mary, which is denied in the end zone with ease. We win the game with a score of thirteen to fourteen and get to boast the best record in the division, at least for now. It's only been two weeks, so we might not have long, but every win deserves a celebration.

I congratulate my guys, laughing and joking with them, until I hear a familiar voice yelling behind me.

"You stupid motherfucker!" Riggs shouts, jumping from the first row of seats, over the railing and onto the field. My eyes widen, first of all, because I haven't seen him in a while, and secondly, because of the look in his eyes as he approaches me. His face is red and the veins in his neck and forehead are visibly pulsing as he runs up on me with no sign of slowing down.

Dalton notices what's happening and goes to step in front of me as a line of defense, but I put my hand on his chest, giving him a tight nod as if to say *let him*. I deserve whatever happens, and he deserves to give it to me.

I put my hands behind my back, raising my chin as he takes the final few steps to close the distance. Even though I'm ready for it, I'm knocked back at the first slam of his fist against my face. Pain explodes behind my eye, but I stay upright, not moving as I prepare to eat another. My teammates rush over to help, but Dalton holds them all back, watching as Riggs punches me again, this time taking me to the ground. He follows, delivering more strikes as he finally speaks.

"My fucking *sister*?" he grits out, spit flying from his lips as he lands a shot to my side. "She was a shell of a person for months! There were nights when she'd lock the bathroom door and sob until she puked because of you, but she refused to tell any of us why!" He punches me again and this time, I push back because I can feel the skin around my eye beginning to swell shut. He stops, scowling at me and shaking his head in disgust.

"Not only did you leave her to put herself back together, but you left *us all*," he says, chest heaving while he clutches the collar of my jersey. "You're chickenshit, Lake. And you'll never be good enough for Grace. We're done."

He shoves his fist into my chest as he stands, walking backward a few steps before bumping into two large security guards that are just now arriving to the scene. They grab him by the arms, hauling him off down the tunnel while fans behind us cheer in the stands. I sit up slowly, wiping the blood from my lip and taking Blaze's outstretched hand that he's offering from above. I wince as he pulls me up, grabbing the towel Dalton is holding out to clean my face with. Everything is numb, and I'm pretty sure he broke my orbital, but the pain of his words hurts way worse than any of the physical damage he did.

When I left Hope Harbor, my only concern was doing the right thing for Grace. I wanted her to be safe and happy, able to live her dreams the way she had always planned. But things changed for us both that summer. What was important to us before we fell for each other shifted, and I don't think I'll ever forgive myself for not acknowledging it back then. I'd give anything to go back and do it differently because after that, things snowballed, and I got to a point where I couldn't return for my own selfish reasons. I knew she'd eventually move on. I was terrified of having to bear witness to her being loved by another man when it should've been me all along.

My biggest regret in life is all the time I wasted being

scared, and now that I have her back, I'm never letting her go again. I'll give Riggs some time to cool off, then I'll reach out to apologize for all the hurt I caused. I'll earn his trust back the same way I did hers. By loving her so loudly, he'll see that nobody on this earth will cherish her the way I do. Because I know what it's like to live without Grace Valentine, and there's no way I'm doing that again.

"Tan!" Grace says, running onto the field and throwing her arms around my waist. "Are you okay? What the fuck was that?" She pulls back, taking my face in her hands, her expression twisting like she's the one in pain as she sees her brother's handiwork. But now that she's here, nothing really hurts anymore.

"How'd you get down here?" I ask. They're pretty strict about letting people on the field without credentials, but when she reaches down and lifts the press pass around her neck, I realize Mads must be behind this. They don't even look remotely alike, but I'm assuming Grace was running so fast, security couldn't get a look at the photo anyway.

I chuckle. "You girls are going to be trouble together, aren't you?"

"Probably," she replies. "Think I can get them to jump my brother in the parking lot with me? What the fuck was he even doing here?"

I blow out of breath. "My guess is that he talked to one of your parents and they told him everything." Now that I know our moms knew what happened between us that summer, I'm not surprised that he would have gotten the information from them. I was gone for too long for there not to be questions about why I came back.

"I hate him," she mumbles.

I put my arms around her waist, bringing her into my body and kissing the top of her head. "No, you don't. He missed a playoff game to come beat the shit out of me because

I broke your heart. He's a good brother and he loves you. Besides, I had that shit coming."

She purses her lips in thought. "Yeah, you kinda did. Didn't you?"

Such a little brat.

I huff a laugh, poking her in the side and making her giggle. "Come on, Bunny. Let's go home so you can make me feel better."

FORTY-TWO

GRACE

"YEAH, thanks Twyla. I'm sticking with my initial statement. I don't want the fans to be mad at Riggs. I deserved everything that happened," Tanner says to the head of the PR company he signed with this week. After everything that went down with my brother, he needed some extra help, and Maverick swore Twyla was just the bulldog he needed to make all of this drama go away.

It probably wouldn't have been nearly as bad if it weren't for all the videos that were posted to social media. Fans captured the fight from every angle, but with all the noise in the stadium, nobody heard the things Riggs was saying about why he was angry. I'm not justifying his actions because I'm still disgusted with my brother, but the media is making it look like he just randomly attacked Tanner for no reason. And although he made a statement saying he was in the wrong, the court of public opinion has already made Riggs the bad guy.

I continue listening to his conversation because nosiness will always be my most dominant personality trait.

"No, I don't think we'll be able to pull off a joint press conference. Like I said, I understand the reasoning behind everything, but we're not at a point where you'd be able to get us in the same room, agreeing on a common ground. I need more time to make that happen."

He pauses while she speaks for a minute.

"Okay. That sounds good. Let me know if you need anything else. Thanks." He ends the call, tossing the phone down on the table before dragging his hands down his face.

"What a fucking mess," he says on an annoyed exhale. "Everyone thinks I'm a perfect angel and that Riggs is just a shitty person for attacking me. Short of me renting a billboard that says *'Hey, Valentine. Sorry I fucked your sister.'*, they're going to continue making him out to be the villain."

I laugh, moving to sit on his lap. "Are you sorry you fucked his sister though?"

"No," he says, gripping my cheeks in one hand and smacking a kiss to my lips. "And I'll do it again." He reaches up, pinching my nipple through his Harvard hoodie, making me moan in the back of my throat.

"My innocent eyes!" Monroe says, slapping a hand over them as she enters the room, stopping to peek at us between her fingers. "Where do you want the paint cans?"

I scoff playfully, because she's anything but innocent. My best friend is known for making grown men weep, and I love that for her.

"Over by that wall," I say, directing her as the door to the lighthouse swings open and my dad walks through with a large package of new floorboards. Now that everything has had time to dry in here and we don't have to be concerned about mold growing, we're repairing the damage caused by the storms. We were going to hire contractors to do it all, but Tanner and I thought it might be fun to do it ourselves.

I've been traveling to work one day a week, then doing everything else remotely because the boutique has been slower than usual lately. I plan on staying at Tanner's place in Boston while I try to get back into the swing of designing clothes. I'm designing game day outfits for the Blizzard girls now, so it's better that I'm closer to them while I work, in case I need to measure or have them try things on as I go. Plus, sleeping next to my guy every night isn't a bad perk, either.

"The new chairs are set up by the firepit if you guys want to go sit out there!" Tanner's mom yells through the window as she pulls the utility gloves off her hands and shoves them into her back pocket. When Monroe and I got here after we closed up the boutique for the day, we were shocked to see everyone pitching in. We immediately changed into more comfortable clothes and started helping, moving around each other like this is the way it was always meant to be.

"What do you say, Bunny?" Tanner says, his eyes locking on the old hoodie that's still so long, you can't tell that I'm wearing shorts under it. "Wanna go make out by the fire for old times' sake?"

"Mmm," I reply quietly. "I'd rather go break in the new mattress while everyone's outside." I lean in, pressing my lips to his. It starts innocent, but as usual, it doesn't take long before he's using his tongue to massage mine while I whimper into his mouth.

"Well, I can promise I'm *never* going to be okay with you two tongue fucking out in the open," a voice says, prompting us both to whip around. My brother stands in the doorway, both hands in his pockets as he looks down at his feet.

"That's fair," Tanner replies, a hint of a smile tipping up the corners of his lips that are both still split but starting to heal. Riggs looks up, finally seeing the bruises his punches left behind.

"You okay?" he asks quietly, remorse showing in his expression.

"Yeah," Tanner says. "No fracture. I'm out for a week, but it looks worse than it is."

I sit quietly on Tanner's lap as long as I can, but when the silence becomes awkward, I have to say something. "Oh my

God, you guys are best friends. Would you just apologize and get over it?" Riggs goes to argue, but I point my finger at him, making him close his mouth. "Tanner hurt me. Really fucking badly. And I'm sorry I didn't tell you what happened between us. But I love him, and I know that he would die before he ever breaks my heart again. We worked through everything and we're moving forward. So quit your whiny baby bullshit and make up already, because I want both of you in my life just like it used to be."

Tanner lifts me off him, pushing his chair back so he can stand. I hold my breath as he closes the space between them, stopping when he's about two feet away from Riggs.

"I fucked up," he says. "I betrayed you by going behind your back and hooking up with Grace, but I can't apologize for falling for her. I deserved to have my ass beat for leaving her...for leaving *all of you*, and I'm so sorry about that. I ran like a bitch because I didn't think I could ever be good enough for her. But I know now, and can promise you with absolute certainty," he turns to me, "that nobody will love that girl the way I do."

Tears fill my eyes, emotions overwhelming me at his words. This is what should've happened all those years ago. If it had, we wouldn't have lost so much time. But what matters most is that it's all over and we have a second chance to do it right. To see where our love story takes us.

My brother nods. "You've always loved her. Even before you knew what that meant. Doesn't make it any easier of a pill to swallow, but I'll try. As long as she's happy, I'm happy." He extends his hand. Tanner looks at it for a second before finally reaching his out and clasping it around Riggs', pulling him in for a hug. They pat each other on the back before backing away.

"Sorry about your face," my brother says sheepishly before raising a brow. "But if you hurt her again, I have no problem beating your ass a second time."

Tanner laughs. "That'll never happen, but if it does, I'll let you."

I walk over, hugging my brother before I punch his shoulder. "You need to get your temper under control, you heathen."

He rolls his eyes. "Whatever. I'm a goddamn delight unless I'm provoked."

The door opens behind him, prompting us all to turn as Monroe comes through the door with her arms full of the painting supplies that we had loaded into the back of my car. As soon as she sees Riggs, a mask of disgust casts a dark shadow over her expression.

"Val," she says in a mocking tone. "To what do we owe the pleasure?"

"Mayhem," he replies flatly. "We both know it's never a pleasure when you're involved."

My shoulders sag in annoyance as Tanner looks at me, clearly very confused. I shake my head as if to say *don't ask* before I take his hand and pull him outside, where our moms are planting flowers, and our dads are taking measurements so we can get the dock repaired.

"What the hell was that about?" he says, nodding back toward the house.

"I wish I knew," I reply. "You've heard of love at first sight. Well, Riggs and Monroe are the exact opposite. They met for the first time last year at the boutique, and they instantly hated each other. I gave up on trying to make them get along."

He looks back toward the house and I can tell the wheels in his head are turning, trying to figure it out, but there's no use. Those two are like oil and water. It's just the way it is.

He sits in a chair, pulling me down to sit in his lap as we watch the sun slowly lower on the horizon. I lean into him, remembering that summer, where we sat in this very spot, unable to stop ourselves from falling.

Maybe Riggs was right. Maybe we loved each other long before we knew what that meant. Tanner Lake is a part of me, just as I'm a part of him. It never mattered how many miles there were between us, or how many years we spent away from each other. We were always going to find our way back here.

This lighthouse has seen the best and the worst of our journey. It may have had to weather a few storms, just like we have, but it still stands strong after all this time. No matter what happens in the future, it'll always be the place we fell in love, the place we fell apart, and the place that saved us. And I've never felt more at home than I do right here, wrapped up in the arms of the boy next door.

EPILOGUE

GRACE

"OH MY GOD, NOOOOOO!" Bella says, waddling out of the bathroom like her ass is on fire. "Grace, help!"

I turn from where I'm helping Mads fasten her shoe just in time to see Bella bend at the side, showing a giant hole in the seam of her bridesmaid dress. Her pregnant belly peeks through the material as her jaw drops in horror.

Dia doubles over with laughter. "How the fuck did you do that?"

Bella pushes her lip out in a pout. "I'm a whale, that's how. I'm growing Maverick Moran's spawn. This kid is already probably bigger than I am, and he isn't even born yet!" she whines, making Dia laugh harder.

"It's all fun and games until the monster cock puts a monster baby in you and you can't even go pee without hulking out in your clothes."

Bella's shoulders fall. "It's not funny. I can't go out there like *this*," she says, gesturing at her dress.

I stand. "I'll fix it. I have a sewing kit in my bag. Just take it off and throw your robe on. I need to repair it from the inside." I unzip her, and she goes back into the bathroom while I rifle through my bag, finding the emergency supplies I always carry. I'm making custom game day pieces full-time now, and I also have a line of affordable, ready-to-wear designs that are licensed by the NFL and can be purchased on my website by the public. I never thought I'd get here, but with the support of these women and my amazing husband, it was as easy as breathing.

Tanner and I didn't waste any time after we got back together. We took a page out of Dalton and Dia's book, visiting the same Vegas chapel they did almost a year to the day later. We figured the best way to top their second Super Bowl win was to tie the knot in true Boston Blizzard fashion. That was the day Blaze and Mads got engaged, and now it's their turn. They chose a more traditional route, getting married in the summer at a beautiful vineyard in Nantucket.

"Here you go," Bella says, setting her dress in my lap. I carefully turn it inside out, thankful that the seam is just pulled apart and that the fabric isn't actually ripped. I do my best to go over every stitch twice, since the girl is ready to pop and this dress was fitted two weeks ago. It's a snug fit, but once we get through the ceremony, she can change into something that'll be more comfortable.

I give it back and she disappears to change just as the door to the room inches open. "Baby Doll, are you in here?" Blaze says, making us all jump up to shield Mads.

"I'm here," she says quietly, her voice wobbling with emotion. Dia and I share a look because as the married ones in the group, we know how emotional your wedding day can be. Although we both had varying circumstances, we understand what these two are about to experience.

"Blaze, it's Grace," I say softly, still shielding Mads in case he peeks in. "It's bad luck to see her right now, but stick your hand through the crack in the door, okay?" He does and I lead Mads to it, putting her hand in his. Other than the bathroom, where Bella is currently changing, there's nowhere else for us to go to give them space, so we try to busy ourselves.

But of course, I'm still as nosy as ever, so I listen while they talk.

"You okay, baby?" he asks. I can see his grip tighten when she sniffles, which makes her tears fall freely down her cheeks.

"Yeah," she replies. "Never better. You?"

It's his turn to sniffle, and I'd bet any amount of money he's crying on the other side of that door. At this point, Dia and I are just sitting on the edge of the bed watching this beautiful couple show each other their hearts.

"Do you remember the pop-up shop?" he says, making her smile through her tears.

"Yeah. I remember that blonde girl with the big boobs trying to press them up against you before I ran out. I was so jealous," she says with a laugh.

"That was the day I knew I wanted to marry you," he says. "The moment I walked in and saw you in my hoodie, I realized that I'd never want another woman ever again. I'm the luckiest man in the world, Madison. Thank you for being mine."

She hangs her head, her shoulders shaking as she lets her emotions take over. There isn't a dry eye in the house as Bella stands in the bathroom door with a wad of toilet paper in her hand to blot her soaked cheeks.

Dia grabs my hand and squeezes, and I realize that this found family of ours is unlike anything else I've ever been lucky enough to be a part of. We all have different stories and journeys that brought us to one another, but this group is so full of love and support, and I'll never be able to express how grateful I am for the way they welcomed me when I was so lost and unsure of who I was. This may just look like a group of football players and their significant others, but it's so much more than that. Every one of these people is a part of me, and they make me feel like my heart could burst at any second with the love I have for them.

Twenty minutes later, I'm making my way down the aisle to stand next to my friend as she marries the love of her life. My eyes immediately lock on my husband, who's standing with Blaze, looking at me like I'm the only girl in the whole world. Tanner has made our second chance more than I could've ever hoped for. I wake up every morning with so much gratitude that he came back home to me.

"*I love you,*" he mouths.

"*I love you, too,*" I mouth back, winking at him before I have to take my place at the other side of the altar.

We all turn to watch the bride as she makes her way toward her future husband. Blaze is an absolute mess when he sees her, not even attempting to hold back his tears. Dalton smacks his shoulder playfully with a goofy smile stretched across his face, because that man is straight-up giddy at weddings.

For the rest of the ceremony, I don't take my eyes off of my husband. I think back to everything we've been through; from bike rides to the end of our street, to him kissing my scrapes and bruises, to falling in love and every other milestone we've shared along the way. Some of them were hard. Others were amazing. But every single one of them was worth it to be able to call him mine.

Curious about Riggs and Monroe? Turn the page to read the prologue of their book, Wild Pitch!

WILD PITCH - PROLOGUE
MONROE

"GOD, you have pretty tits. What did you say your name was again?"

"I didn't," I reply on a breath, grabbing him by his collar and jerking him to my mouth. As soon as our lips meet, just like they did in the back of the car on the way to this swanky ass hotel, fireworks explode around us. I moan into his mouth, and I realize that this is way out of character for the girl I'm trying to be, but I want to melt right into his kiss.

I'm not here to fall in love.

I'm here to get some strange dick.

He pulls back. "You're not going to give me anything?" he questions. "What am I supposed to yell out while I'm fucking you?"

I bark a laugh, surprised by his candor. "Who says I'm going to let you fuck me?" I ask.

"Babe, you're topless in my hotel room and the muscles in your stomach are quivering. We're fucking," he says with a cocky smirk.

This guy is too hot for his own damn good.

I step back, slapping both hands over my abdomen, that is, in fact, trembling. I can't let my body react like this. I need to stay in control. I gave all of myself to someone once, and it ended with me having to skip town and start all over. I just got here. I'm not doing that again.

"Listen, Val," I say as he steps back toward me and digs his long, thick fingers into the flesh of my waist. My body goes hot all over again with the way his touch is so firm, biting into me in the most delicious way. As soon as he traces his tongue in a wet line from the base of my throat to my earlobe, I moan loudly, almost losing my train of thought. "I..." I breathe, "I need this to be a one-time thing. No personal details. Just sex."

He trails kisses over the side of my face, working his way back to my mouth. "I already gave you details," he murmurs. "I told you I'm in town for work, that I live in Florida, and that I'm going to blow your fucking mind tonight. The least you can give me is your name."

"How about I just suck your cock instead?" I say, dropping to my knees and bringing my fingers to the button of his dress pants. Hopefully the distraction will make him stop asking so many questions.

"Fuck," he groans, gripping my long, newly chocolate-brown hair. "I'm going to call you Mayhem. Because that's exactly what you look like down there. Chaos. Trouble. Like a riot I know I should run from, but I can't fucking look away."

I keep my gaze on his as I pull his pants and boxer briefs down in one go. My eyes widen and my mouth waters as his cock springs free. It's big and hard, with wide veins wrapped around it and a bead of precum sitting at the tip, waiting for me to lick.

I don't waste a fucking second. I need this so badly after everything I've been through in the past week. Packing everything you own into your small car and leaving the only place you've ever known to start all over by yourself takes a toll on you, and I just want to let go. The old Monroe needs to die so the new one can be born. I have a chance to be anyone I want now, and I'm choosing to be a bad bitch that takes what she wants and doesn't let anyone use her as a doormat. As far as everyone here knows, that's exactly what I am.

I lean forward, lapping at the head of his dick before sucking it between my lips. I moan at the way he tastes as I feel my pussy getting unbearably wet under my panties. I squeeze my thighs together for relief, but it's nowhere near enough.

"Holy fuck," he rasps, gripping my hair tighter in his fist. "That's it, baby. Suck my cock." The sound of his voice, plus the way he's got his fist clenched tightly to my scalp has me taking him as far back as I can go, fighting against my gag reflex that's telling me to pull back. I've never done anything like this before, especially with someone I just met, but I've never felt more alive.

Looking up, I almost orgasm without even being touched at the sight above me. Val's face is pointed up to the ceiling in pleasure, and I watch his Adam's apple bob as I suck his cock like it's the most delicious thing I've ever tasted. It's not far off. I could live off the flavor of his skin.

"You suck me so good. *Fuck*," he grits out, thrusting his hips into my face. I feel powerful and owned at the same time, and it's making my blood run like lava through my veins.

I feel him get impossibly hard against my tongue and he pulls away with a jerk. A string of saliva connects us as I look up at him through my lashes, both of us gasping for air as we stare into one another.

"Up," he growls loudly. The tone of his voice has me on high alert, and while I should be running for the hills, it makes the throb between my legs intensify almost to the point of pain. I scurry to stand, willing to wait for further instruction, but I don't even get a second to think before I'm lifted off my feet and tossed onto the bed. I push up onto my elbows, watching as he stalks my way with a look in his eyes that I can only describe as predatory. Prowling toward me, I stare, not blinking a single time as he crawls over my body and leans down, pressing his mouth to my throat. I arch up to him, throwing my head back as he licks and sucks, but when he sinks his teeth into the sensitive skin of my neck, I hiss a breath through my teeth as pain radiates down toward my shoulder.

"I want to take you rough," he says. "Are you okay with that?"

I shouldn't be. His voice is dark and chilling...and it's possible that he just broke through my skin when he bit me. But, *fuck*. I want more.

"Yes."

I blink my eyes rapidly, waiting for them to adjust to the early morning sun that's peeking through the blinds of the hotel room. Memories from last night slowly come back to me as I lie there, trapped under Val's muscled arm. The biting. The clawing. The way he worked my body until I was a desperate, writhing mess, begging for more pain to go with the pleasure he was giving me.

It was *everything*.

But I can't stay here. I need to sneak out somehow without waking him. He already had a million questions that I wasn't willing to answer last night, so I know if he gets the chance, they'll start right back up. Plus, I don't want to be late for my first day at the boutique, so I need to skedaddle.

Wiggling down the bed, I inch myself out from under his gigantic arm. Whatever this guy does for work, it has to be some type of manual labor. I bet he can pop someone's head right off their body with the inside of his elbow while chugging a beer with the other hand. I try to hold in my laugh at the mental image as I continue working my way down the mattress.

As soon as I'm out from under him, I rush around the room, picking up my clothes. My shirt and bra are right by the door where he pulled them off of me as soon as we entered the room, unable to wait a single second. I get them on, spinning quickly to look for the rest of my clothes. The pink linen micro skirt I wore to the hotel bar last night is tossed over by the window. I run over, swiping it and sliding it up my legs before tiptoeing over to where my panties lay bunched up by the bed. But when I go to put them on, I realize they're completely ruined. Memories of Val literally ripping them from my body flood my brain and I want to swan dive right the fuck back into the bed with him for another round. But I'm just going to have to settle for keeping last night's festivities in my spank bank for future use, because this can't be anything more.

I grab my clutch off the back of the armchair before moving to the door, taking one last look back at Val before reluctantly leaving him without saying goodbye.

Forty-five minutes later, I pull into the parking lot behind Praya, the luxury boutique I just got hired at. The drive from Boston to Hope Harbor wasn't too bad since I made it through the city before rush hour. I had to touch up last night's makeup and steer with one knee while I brushed the wild knots out of my hair, but I managed to make myself presentable.

And keeping an emergency pair of panties in my glove box?

What a power move.

I rush to the door with about ten minutes to spare before the store opens, smoothing my clothes down and walking in like a normal, confident individual that has her life together, even though I definitely don't.

"You must be Monroe!" an adorable blonde girl says as

she stands and comes my way. "I'm Grace. I'm the assistant fashion buyer here. It's nice to meet you." I take her extended hand, returning her smile. She can't be more than a couple of years younger than me, if that, and I have a feeling we're going to get along really well.

"Likewise," I say, looking around. "Where is everyone?"

"Oh!" she replies. "The ladies always meet for tea time on Monday mornings before they come in, so they'll be a little behind. It's just us for about an hour. Until my brother gets here. He's a professional baseball player and his team is playing in Boston tonight, so he's dropping in to say hello before he has to be at the stadium."

"Oh, that's cool," I offer. "What's his na—"

"Riggs!" she squeals, cutting me off as she runs to the door. She jumps into her brother's waiting arms as I turn around, smiling while I watch them embrace one another.

"Hey, Bunny," he says, and my blood goes cold when I hear his voice. As soon as she steps back, our eyes lock. Eyes that I was just looking into hours ago as he ripped orgasm after orgasm from my exhausted body.

This lying motherfucker.

Wild Pitch, Book 1 of the Daytona Fury series, is coming to Kindle Unlimited and paperback this fall.
Preorder on Amazon
Add to Goodreads

AFTERWORD

I can't believe the Boston Blizzard series has come to an end.
insert ugly cry here

This series and these characters will always hold a special place in my heart. They're my first babies and their stories truly changed my life. I've learned so much from them, not only about how to write, but also about myself as a person. I started as a self-conscious, unsure wannabe author who had no idea what she was doing. Four books later, I still have no clue wtf is going on half the time, but I'm one hundred percent sure I was meant to write these books.

Thank you so much for coming on this journey with me. I'll never be able to express how much it means to me that you love Blaze, Mads, Maverick, Bella, Dalton, Dia, Tanner, and Grace just as much as I do.

Thank you, from the bottom of my heart.

Love,

Candice

ACKNOWLEDGMENTS

My husband - You make writing about love easy with how openly you show yours for me. The endless hours you spend listening to me ramble on and on about these characters and their stories, even when you have no idea what I'm talking about, will always be some of my favorite moments with you. Not because you help me figure stuff out, which you do, but because I can feel how truly excited you are watching me on this journey. I couldn't do any of this without you. I love you.

My kids - For the love of God, I hope you never read these books. But if you do, I love you both more than you'll ever know.

My mom - Your love and support is unmatched. I am the luckiest girl in the world to have you in my corner, always reminding me that I can do anything. As much as I joke around about trying to get you to stop reading my work, I hope you never do. You build me up every day and I love you.

Breanne - Every time we do this, you amaze me even more. You're the perfect editor for these books, and I wouldn't trust another soul to do the things you do for them. In all the years we've known each other, this has been my favorite part of our journey. I can't tell you how thankful I am to have you. I'm so proud to call you my sister.

Hannah Gray - Thank you for being my other half in this crazy world of writing. I don't know what I did to deserve you, but there will never be enough words to show my gratitude. I love you!

Lexi James - The way you just take my crazy plot rants and help me turn them into these stories that I'm so proud of still amazes me, even after four books. I would be a mess without you. I love you to the moon and back…and I can't wait to see what's next for us!

Jaime Rayyan - Thank you for always letting me be a literal basket case in your VMs. It's become such a huge part of my writing process and I am beyond grateful for the care you put into making sure my stories are perfect.

Maggie Marrero - I can confidently say I wouldn't have made it through this release without you. From everything you did to keep my life together, to giving me ideas on how to make Tanner and Grace's story complete, to making sure I didn't spiral…I'm so grateful for all of it. You are a gift.

Amanda Mudgett - My little flower. You'll always be my biggest cheerleader and the President of my non-existent fan club. I know if I need anything, whether it's a bomb-ass edit or someone to drop everything to read my book for the fifteenth time just to remind me that it still doesn't suck, you're always there. I only hope that someday I can make as big of an impact on your life as you have on mine.

My FSBB girls - I will never have the words to tell you how you've changed my life. Your support is something I'll never feel worthy of, but I'll continue to be so grateful that you bless me with it every day.

Autumn and the Wordsmith Publicity team - Thank you for doing all the heavy lifting for these releases. I'm so thankful to be part of such an amazing group of authors and professionals.

My beta readers - Your love and encouragement while I write these books makes me push through, even when I think I can't. Thank you so much for the time and dedication you put into helping me create such complete stories.

My ARC team - To my OGs and my newbies, I love you all so much for taking a chance on me. I can't wait to bring you along wherever this journey takes us!

Bookstagram/BookTok girlies: Thank you for continuing to give me a safe place to land. Your reviews, edits, and messages mean more to me than you'll ever know.

My readers: You make my dreams come true every day, and I'll never be able to show you how grateful I truly am. I love you all.

ABOUT THE AUTHOR

C.L. Rose is a wife and mother of two. She lives in Northeast Ohio with her husband, son, daughter, and dog, Tank. When she isn't writing, you can find her reading in front of a space heater, wrapped in a thick blanket, probably complaining that she's cold.

authorclrose.com

MORE FROM C.L. ROSE

Hot Route
The Stunt: A Boston Blizzard Novella
Run Game

Coming Soon...
Wild Pitch